MATCHMAKING *for* PSYCHOPATHS

ALSO BY TASHA CORYELL

Love Letters to a Serial Killer

MATCHMAKING *for* PSYCHOPATHS

TASHA CORYELL

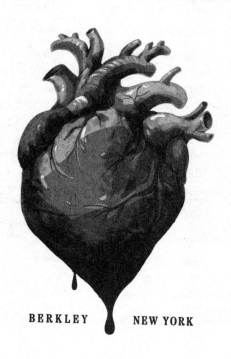

BERKLEY   NEW YORK

BERKLEY
An imprint of Penguin Random House LLC
1745 Broadway, New York, NY 10019
penguinrandomhouse.com

Copyright © 2025 by Tasha Coryell
Penguin Random House values and supports copyright. Copyright fuels creativity,
encourages diverse voices, promotes free speech, and creates a vibrant culture. Thank you
for buying an authorized edition of this book and for complying with copyright laws by not
reproducing, scanning, or distributing any part of it in any form without permission. You are
supporting writers and allowing Penguin Random House to continue to publish books for
every reader. Please note that no part of this book may be used or reproduced in any
manner for the purpose of training artificial intelligence technologies or systems.

BERKLEY and the BERKLEY & B colophon are registered trademarks of
Penguin Random House LLC.

Book design by Daniel Brount
Interior art: Heart © GoodStudio/Shutterstock.com

Library of Congress Cataloging-in-Publication Data

Names: Coryell, Tasha, author.
Title: Matchmaking for psychopaths / Tasha Coryell.
Description: New York : Berkley, 2025.
Identifiers: LCCN 2024046052 (print) | LCCN 202404 (ebook) |
ISBN 9780593640302 (hardcover) | ISBN 9780593640326 (ebook)
Classification: LCC PS3603.O7984 M38 2025 (print) | LCC PS3603.O7984
(ebook) | DDC 813/.6--dc23/eng/20241021
LC record available at https://lccn.loc.gov/2024046052
LC ebook record available at https://lccn.loc.gov/2024046053

Printed in the United States of America
1st Printing

The authorized representative in the EU for product safety and compliance is
Penguin Random House Ireland, Morrison Chambers, 32 Nassau Street,
Dublin D02 YH68, Ireland, https://eu-contact.penguin.ie.

To anyone who has ever been called "crazy"

MATCHMAKING *for* PSYCHOPATHS

PROLOGUE

THE WEDDING WAS THE end of the story. That was true in romantic comedies and classic novels alike. There was a woman (overworked and undersexed) and a man (rich and hot) who underwent a series of trials and tribulations until they finally found their way together.

I grew up on stories like that. My mother loved romantic comedies. It was a facet of her personality that might have been surprising for people who were familiar with her only from tabloid stories or podcasts that described her as someone who was beautiful and terrifying in equal measure. We would spend evenings together in front of the television—just the two of us—curled up on the couch with a pile of snacks, watching the hilarious escapades of people falling for one another. I'd never bought into the moral panic surrounding television consumption, whether it was in response to too much violence or to too much sex. People were more than their viewing habits. Still, those nights with my mother were some of the most influential times of my life, impacting not only my romantic dreams but my career aspirations as well.

"Was it like that when you and Dad met?" I asked her once after we finished watching *When Harry Met Sally* or *Sleepless in Seattle*. After a while, all the films started to run together. Two people met; they fell in love; the end.

She smiled. For most people, smiling was a friendly gesture, but there was a viciousness to my mother's grin.

"What your father and I have can never be captured," she told me.

I'd idolized the two of them, their love, even as I'd witnessed the brutal conclusion of their relationship.

My own wedding took place on the kind of perfect spring day that looked like it had been orchestrated by a production crew. Like in the romantic comedies that my mother and I were so fond of watching, the pathway to the altar had been circuitous. There was drama, heartbreak, and even a little death, but it was all worth it, because I'd landed exactly where I was supposed to be.

"Do you want another mimosa?" the maid of honor asked.

"I'd love another one," I told her. "Go light on the orange juice. Very light."

Downstairs, I could hear guests filtering into the chapel. It was exhilarating to consider that not only did a man love me enough to legally declare his devotion to me but there was a whole crowd of people who wanted to witness it happening. I'd experienced an enormous amount of loneliness in my youth, isolation that I worried marked my skin like smallpox. The sound of chatter below served as reassurance that all of that was behind me. I'd witnessed things that were horrific, had been mocked and terrorized by my peers, and I'd come out the other side of everything as a bride in her wedding gown.

Neither of my parents were in attendance, for obvious reasons.

"Are you nervous?" the maid of honor asked as she handed me my drink.

"No."

It wasn't exactly true. I wasn't nervous about the groom, as there had never been two people who were more right for each other than us. The issue was more that I was eager to get the ceremony over with. The wedding was the end of the story, but only once the couple said *I do*. Before that, anything could happen.

For the first time that day, I was left alone in the room, and I examined my reflection in the mirror, admiring the way the dress flattered my curves. Generally, I considered myself to be an attractive person. My face was nice enough, with deep brown eyes that men liked to call "mysterious," and I had brown hair that refused to be categorized as either curly or straight. My body was passable as well, though I'd never been one of those people who threw themselves into strenuous fitness routines. I preferred to spend my free time on the couch, reading books or watching reality television. My real strength was my ability to read people. I could look at someone and understand what it was they wanted, a skill that came in handy both in the workplace and in personal relationships.

Despite that skill, finding true love hadn't been an easy venture. If I saw others as transparent panes of glass, I was a brick wall. I didn't know how to open up, let people in, and as a result, most of my connections remained at surface level. It was the rare person who could breach my boundaries to become a friend, and even rarer to find someone worthy of romance. The events that ultimately led to my wedding day were so tragic, so comic, that no screenwriter could've plucked them out of their head. Then again, that was how a romantic comedy functioned—a series of increasingly embarrassing escapades until two people realized they were in love.

There was a knock on the door. I opened it with a smile, expecting to be greeted by a friend or my future mother-in-law. Instead, there was a box.

The box was the same shade of white as my dress, and secured with a pink bow on top. I looked around to see who had left it, and found the hallway empty. I pulled it into the room with me, noting that my hands had begun to shake. It was possible that I was nervous after all. It was probably better to cut back on the champagne until the ceremony was completed.

The box was awkwardly large, and I sat down, then placed it across my legs, untied the bow, and slowly removed the top. I reassured myself that everything was still good. It was ordinary for a bride to receive gifts on her wedding day—or at least that's what I'd gleaned from dating shows that I'd watched. Maybe the groom had written me a poem or gotten me a monogrammed keepsake.

However, as I rooted through the tissue paper inside, it became apparent that the question was not so much *what* was in the box but *who*. A shriek came out of my throat as my fingers touched something hard that revealed itself to be bone. The distance between a romantic comedy and a horror film was never as great as people wanted it to be.

1.

Four months earlier

MOLLY AND NOAH WERE already seated at the table when I arrived at the restaurant. I was underwhelmed by the presentation. There were no gifts waiting, no bouquet of flowers, nothing to indicate that we were celebrating my birthday rather than having an ordinary meal.

I swallowed my disappointment as I pulled out a chair and joined them.

"Oh wow," I said. "My two favorite people. What are we drinking tonight?"

The setting was so mediocre that I decided it was a fake-out before the surprise party that I'd spent the previous two months hinting to my fiancé, Noah, that I wanted.

"I'd love a surprise party," I told him while we stood in the corner at a housewarming for one of his friends.

"Maybe you'll throw me a surprise party," I whispered into his ear while we made love.

"I told Noah that I want a surprise party," I texted his mom.

My favorite birthday party ever—my last real party—had been a surprise. I was turning ten, and I came home from school to find the living room full of people. None of them were other kids. I didn't care. I didn't have any friends my own age anyway. I claimed that I preferred the company of adults. "Kids are stupid," I used to say to my parents, and the three of us would laugh and laugh. There was no better feeling than entertaining them like that.

What I couldn't admit was that I felt excluded. The other girls were enrolled in dance lessons, soccer, and horseback riding, and developed languages that I was unable to speak. They didn't care about the films that I'd watched over the weekend or the chapter books that I'd completed. My parents didn't seem to understand that children's extracurriculars existed, and wouldn't have been able to afford them if they had understood. "What could be better than the three of us?" they said, which was a statement that I wanted to be true.

My tenth birthday fulfilled fantasies that I didn't even know I'd had. Instead of one big cake with cursive icing spelling out *Happy Birthday, Lexie,* there were trays of exquisitely decorated petits fours and a tower of cocktail shrimp. Someone gave me a flute of champagne, and thought it was hilarious when I took a sip and grimaced before setting it down. The air grew smoky with a scent that, years later, I would realize was marijuana. We pushed the couches out of the way to make a dance floor, and I grew light-headed as I spun in circles, the guests cheering my name. I was so ecstatic that I failed to notice the lack of presents. I ended the evening with the assumptions that all adult parties were like that and that age ten was going to be the best year ever. I was horrendously wrong on both counts.

When I woke on the morning of my thirtieth birthday to find on my bedside table a note from Noah that said *See you tonight @ Antonio's 7pm* in Noah's messy doctor's scrawl, I took it as confirmation that the surprise party was happening as requested. I looked up Antonio's online and saw that they had a private room available for rent. I scrolled through photos of the space, building in my brain a vision of the night to come. Couples were always throwing each other elaborate theme parties on my favorite reality shows—gatherings with themes like "cowboy," "luau," or "1920s murder mystery," filled with dozens of the friends who served as extras in their lives. That was the kind of thing that I was envisioning, except the theme was "my parents' house twenty years ago." Before everything went wrong.

I spent the day primping. I got a facial, followed by a manicure and a blowout.

"It's my birthday," I told the aesthetician.

"It's my birthday," I repeated to the nail tech.

"It's my birthday," I informed the hair stylist.

It was the kind of thing that was allowed only one day of the year, and I was going to take advantage of it.

At home, I opened a bottle of champagne and practiced making surprised faces in the mirror.

Oh my gosh, what a surprise!

A surprise party?! I had no idea!

I can't believe my fiancé is so good at keeping secrets!

By the time I put on the sparkly purple dress that my best friend, Molly, had helped me pick out, I was significantly inebriated. I took selfies against the wall of my town house, with the best lighting, and ordered an Uber to come pick me up, because if Noah's party for me would be anything like the ones that I'd seen on TV, there was no way that I would be in any state to drive later in the evening.

When I'd arrived at the restaurant, I was surprised when the host led me past the private room, which was dark and empty, but I wasn't surprised to see Molly sitting next to Noah at the table. I'd known for weeks that she was in on the secret. On a couple of separate occasions, I'd caught Noah texting her when I'd peeked over his shoulder. Molly and Noah had conspired together before— she was the one who had told him my ring size and preferred stone cut before he'd proposed—so when I saw the messages, I knew something good was in the works.

Then, two weeks prior to the dinner, Molly had invited me to the mall. She'd ordered a dress online that turned out to be too small, and rather than mailing it back, she decided it would be easier to return it to the store directly.

"It would be a good opportunity to buy a dress for your birthday," she said, with a wink.

That was the kind of friendship that Molly and I had—we existed together. If I wanted an afternoon coffee as a pick-me-up, she swung by and we went to Starbucks. If Noah had a late shift at the hospital, Molly came over with a pizza and we watched reality television. Having Molly was what I'd imagined having a sister would've been like, had my mother ever listened to my requests for a sibling.

Molly was the first friend I'd ever had who provided the kind of bond that I'd witnessed in movies. I'd had acquaintances, of course. People I saw at work or the gym. We said hello to one another and exchanged pleasantries, but we didn't really *know* one another. It was like there was some invisible fence that everyone had the access code to except for me. I blamed my mother. She hadn't been close with anyone either, except for my father, and that had ended catastrophically.

Things with Molly were different. She was fun and pretty and, most important, she liked me. She made me want to tell her things, real things, not the mindless chatter I gave other people.

When she picked up the sparkly purple dress and said, "This would be perfect for your birthday," I listened between the lines to hear *This would be perfect for your surprise party.*

That was why I was certain that the table at the restaurant was the beginning of the night rather than the end. Surely there was something more than a simple birthday dinner afoot. If about nothing else, I was right about that.

As I approached the table, Noah's gaze drifted in the direction of my cleavage. I did have nice breasts, an attribute that I didn't take for granted.

"You look good," he said.

As a medical resident, Noah spent a lot of hours at the hospital, which meant that he had to tend to our relationship in other ways. He gave frequent compliments, had a standing weekly flower delivery, and knew my favorite meal at all our regular take-out spots, so that I wasn't stuck cooking for myself every single night. Molly sometimes asked me if I was lonely spending so much time by myself, but I didn't mind. After all that time alone in my youth, being with others too much could be overwhelming.

"Thanks," I said.

I noticed that Molly had also donned a sparkly dress, which seemed a little tacky considering that she'd helped me pick out my outfit for the evening. Molly could be like that sometimes, stepping into other people's spotlights when given the chance. I knew it was because she was insecure. She needed the reassurance of having everyone look at her.

"I think I'm going to get a martini," I announced, thinking of the glasses that had floated in guests' hands at my tenth birthday party. "I don't usually drink martinis, but it seems like a good night for one."

"I think I'll get one too," Molly said.

Noah, who didn't ordinarily drink, because he was nearly always on call, ordered straight bourbon. He kept glancing in my direction in a way that made me worried there was something on my face.

"We have something to tell you," Molly said when our drinks arrived.

"Oh?" I took a sip of my martini. It didn't taste the way that I thought it would when I was a kid. That was true of a lot of things. Coffee, cigarettes, oysters. Everything about being an adult was at least a little bit worse than it looked from a child's viewpoint.

Molly glanced at Noah, who was staring intently at his drink.

"Noah and I are in love," she said.

I giggled. It was the only reasonable reaction to such a joke.

"With me?"

"No, with each other."

It might've been an effect of the candlelight, but she looked almost gleeful. She was so unlike the Molly I thought I knew, the Molly who came off as meek until her shell was cracked. I considered myself to be a good judge of character. After all, I'd detected the wrongness within my parents before anyone else had. There hadn't been anything sour or vindictive in Molly, or at least I hadn't thought there was. The possibility that I'd been mistaken made me panic.

Meanwhile, Noah was somehow shrinking, his body deflating like an air mattress over the course of a night.

I giggled again. The sound irritated me, but I couldn't stop myself.

"What are you talking about?" I asked.

"We've wanted to tell you for a while now. I swear, we didn't mean for it to happen. We ran into each other at a bar. We were drunk and, well . . ." Molly's voice trailed off as she waited for me to put the pieces together. She had the tone of someone pretending to be apologetic, which I was well acquainted with from all the reality shows that we'd watched together. *I'm sorry if I made you feel that way, but I was being my authentic self.*

"Noah doesn't go to bars. He's always at work." I lost confidence in the words as they came out of my mouth. I was operating in a dream space, where I wasn't sure what was real. It seemed strange that my arms were still connected to my body, that I was able to maintain my hold on the glass.

"There are things that he doesn't tell you," Molly said.

I looked at Noah, who was now the size of a mouse. I couldn't figure out why I'd ever thought him tall.

"Did you forget how to speak?" I asked.

I'd never seen him like that before. He usually had the obnoxious confidence of a man with a degree in how bodies worked.

"Sorry, Lexie," he whispered into his bourbon.

"That's it? That's all you have? Your job that involves telling patients that they're dying, and you can't look me in the eyes and tell me that you've been cheating on me?"

I stared him down. He refused to meet my gaze.

"This is a joke, right? One of those pranks? Well, you got me. I'm so sad, boo-hoo. You're having an affair, are deeply in love, all that. Can we skip to the end, where you tell me that none of this is real, and then celebrate my birthday?"

Noah's head shot up like someone had just stuck a needle in his side.

"It's your birthday?"

His eyes were red. Had he been crying? I hadn't noticed.

"Of course it's my birthday. That's why we're here. This is my birthday dinner."

Noah looked at Molly.

"Did you know?" he asked.

"Yeah, I mean, I guess I thought it was a little weird that you wanted to tell her on her birthday, but I went along with it because that was what you wanted," she said.

Noah shook his head.

"No," he insisted. "No, I didn't know. You should've told me, Molly. I wanted to let her down gently; you knew that."

The joke was going on too long, too seriously. I needed it to end. I looked around for hidden cameras, for the rest of the party to pop out and say, *Surprise!* It wasn't the kind of thing that was ever supposed to happen with Noah. Above all else, he was supposed to be safe.

"It's better that she knows," Molly said. "Now she can get on with the rest of her life."

"Noah *is* the rest of my life," I said. I thought about the house we were going to buy, the children we were going to have. The last time I'd seen Noah's mother, she'd handed me the smallest onesie that I'd ever seen, stating that she'd found it in the store and couldn't resist. It had been an act as meaningful as when Noah had slid the engagement ring onto my finger.

"We have a wedding date, a venue. I bought a dress. It's being tailored. What about the *house?*" Noah and I had been casually house hunting for the past couple of months. He'd moved into my town house shortly after we started dating, and we'd decided that it was time to move into something bigger and jointly owned. Just the previous weekend we'd toured a suburban four-bedroom, five-bathroom house that he'd called his "dream home." For some reason, I'd thought my presence was implied within that dream.

"Lexie, I'm sorry. It's over," he said sadly.

There was a rushing in my brain. The sound of a dam lifting, a waterfall set free. They were serious, or at least Molly was. She sat with her martini glass pinched between two fingers. She looked so good. Had she lost weight? I'd thought her dress was similar to mine, and now I realized that it was exactly the same, only hers was bright red instead of purple.

I thought back to our shopping trip. She'd known. She'd directed me to buy the dress and then purchased one of her own. The whole situation had been engineered to obliterate me. Why go for a gunshot wound when you could send a bomb?

"Why are you doing this to me?" I asked.

"It's not about doing anything to you," she said. "It's about Noah and me. We're in love."

"No, you're not. I know all about love, and this isn't it."

I looked at Noah.

"You don't really want this. I know you don't. I know everything about you, Noah. We're meant to be together. The perfect couple. You might be happy with her right now, but it won't last. Trust me on that—I'm an expert. There's still time to fix this. You can leave with me, right now, the two of us. We can go home and make things right. You don't have to go with her."

He almost went with me. His body didn't move, but I could

sense that he wanted to go. At his core, Noah was a rule follower. He did what people told him to do, because historically that had worked out in his favor. He'd gotten into a good college and medical school, and had matched with a residency. He wasn't used to people delivering advice in anything less than good faith.

"Sorry, Lexie," he said again.

I wanted to claim that what I did next was an original action; however, it was something that I'd seen a character do on one of my favorite reality television shows. One of the cast members was in a fight with another cast member because she'd had a make-out session with a guy whom neither of them were dating but both had previously slept with.

"That was so shady of her," Molly had said when we watched the episode. She then clapped and cheered when the wronged woman threw wine at her castmate's face, staining her expensive outfit.

I didn't have wine, but I did have a half-drunk martini.

I stood up, wrapping my fingers around the glass, and tossed the remaining liquid at Molly's face. Something that I knew, and Noah likely didn't, was that Molly wore a lot of makeup. She'd had bad acne as a teenager, and she'd carried insecurity about that with her into her adult life. Whatever holding spray she might've applied was no match for the liquor from my glass, and lines began to streak through her foundation. My only regret was that I hadn't ordered red wine, which might've stained her cursed dress.

Molly gasped.

"Bitch!" she said.

I grabbed my jacket off the back of my chair and marched out of the restaurant. When things were particularly bad, I liked to step outside myself. I was no longer in my body, but was a woman

I was watching on a reality television show. Rather than a participant, I was a member of an audience to my own rippling pain. I narrated my life through "confessionals," in which cast members provided exposition on events depicted on-screen. *Yeah, I was definitely shocked when Noah and Molly told me they were in love. They were the two people I trusted most, and they betrayed me. You'd think it was something I'd be used to by now, but you never really adjust to being hurt by the people you love.*

The distance made the pain manageable. Performing the motions of being a strong person was almost the same as actually being one. I understood why reality television stars wore full faces of makeup while lounging around the house. They needed to appear put together even when their lives were falling apart.

2.

———

ANOTHER THING THAT I'D learned from television was that in times of crisis the appropriate action to take was to get very, very drunk. There was a bar down the street from Antonio's, a place that earlier I'd imagined we'd drunkenly stumble to for an after-party. I entered alone, a state that normally didn't bother me, but that night I felt conspicuous. I made a beeline for the bar and ordered a Long Island iced tea from the himbo bartender. I wanted to be obliterated.

I tried to think of someone I could call. A friend who would make indignant declarations on my behalf, like *How dare they! She was your best friend!* I thought of all my followers on social media, people who made comments like *So cute!* or *Send me the recipe!* when I posted pictures from my day-to-day existence. I labeled them "friends," but none of them were people I could call on in times of crisis. All they wanted from me were flattering photographs, shots of food that I'd eaten, and glimmers of my work life. They didn't want the real me. Molly was the only one who knew who I actually was and still loved me for it. Or at least I thought she'd loved me.

Before Molly and I became friends, at the age of twenty-four, I spent most of my time alone. I went out, sure. Attended parties, slept with men, had relationships that never went beyond the surface level. It was a condition that I'd adjusted to at a young age, as I was an only child and my parents weren't interested in arranging playdates or engaging with me themselves.

Everything got worse after the arrest.

Seemingly everyone knew what had happened, and avoided me as though that kind of violence might be contagious. I spent my time watching television and curating an online presence that allowed no one to know who I was or what had happened between my parents. To my followers, it appeared I was living a cool and fun life full of friends who were just out of the frame. In reality, I was nearly always by myself.

When I turned eighteen, I changed my name and went to college in a faraway state, where no one had ever heard of Peter and Lydia Schwartz. I was good at making acquaintances, but I still didn't have a best friend the way that the women I watched on television did. While the other students longed for sex and romance, I was envious of the women who got ready for parties together, held back one another's hair when they drank too much, and confided their deepest, darkest secrets to one another. I tried joining clubs, going to exercise classes, and inserting myself into conversations with women I liked from afar, but I struggled to get past a surface-level relationship. My peers told me stories about themselves, and when I opened my mouth to reciprocate, nothing emerged. They were, I realized, unwilling to give themselves away to someone who couldn't do the same in return.

That all changed when I met Molly.

Molly and I met in a group exercise class. She was new to fitness, preferring to spend her free time on the couch in front of the TV, and struggled to keep up with the other women, who looked like screen-printed copies of one another, down to their matching outfits. After class, everyone went to a café to drink green juice together. Molly and I were never invited. I couldn't figure out what I was doing wrong. I wore the same outfits as them, did my hair the same way. A couple of them even watched some of the same television shows as me, but gave curt responses when I tried to engage them in discussion about them. I thought of friendship as a code I needed to break. If I tried enough combinations, then eventually they'd let me in.

"Do you want to go for coffee?" I asked Molly in the locker room one day when I noticed her staring longingly in the direction of the other women.

She turned toward me. The eagerness in her expression nearly broke me in two.

"Yes, I'd love to," she said.

Based on what I'd previously witnessed, I'd expected Molly to be shy, but she started talking the moment we sat down.

"Can we talk about how snotty everyone in our class is?" Molly said. I was surprised by the force in her voice and reconsidered my earlier judgment of meekness. She was also cuter outside of the exercise class setting, with big blue eyes and fashionable clothing.

"Oh my gosh, I thought it was just me," I told her. I'd put so much of my energy into trying to get the women to like me that I was excited by the opportunity to vent.

"They act like they're superior to everyone because they're in good shape," Molly said.

"Don't let them fool you. Those matching sets they like to wear cover up a lot of flaws," I replied. "Why d'you think I bought them?"

"And what's with the green juice? It tastes like grass, in my opinion."

"Ugh, yes. They're scared to eat food."

"That's because they don't have a personality outside of their bodies. I don't know what they're going to do when they get old."

As it turned out, a shared focus of dislike was a solid basis for a friendship.

The following week, the two of us got drunk at a tequila bar, where we discovered that we had a lot in common. Molly also had a penchant for romantic comedies and reality shows about women who were wealthy disasters.

"I love all the *Real Housewives* franchises, *Love Island*, *Love Is Blind*—you name it," she told me. "I used to be embarrassed about the things that I liked. Then I realized that all the things we're supposed to hide, all the stuff we're supposed to feel guilty about liking, are things that are geared toward women. It's so stupid. That's why I get so mad about the women in our exercise class. Society pressures us into being these perfect little things, and that's just not who I am, you know?"

Yes, yes. I did know. I'd spent so many years of my life trying to fit in that it was freeing to be around someone so open. Suddenly, we were spending all our time together. It was the friendship version of a whirlwind romance. We cooked healthy meals, and then splurged on pints of ice cream while catching up on our favorite shows. We quit our original exercise class and tried out gyms across the city, none of which could compete with the seductive draw of the couch. We got second piercings in our earlobes, and I was Molly's caretaker when she got her wisdom teeth removed. I finally had the kind of friendship that I'd always longed for, the kind that I'd seen on TV. I told her about what had happened with my parents, because telling secrets to each other was what friends did. Unlike the kids in my youth, she didn't judge me.

"That must've been so hard," she said, then hugged me and insisted that we eat a pint of ice cream.

Our relationship changed after I met Noah. By that point, Molly and I had been friends for three years. She was with me when Noah and I met, because she was nearly always with me. We were at a bar, drinking cocktails, something pink and girly, when Noah and his friends walked in. Molly watched the way that my head swiveled to follow his form across the room.

"You like him," she said.

I wasn't usually shy, but something about Noah made me that way. He was so wholesome, like a loaf of bread, with his blond hair and preppy style, which I would later learn was out of apathy more than anything else.

"He's cute, I guess," I replied.

"Let's get closer," Molly said, grabbing my hand.

I could hear them talking.

"I had this one patient today who was so difficult. She kept interrupting me to tell me that I didn't understand," one woman said.

"I had one of those last week," a man replied.

From their conversation, I pieced together that they worked in the medical field.

"I think he's a doctor," I whispered to Molly. I wanted him so badly that I began to feel physically ill. It made me uncomfortable to desire things that only other people could give me, because my childhood had taught me that it was best to stick to things that I could provide for myself.

"Talk to him," Molly urged.

"No."

Noah wasn't like the other men I went for. The muscular guys with their slicked-back hair who avoided committed relationships like they were a venereal disease. Sex was easy. Sex meant that I didn't have to think about my parents' relationship, even though deep down I longed for that kind of romance. Noah, I correctly identified, was a boyfriend guy. I'd later learn that he hadn't been single for longer than a month since he was thirteen. Unlike me, he'd never been alone in his life.

Molly didn't care about the psychoanalytic reasoning that held me back. She was my best friend, which meant that she was my wing-woman in dating, and she gave me no choice in the matter by shoving me in the back hard enough that I fell down right in front of Noah.

"Ow," I cried out involuntarily.

It irked me when female protagonists in books described themselves as hopelessly clumsy and yet men were drawn to them like bees to honey. Men, I thought, wanted graceful women with legs that extended to the sky. That was until Molly pushed me in front of Noah and made him love me.

"Are you okay?" he asked, rushing to my side. "I'm a doctor. Does anything hurt?"

His opening line was technically a lie—he was a first-year resident rather than a full-fledged doctor. The difference didn't matter to me in that moment, as my ankle really hurt.

Noah insisted on taking me to urgent care because Molly was too drunk to drive. We bonded in the waiting room of the clinic, where Noah told me why he wanted to become a doctor ("I wanted to help people; plus, the paycheck doesn't hurt") and I told him about my favorite romantic comedies ("*When Harry Met Sally*. Also, it's become cool to hate on *Love Actually*, but I think that it hits a lot of good notes"). I almost resented it when the nurse called me back, because I wanted to spend more time talking.

As it turned out, I'd fractured my ankle in the fall, a break that would require surgery and a several-weeks-long recovery. Surgery was difficult for people without spouses or family members to act as caregivers, but Noah took up the role without needing to be asked.

"You know, you don't have to do this," I told him.

"I know," he replied. "I'm doing it because I want to."

He learned my favorite Starbucks order, and watched episodes of reality television next to me in bed. When I started physical therapy, he helped me practice the motions. We practiced other things too, hours spent between the sheets that had nothing to do with healing. By the time I was walking without a cast, Noah and I were in a committed relationship.

It wasn't lost on me that our meeting was like something out of one of my beloved romantic comedies—the clumsy woman falling into the arms of the handsome doctor. It seemed a side note that Molly was the one who had pushed me.

Sometimes I thought that Molly regretted setting the two of us up, because it took part of me away from her. There were nights when she wanted to hang out after Noah was off work and I prioritized my time with him. When we were together, I was distracted by his texts on my phone. When I complained about him she seemed to relish it, happily bringing me pints of ice cream while I vented. That was, she liked it until she took him away from me.

I was sitting at the bar, sipping my Long Island iced tea, when a man approached me. He was handsome, the kind of guy I'd gone for before I met Noah. He wore a black sweater that flattered his muscular chest. He had a scar that cut through one of his eyebrows; on a lesser man it might've been a flaw, but it served only to make him more appealing. I smoothed out the wrinkles in my sparkling dress. There was no situation so bad that it made me entirely vacate my vanity.

"Hi," he said.

I knew that, logically, I should be wary of people who approached lonely women in bars. However, it was my birthday, and my best friend and fiancé had just announced that they were having an affair, both of which allowed for some socially acceptable recklessness.

"Hi," I replied.

"My friends and I saw you standing over here all alone and thought you might like some company."

He gestured toward a group of people at the dartboards. The men were all almost as attractive as the one standing next to me, and the women were dressed in revealing outfits of a type that I was used to seeing primarily on reality dating shows. It felt good that despite his company, the man was drawn to me.

"As a matter of fact," I told him, "it's my birthday."

"Is it? Happy birthday. What's a girl like you doing alone on her birthday?"

I wasn't ordinarily a candid person. While I had a penchant for imagining myself as a reality show cast member who displayed her truths for all to see, my life contained no room for confession. I told Molly things, and occasionally Noah, and everyone else received the filtered versions of events that I presented on social media. However, there was something about the man in front of me that was like a camera in my face. He made me want to spill all my secrets, with no regard for the future—or maybe that was the alcohol coursing through my veins.

"My fiancé invited me out to dinner and then told me that he's leaving me for my best friend," I said. The words tasted rancid. They made me want a shot.

"You're joking," he replied. He looked me up and down, trying to figure out what about me might inspire such an act. What he didn't realize was that such things weren't visible on the skin.

"Dead serious."

"Wow. Oh wow. That's a terrible thing to happen on your birthday."

"It's okay," I assured him. "He's going to come crawling back to me."

The words surprised both of us, but as I said them, I recognized the truth embedded within. I couldn't erase from my brain the Noah I thought I knew. The one who sent me flowers, who brought me breakfast in bed when I was hungover, who nursed me back to health when my bones broke. People didn't change so dramatically overnight, and neither did my emotions.

There was a character on one of my favorite reality shows whose boyfriend had cheated on her and she'd taken him back. They were engaged a year later, followed by marriage, and had a baby on the way. I hadn't understood it at the time. Molly and I had yelled at the screen.

"I would never stay with someone who cheated on me," Molly said.

I got it now. I'd first realized sitting in the waiting room on the night we met that Noah and I were going to get married. No one had ever *cared* for me like that before. When I was a child, my parents had once neglected to take me to the doctor for a UTI, and the infection had nearly spread to my other organs when I was finally seen. Noah recognized my needs. He provided food when I was hungry and medicine when I was sick. On top of that, we'd made the down payment on a wedding venue, my dress was being tailored, we had appointments to meet with caterers and bakers, and we'd even found our dream house. Forgiveness would not come easily or quickly. However, I would let him tend to the wounds he'd left on my heart the same way that he'd tended to my ankle.

Things with Molly and Noah wouldn't last. They weren't meant to be, not like Noah and I were. He would grow tired of her and then come crawling back to me, begging for forgiveness. It wasn't ideal, but then, love never was, was it? It was the difficult times that made the story.

"You would take someone back after they did that to you?" the handsome man asked.

"I've lived through worse," I told him.

He moved his eyes across my face, staring at me the way that I'd stared at spoons as a child, trying to bend them with brainpower alone. I wondered what my cheekbones were telling him, what truths he could glean from my eyelashes.

"Let me help you forget about it for a night," he said.

He held out his hand, an invitation. I stood up from the stool and took it. It was as though he were asking me to the dance floor, his feet leading the moves.

"Okay," I said. "A night."

That was all it was supposed to be, a single night with a handsome man—a naïve assumption. All my television viewing should've helped me realize that a chance encounter with a charming stranger was always the beginning of the story rather than the end.

3.

—

THE HANDSOME MAN AND I took a shot before he brought me to meet his friends. The lick of salt, the sting of tequila, the lime squeezed between my teeth . . . Everything was so much more physical when I couldn't tolerate being inside my own head.

His friends were the kind of beautiful people who were friendly because they'd had no reason ever to be mean. They accepted me like I'd always been one of them. I met the women, whose names I quickly forgot, and the other men, who gently vied for my attention with the knowledge that I already knew who I wanted. At some point the handsome man gave me his name, but it seemed unimportant. I had no intention of going home with him, even as something so simple as a brush of his hands across my waist made me feel electrified. I didn't want to write about him in my diary. I wanted to make Noah feel like shit for cheating on me. Besides, it'd been so long since a man other than Noah had touched me that probably any good-looking man would've elicited such a reaction.

I liked the feeling of being one of the gang, even if it was for only a night. I won a game of darts, or they let me win. Someone bought a round of shots, and included me within their ranks without needing to be asked to. When he wasn't directly next to me, I caught the handsome man staring in my direction as though he was captivated by my beauty. I stared back. I wasn't scared of a little eye contact.

The gathering at the first bar was a pregame. They hadn't even had dinner yet, which was good, because I'd marched out of my birthday dinner before my entrée arrived. I lamented missing out on the seafood linguine that I'd spent the day anticipating.

No matter. I followed the handsome man and his friends down the street to a steak house.

"It's on me," he said as I perused the menu. The two of us were like prom dates, except I hadn't attended my prom.

I ordered a bloody steak the size of my head, and a baked potato. I didn't even like steak, but I liked the feeling of sawing into the meat with the knife, the pink juices melding with the butter from the potato. There were cocktails too, of course, an endless stream that appeared without my asking.

"It's my birthday," I said as I shoved meat into my mouth.

"It's my birthday," I told the server who brought out their coworkers to sing "Happy Birthday" over molten chocolate cake.

"It's my birthday," I said to the bouncer when I handed him my ID at our next stop.

"It's my birthday," I repeated to the handsome man before he gave me a kiss.

Somehow, I found myself standing on a table and dancing. There were a lot of factors that worked against me as a dancer. I was gangly, with long limbs and a flat ass. I'd never had a good sense of rhythm, and I'd been unable to convince my mother to sign me up for ballet classes. However, dancing was a lot like being hot, in that confidence was the majority of the battle.

"It's her birthday!" the handsome man shouted.

"Woo!" everyone cheered.

When thoughts of Noah and Molly entered my brain, I shoved them inside that little box I kept in my chest for my darkest memories, the same place within me where my mother resided. No one watching would've suspected what had happened earlier in the night. All anyone would see was a woman having the time of her life.

The handsome man easily lifted me off the table, as if he carried bodies around as a job, and set me on my feet. I ground my butt into his crotch as his hands ran their way over my hips. I almost felt bad that I wasn't going to fuck him. I almost reconsidered.

Somehow, I found myself in the back of an Uber. There weren't enough seats, so I sprawled across several men, none of whom seemed to mind. My head was in the handsome man's lap. He gazed down at me like I was a gift.

"Where are we going?" I asked.

"His house," the handsome man said. He gestured to the man whose legs held my feet. I was positive that I'd never seen him before. He must've joined the group later in the evening.

"Cool," I said.

It didn't occur to me that I might be in danger. I'd always been good at reading people, and I didn't get the sense that any of these people might want to cause me harm.

Somehow, I found myself in a bathroom, snorting cocaine with one of the most beautiful women I'd ever seen. She was so gorgeous that she transcended any jealousy I might've had. I wanted to touch her face.

"Where did you come from?" I asked.

"Oh, Lexie." She laughed. "You're so funny."

"Is it still my birthday?"

"It's your birthday for as long as you want it to be," she said.

She paused in the bathroom doorway. Maybe, I thought, she could become my new best friend. I already missed Molly. I wanted to tell her about my night.

"Are you going to hook up with him?" she asked.

It was implied that she was talking about the handsome man.

"No," I said. "I have to get married."

A look of confusion crossed her face. I offered no clarification.

"He likes you. I can tell," she told me, and disappeared into the night.

Somehow, I found myself in a hot tub. I was wearing a bikini that didn't belong to me. I was sitting in the handsome man's lap. I was pleased to be there. Glamorous reality TV stars were frequently getting into hot tubs after a night out.

"What do you do for work?" the handsome man asked me.

"I'm a matchmaker," I replied.

"Like on those Netflix shows?" he asked.

It was a common reaction when I told people what I did. Matchmaking was becoming a lost art, with everyone dependent on dating apps or, worse, alone forever. We could conceive of love only as something mediated through a screen. What I did was real and important. There were so many lonely people in the world.

That was the other reason why I was so confident that Noah and I would eventually end up together. Not only was I confident in the strength of our bond; I had professional qualifications that meant I knew when two people were right for each other and when they weren't.

"It's kind of like those shows," I told him, though I thought they failed to capture the nuances of the field. Matching people was about more than pairing people who looked good for each other on paper. Most people, in actuality, were unable to voice the traits that they desired in a partner. Matching was about careful cultivation, more like growing a garden than like making a sandwich.

"You wouldn't necessarily see my clients on TV," I continued.

"Why?" he asked. "Are they ugly?"

I smiled.

"No, they're not ugly. They're . . . well, they're special."

"What does that mean? 'Special'?"

"I'm a matchmaker for psychopaths."

"Psychopaths?" The handsome man raised his eyebrows. Everyone in the hot tub leaned in closer. I liked the way that they were looking at me, the same way that Molly and I perched on the edge of the couch, careful not to rustle our bags of food, when a particularly heated scene was playing out on one of our favorite shows. The cast members were so used to being on camera that they didn't acknowledge its presence, but surely they knew when it was their time in the spotlight, just as I knew I was the center of attention in that hot tub when I invoked that word: "psychopath."

Technically, I wasn't supposed to use that term. First and foremost, it wasn't listed in the *Diagnostic and Statistical Manual of Mental Disorders*, the manual used by mental health professionals. "Psychopath" was what people called their exes, their shitty bosses, or their estranged parents. Secondly, my boss, Serena, insisted that we weren't in the field of diagnosing people. Just because we knew intimate details about our clients' lives—including those revealed by an intensive intake questionnaire that was capable of detecting a variety of mental health issues—didn't mean we were allowed to label them in that way. Finally, it would be catastrophic if clients knew how they were being sorted. *Yes, your matchmaker is Lexie, who works with all the psychopaths who come to us looking for love.*

When I interviewed for the position, I didn't know who my clients would be. I'd applied to Better Love after burning out in a series of corporate jobs that paid well but were intellectually and emotionally unsatisfying. I was bored in the office, spending most of my time shopping online rather than doing work. Worse, most of my coworkers were bros who loved wearing name-brand fleeces with the company's logo on the front. They talked incessantly about the women they'd fucked, while simultaneously being hugely uncomfortable around women, members of the LGBTQ+ community, and especially people who weren't white. On occasion, they unsuccessfully tried to proposition me for sex.

When I saw the job ad that called for someone "devoted to helping others find love," with "experience in psychology," I knew that I was meant for the position, the same way that I knew Noah and I were meant to be together. Moments spent watching romantic comedies with my mother were some of the only cherished moments of my childhood, and I figured that becoming a matchmaker would be the equivalent of immersing myself in one of those films.

"We have clients with all sorts of backgrounds," Serena explained during the interview.

I was taken by her immediately. She was one of those older women who didn't let age stop them from looking hot and glamorous.

Even in the wintertime she favored shoes with heels so sharp that they could pierce the skin.

"Some of them have been married before; some have physical disabilities; others have children," she elaborated. "What they all have in common is that they're tired of dating the way that it exists today. We do two things at Better Love. We assist people in presenting the best version of themselves, the one most capable of receiving love, and we help match them with their person. The role that you would be filling—well, that's for our clients who have certain personality traits."

"Psychopaths," Oliver confirmed later. "You're working with psychopaths."

Oliver was the LGBTQ+ specialist, and the keeper of Better Love lore. The story that Serena told of the founding was this: her son was having difficulty finding a girlfriend using dating apps. He would message with someone for a couple of weeks, only for her to disappear when he suggested meeting up in person; or she'd go on a date, expect him to pay for the meal, and then never talk to him again. Serena didn't get it. Her son was educated, good-looking, and well-dressed. She decided that the apps were the problem. The algorithms couldn't predict what he wanted or needed out of a partner, not the way that she could.

On paper, Serena was a stay-at-home mom. In practice, she was the genius behind her husband's successful businesses. Starting a matchmaking company was a no-brainer. She would find her son the love of his life and, in the process, make some money. She hadn't anticipated how large the need would be. There were so many people who were fed up with dating in the modern world. They were tired of people who didn't look like their pictures, or who were attractive without any personality behind the pretty face. They were exhausted from all the dates they'd gone on, all the times that they'd been ghosted, and felt guilty about the times that they'd ghosted others themselves. Surely there was an easier way.

The part of the story that Serena left out, the portion that was later filled in by Oliver, was the origin of the intake questionnaire, and with it, my specialty. Though she disliked the format of dating apps, she saw the value of getting to know clients before they ever walked through the door, and thus, she devised the intake questionnaire. Serena wasn't a psychologist. She was a businesswoman and mom, and the questionnaire, like much of the operation, was built from her intuition. She borrowed language from various personality quizzes, and somewhere along the line she came across the Hare Psychopathy Checklist. Things like *Do you frequently lie?* and *Did you frequently get into trouble as a child?* were scattered among queries such as *Do you prefer dogs or cats?*

Serena's son was one of her test subjects for the intake questionnaire. When she first saw the results and realized how closely his answers aligned with psychopathy, her first reaction was denial. It was difficult to accept that the person she'd birthed, whom she cherished above everyone else, might reside in a different kind of emotional reality. The more she thought about it, the more it made sense. Her son, though very bright, struggled to hold down jobs for long periods of time. He made friends easily and lost them just as fast. On several occasions, she'd overheard him making the kinds of cutting remarks that could destroy a person, with seemingly no understanding of how they were hurtful. Suddenly, his difficulties in dating made more sense.

Because he was her son, and because she loved him, Serena refused to see the questionnaire results as a reason why her son shouldn't have a relationship. Many psychopaths had successful relationships, or so she assumed. From her research, she learned that a lot of professionals ranked highly on the psychopathy scale. She decided that rather than rejecting clients with these traits, it was simply a matter of tailoring her services to such people. That was where I came in.

"I'm looking for someone strong, someone who isn't easily manipulated," she told me during the interview.

I described my previous work experience, the corporate bros, my psychology minor, how for many years I'd thought I was going to become a therapist. I told her about watching romantic comedies with my mother. Saying the words was a pointless exercise. We both knew that she was going to hire me. Every experience of my life up until that point had been leading to that moment. Serena was all about gut instinct, and her gut told her that I was right for the job.

Three years in, my specialty had proved to be in high demand. That was the thing about psychopaths: they were everywhere. In every racial and ethnic group, sexual orientation, and gender. There was no single identity that could inoculate a person against that brain chemistry. I even helped her match her son, and he'd since married, in a lavish ceremony.

I didn't explain all that to the handsome man and his friends. I just smiled as they looked at me with rapt attention, like I was a guest on a podcast.

"Are there a lot of psychopaths out there looking for love?" asked a man across the hot tub. I couldn't quite tell beneath the bubbles, but I was pretty sure that he wasn't wearing a swimsuit.

I leaned forward, and everyone else mimicked my movement, so that our heads gathered in the middle of the tub in a meeting of the minds.

"There are some estimates that as much as twenty-five percent of the population could be categorized as psychopaths."

One of the women snorted.

"I think I've dated a few of your clients," she said.

The other woman nodded knowingly. That was a common reaction. Men were constantly calling women crazy, hysterical, criticizing them for their outsized emotions; whereas men were described as psychopaths for their seeming lack of feeling, for the games that they played to woo sexual conquests. Little did they know that women were just as likely to be psychopaths as men; they were just better at masking it. Men were so scared of women with too many feelings that they never stopped to consider what happened when there were none at all.

"That's so interesting. You're so interesting," the handsome man said.

He kissed my neck. He had soft lips, and a body that made me want to relent, but he wasn't Noah. I pushed him away and took another shot of tequila.

SOMEHOW, I FOUND MYSELF IN THE BACK OF A CAR. THE CROWD had been reduced to just me and the handsome man. There was a map loaded on the driver's GPS. I didn't recognize the destination. I wasn't afraid, though maybe I should've been.

"You know, this isn't the worst birthday I've ever had," I told him.

"What was the worst birthday you've ever had?" he asked.

We weren't wearing seat belts. I was so deep into liquor and riding in a car with a near stranger that safety precautions seemed ridiculous.

"I was nine. My parents forgot. I spent the whole day waiting for them to give me a cake, presents, anything at all. They didn't come home that night. They did that a lot—left me by myself. They only realized what had happened when I told them a few days later. They gave me a puppy as an apology, and then gave the puppy away when they decided it was too much work to take care of it. They made it up to me the next year though."

"I can't believe you've had people forget your birthday on more than one occasion," he said. "You're such an unforgettable person, Lexie."

He was so good-looking that I almost disliked him, because I felt manipulated by his face. There was a kind of pleasure in knowing that no matter what he said or did, he couldn't have me. I was already reserved for someone else, even if that person had temporarily left me for my best friend.

Somehow, we ended up in a hotel room. I didn't remember checking in or walking down the hallway. Extreme intoxication was the closest I got to teleporting. We weren't having sex. All of our clothes were still on and we were sitting on the edge of the bed.

"I had a really messed-up childhood," I told him.

He laughed.

"Who didn't? No one makes it to adulthood unscathed."

"No, it was really, really bad," I insisted.

"What happened?" he asked. His eyes roved my face, traced the shape of my lips.

"I can't tell you."

"Why not?"

"Because you'll look at me differently, and I want you to keep looking at me exactly as you are right now."

"What if I tell you my secret?" he asked.

He had a face that was difficult to resist, and as much as I knew there were no trauma Olympics, I couldn't help but make childhood trauma into a competition.

"Fine," I agreed. "I'll tell you mine if you tell me yours."

I told him stuff then that even Noah didn't know. The thing about heartbreak is that it reveals the ways in which all tragedy is connected. I was wounded as a child, and those wounds, though long stitched shut, continued to impact the way that I moved through the world. Damaged tissue wasn't the same as healthy skin. The final girl in a horror movie could never be the same thing as a romantic-comedy protagonist.

At that point I blacked out. It was the alcohol or it was the honesty. I didn't remember what he'd told me or what I'd said after that. There were things people knew, things that had been reported to the public, stories that I'd told Molly, and then there were things that were buried so deep that a shovel was needed even to penetrate the surface of my trauma. My memory understood what reality television did, which was that life required some editing in order to be palatable. There was no suspense or mystery when viewers were given all the information at once. If only I'd understood the consequences of what we'd said, how our utterances were incantations of death, then I might've just fucked him and been done with it.

4.

I WAS ALONE WHEN I woke in the morning, my mouth so dry
that it ached. I wore only underwear, my sequined dress abandoned in a puddle on the floor. Despite my near nudity, I was
certain by the way that my body still hungered that the handsome
man and I hadn't slept together. People should get awards for that
kind of restraint.

I wasn't embarrassed by my actions. People in rom-coms and
reality television treated wild nights out as a kind of therapy. The
worse things were in their lives, the more they deserved recklessness. They got drunk and kissed people. They got drunk and
screamed at the sky. They smashed plates and went on adventures
late into the night. Irresponsibility was a rite of passage in times of
tragedy. Though it would've been preferable if I hadn't spilled my
deepest, darkest secrets to a man whose name I couldn't remember.

What surprised me was how ineffective my wild night had
been. I'd hoped that the experience would be a kind of cleansing,
after which I would wake with a new kind of clarity, and instead,

my head was pounding and there were several bruises on my legs—probably due to my attempts at dancing. Worst of all was my heart, which ached so badly that I examined my breasts, looking for signs of trauma.

I wanted to text Molly and tell her what had happened. Outside of the handsome man, she was the only person in my life who knew the truth about my childhood, or at least the amount that was safe for me to tell. I wanted to cuddle up next to Noah, have him stroke my hair and tell me to drink some electrolytes to cure my hangover. I couldn't do either of those things, because the two people I'd loved and trusted most in the world had betrayed me in order to be with each other.

I'd never been heartbroken before, at least not by a man. Prior to Noah, I'd avoided serious relationships. It was safer to keep my distance. But I wanted what I saw in movies. The doting husband. Cute kids who performed in school plays. The mother-in-law who said things like *You can call me Mom*. That was one of the things I hadn't previously understood about breakups, that in addition to losing the person, you were also losing the entire universe they existed in. It had been only twelve hours, and already Noah's absence hurt so badly that I longed to crawl out of my skin.

Infuriatingly, unlike for an external injury, there was no Band-Aid that I could apply, no healing ointment. All those scientific advances, and still there was no cast for a broken heart. My own body was out of my control, and the only way I could conceive of to fix it, regardless of whatever forgiveness and humiliation it might entail, was getting Noah back.

I found my purse on the floor, my phone inside of it. A small relief. On the dresser there was a key card with the name of the hotel, and I called the front desk.

"Can you tell me the credit card on file for this room?" I asked.

The receptionist rattled off an unfamiliar train of digits.

"Thank you. And what's the checkout time? Late checkout? Great. Can you transfer me to room service?"

I ordered a full breakfast and enough coffee for two. I took a shower while I waited for the food to arrive, and dressed myself in one of the robes hanging in the bathroom.

I ate in bed, not caring whether I got crumbs on the sheets, and looked through my phone to see if there was any evidence of what had happened the previous night. There were a couple of "happy birthday" texts, including one from Noah's mother. I took that as a sign that he hadn't told her what he was planning on doing.

Thank you! I replied. I wasn't going to be the one to tell her. Noah was going to have to do that himself.

Noah's mother and I were close. That's what I told people. *We're close*, I said smugly. A man was the goal, yes, but his family was equally important. There was a whole genre of movies about that. The son bringing the daughter home for the holidays. The awkward interactions, followed by eventual welcoming. When he first brought me home after six months of dating, I'd prepared myself for the familial hazing that the screen had warned me of.

It never came. Noah's mother screamed when she saw me.

"You're so cute!" she said.

"I can't wait for grandchildren!" came out of her mouth only ten minutes later.

I soon figured out that I'd confused my genres. She wasn't a mother from *Meet the Parents* or *The Family Stone*. She was from a Hallmark movie. All she'd ever aspired to was having babies and learning how to make the perfect casserole, and now that she'd completed all that, she was ready to pamper some grandchildren.

I was fascinated by her outfits, which looked like they were from a J.Crew catalog spread. The way that she seemed never to swear or raise her voice, even though she had four children. How she always left at least half her meal on her plate, claiming that she was "so full" despite having spent hours in the kitchen. She was the opposite of my own mother, who wore salacious outfits that showed off her breasts, never cooked, and didn't hesitate to take the last bite of food off a shared appetizer plate.

It wasn't that I wanted Noah's mother to replace my own. No, actually, that was exactly what I wanted. I wanted her to adopt me as a daughter. I did everything I could to be like a woman raised in her home. I learned how to cook. I bought a series of conservative sweaters, which Noah found oddly sexual. What really made us click was the one thing that she and my mother had in common—she too liked romantic comedies. She disliked the violence on the news, she said. She enjoyed feel-good stories in which two people met each other and fell in love.

We watched those movies, the ones I'd originally viewed with my mother, and it was almost the same. The bowl of popcorn was smaller, her laughter quieter. Sometimes she cried, which was something that my mother never did. I struggled to pay attention to the films. I spent the whole time thinking *Is this it? Have I escaped from all the trauma that my mother wrought?*

It pained me to think of Noah telling her that he'd left me for Molly. A small, irrational part of me hoped that she would choose me over her son. After all, he was the one who'd cheated on me. I was innocent. I'd been faithful. I'd been the person everyone wanted me to be, someone who was deserving of love. Maybe she would convince him to get back together with me. That was the kind of thing a mom in a movie might do.

I looked at Molly's social media. She'd posted a picture of herself in her sparkling dress, the one that was identical to mine. *Celebrating!!!* said the caption. Because I was looking for it, I found ugliness in the shot. Strands of hair slightly out of place. Wrinkles beginning to form around her eyes, her smile. I wondered what she and Noah were doing, and then I made myself stop. It was best not to think about it.

Before leaving the hotel, I selected one of the selfies I'd taken the previous night. They'd taken on new significance in the hours that had passed. The person in the pictures was young and innocent—she had the face of someone who had never heard her best friend say that she'd stolen her fiancé. I selected one, quickly edited it, and posted it on social media.

Thanks for all the birthday wishes! I captioned it. *I had the best time!!!*

There was no reason that anyone needed to know about Noah and Molly. One kind of pain was caused by what they had done to me. A second would be because of other people knowing about it, and I wanted to avoid that for as long as possible. My embarrassment over the situation was almost as sharp as the heartbreak. At least that had a relatively easy remedy—I simply needed to get Noah back before too many people knew.

I thought briefly of the handsome man, wondered where he'd disappeared to. It didn't matter. He'd served his purpose. It had been nice having a good-looking guy interested in me for the night, but now I needed to resume the path to my destiny.

Back at the town house, I set about cleaning. I put fresh sheets on the bed, helpfully popped Noah's dirty clothes into the washing machine for when he came back, and mopped the kitchen floor. Remnants of the hangover lingered in my body, but as long as I kept moving, I was able to keep the worst waves of heartbreak at bay.

Cleaning wasn't intuitive for me. My parents had never done it. Mess piled up around us until we moved and left everything behind. I still remembered the dolly that was forgotten when I was four.

"I'll buy you a new one," my mother said flippantly, and she bought me an expensive replacement that I hated.

As a result, I was weirdly protective of my belongings, unable to break the paranoia that someone might take them from me. Other people cleaned before their parents came over for visits, but I cleaned so that my house never looked like theirs. I knew how neglect could wear at things until they broke, and thus, by reading books and watching videos of women who looked like Noah's mother, I taught myself to care for my home. I still hated it. The hate was part of the point. It was the reason why I did the bulk of the tasks on Sunday, the day that I talked to my mother each week. I needed one type of unpleasantness to distract me from another.

I avoided looking at Noah's things, which was easier than it might've been with other men, as he left little decorative impression on the space around him. Before he moved in with me, he was living with two roommates who were fellow medical residents. Their house was utilitarian. They ate; they slept; they returned to work. Doctors, I'd noticed, were prone to a kind of pragmatism that could lead to an empty life. Noah moved in with me after only a few weeks of dating. All he brought with him were clothes, and gym equipment that he stored in the garage. It made sense when I visited his childhood home, where his father was a nearly invisible presence. I didn't mind, because it meant that the town house both financially and visually continued to belong to me.

It was my father's death that allowed me to buy the townhome. The money was a surprise, for a variety of reasons. I'd never thought my family was poor when I was growing up, because my parents were prone to extravagance. As a small child, I'd eaten in more five-star restaurants than most people had in their entire lives. In between such meals, however, I often went hungry. My parents were good at bringing in sums of money, and even better at spending them immediately. Neither of them could hold down a steady job for longer than a year, resorting to conning their way into the kinds of luxurious environments that they preferred. They had no retirement savings to speak of—something that would prove to be unnecessary anyway—and whatever was left in their accounts had gone to lawyers during the trial.

The only inheritance I'd received was a stack of handwritten papers with a note labeling it as my father's manifesto and stating that in the event of his passing, it was my duty to get it published. When I was twenty-one I burned all the pages without ever reading them. Some things were better left unseen.

It wasn't until years after his death that I learned about the money. It had been held up in court due to the dubious legality of its origins. I had no doubt that it had been acquired through nefarious means, but eventually it was cleared and made its way to me. I wasn't too proud to take the funds and use them on a town house, though it did cast my hunger in a new light. That there were days when I'd gone without eating, and that I frequently wore clothes that were ill fitting and that my classmates judged weird, was a *choice*.

The sum wasn't so much that I could afford something huge or centrally located, and unfortunately my parents' method of charming their way into housing didn't work on mortgage brokers, but the town house, with its gray walls and neutral floors, was nice in a way that appealed to me. The normalness of it made me feel normal.

"A town house," my mother scoffed when I told her. "Those places have no personality. You should've invested in something classy."

I didn't bring up the roach-infested motel that we briefly lived in when I was seven. There was no point in rehashing the past with someone who refused to acknowledge the wrongs that she'd done.

I was cleaning the bathroom when the call came in. All the calls started the same way, with a robotic voice notifying me that I was receiving a call from the Northport Correctional Facility.

"My darling?" My mother's voice came through the line.

She rarely referred to me by my name, and she absolutely refused to call me by my preferred nickname of Lexie, because, she said, it sounded "trashy." Instead, she used pet names—"honey" or "sweet" or "darling." A stranger might have interpreted it as a sign of affection, but I knew better. It was simply another method of erasure.

"Hi." I struggled with what to call her. When she was arrested, I was still young enough that I called her "Mommy." In the rare moments when I mentioned her to other people, I called her "my mother." Usually I avoided referring to her at all.

"You sound stressed," she said.

I brought the phone into the living room and sat on the couch. The nice thing about Noah's absence was that it meant I didn't have to hide while I talked to my mother. On the Sundays when he wasn't at work or the gym, I'd frequently found myself sitting in my car, in the garage, so that he wouldn't be able to hear her voice through the phone speaker. I wasn't sure if I was worried that she would scare him or woo him, but either way was a situation to be avoided.

"I'm fine," I told her. "Just an ordinary Sunday."

"And how is your fiancé?"

"He's good. Great. At work."

There were no circumstances in which I would admit to my mother what Noah and Molly had done to me. Though she'd never spoken to him, my mother was obsessed with Noah. She called him "your fiancé" because she didn't know his name. I avoided telling her too many details about my life, because I worried what she might do with them. She didn't know which state I lived in or what I did for work. Sometimes I was tempted to tell her that I was a matchmaker, because I thought she would be charmed. *I still think about watching movies with you. I've made helping people find love my entire life, as though I can replicate the experience.* I resisted only because I knew my mother's penchant for destroying people, a hobby that went past murder.

I hadn't intended even to tell her that I was engaged. I'd made it through an entire year of dating before the word "boyfriend" had slipped out during a conversation, and she'd latched on, wanting to know everything about him, or at minimum, everything that I was willing to give.

"A doctor!" she'd exclaimed.

"Tall!"

"Attractive!"

She'd treated him like an accomplishment, something greater

than my degree or career. She filled in the gaps, what I refused to tell her, with plotlines from romantic comedies, sometimes confusing my life with the lives of the protagonists of *Love Actually* or *27 Dresses*. I never corrected her.

When she found out I was engaged, her tone was almost chastising.

"Finally," she'd said. "I can't believe it took you so long." And then she proceeded to ask me a million questions that I couldn't answer about the wedding.

I knew how she would react if I told her that Noah had left me for my best friend. She'd think I was pathetic. *How could you let that happen?* she would say. She tended to blame me for all my misfortunes. So instead of telling her the truth, I lied.

"I picked out a wedding cake," I said.

There had been no cake. No sweetness.

"Wonderful. What kind?"

"Red velvet. I like the color."

"Chocolate is better. You should do chocolate."

From there, she launched into a monologue in which she described all the best cakes she'd ever eaten.

The blood came out of nowhere.

"A woman was stabbed today," she said, without warning.

I was silent. I'd learned that a response would only encourage her. She wanted to shock me. It was the same thing she'd done to the other mothers at school pickup when I was a kid. *Your husband looks like he has a big dick,* or *Oh, you live in that part of town? I knew someone whose sister was murdered there.* She was happiest when everyone around her was off-kilter, because it meant she held control of the situation.

"Someone got ahold of a pencil. Very resourceful. Anything

can be a knife if you want it enough, you know. It was very messy. That's the problem with inferior tools—they do the job, but it's harder to clean up after. They took her to the infirmary. We're still waiting to see if she lived."

I didn't quite trust the "someone" at the beginning of the sentence. It was a way of deflecting. *Someone* could be another inmate. *Someone* could be my mother. I'd learned to read between the lines. I could've authored a biography with all the stories that she'd told me during our phone calls over the years. At times, when I was particularly financially pressed, I was tempted by the possibility. However, I knew that my mother, in any form, shouldn't be released into the world.

I was relieved when she said, "I must go, my sweet."

"Bye."

Neither of us spoke of love. We didn't have a relationship like that.

Mothers showed up on reality television a lot. Viewers enjoyed seeing the people who created the cast members they were obsessed with. Sometimes the mothers were such a hit that their popularity surpassed that of their children. Any strife that might've existed between parent and child was concealed for the cameras. *She's my whole world*, the stars liked to say. More than their fame, their money, their looks, their mothers made me envious. I wanted a mother like that. Someone I could describe as a best friend. A relationship that was palatable enough for television outside of true crime documentary.

When I said that my mother was my world, what I meant was that I couldn't escape her. She tinged everything I did, regardless of the distance between us.

Though we were separated by a multitude of states, part of me was convinced that my mother could see my every movement. I worried that she somehow knew what had happened with Noah and Molly, knew that I had spent my night blacked out with strangers.

You're such a disappointment, I could hear her saying long after we ended the call. It was stupid how much I still wanted to please her. At what age, I wanted to know, did a child stop longing for their parents' love?

5.

THERE WAS SOMETHING UNSETTLING about the ordinariness of taking a seat in the conference room for the Monday-morning intake meeting. No one knew what had happened with Noah and Molly. All anyone saw was what I wanted them to see on social media—a smiling woman dressed for a night out with the love of her life.

I took two doughnuts with heart-shaped sprinkles from the box in the middle of the table. It was still January, but in the field of matchmaking, every day was a kind of Valentine's Day.

"How was your birthday?" Oliver asked, sliding into the seat next to me.

"It was great," I told him as I took a bite of the first doughnut. "Noah got reservations at a fancy restaurant. I went out afterward, drank too much—you know."

Had I been in any other profession, I might've told my coworkers what had happened. As it was, it felt like a dentist opening her mouth to reveal teeth full of cavities. In the workplace, my successful relationship gave me a certain legitimacy that I had no desire to destroy. Besides, I figured that Noah and I would get back together in no time at all. I didn't want him to feel embarrassed at our wedding when all of my coworkers made faces at him like *I know what you did*, which Oliver, fan of gossip that he was, most certainly would.

Nicole came in next. She wore a giant red bow in her hair. I'd once heard Oliver describe her aesthetic as "love vomit."

"Did Noah get you something nice?" she asked. She was obsessed with my relationship. I assumed that was because she was bored with her loaf of a husband.

"He got me exactly what I wanted," I replied.

Nicole and I started working at Better Love at the same time. In my final interview, Serena had described the work environment as being "like a family," which appealed to me, as I had none—or at least none who were legally allowed to reside outside a correctional facility. Nicole, apparently, hadn't gotten the message, because she hated me immediately. She questioned the matches I made, the dates that I planned, and the clothes that I wore for meetings.

"Should we even be helping these people at all?" she'd asked once, wrinkling her nose at the results of the intake questionnaire for one of my new clients. It should be noted that Nicole's disdain wasn't reserved for the people on my list. She disliked anyone who fell outside her notion of "normal," which included those who were socially awkward, not conventionally good-looking, or anything she identified as being "different."

Nicole had been a cheerleader, and she'd married her high school sweetheart, Ethan, the week after she'd graduated from college. She was the kind of girl who had made my life miserable during my teenage years. The only difference was that the girls I'd gone to school with knew about my parents, and therefore felt justified in their taunts, whereas Nicole hated me just because she could.

I did my best to get my revenge through excellence, matching clients to spite Nicole, in addition to satisfying my desire to facilitate love. Sometimes, though, I found myself unable to resist gossiping about her, or taking the last remnants of coffee in the machine right before she went to pour herself some. I wasn't an angel, but I tried hard to be good enough, regardless of how the people around me were behaving.

The sweetness of the doughnut was startling. The shock of what Noah had done had knocked my senses off-kilter, a kind of emotional concussion. Everything took on an artificial quality, like I was moving through a film set.

The other matchmakers filled the remaining chairs, and Serena came in last, taking her place at the head of the table. She wore a pink power suit that she was somehow able to pull off. Her long nails clicked along the side of her coffee mug, and the scent of her trademark perfume wafted through the air. She had my favorite quality that a person could have, which was that when she entered a room, everyone turned to look.

The process at Better Love worked like this:

Clients found us from our advertisements, which lined billboards and the sides of buses, and flashed across social media as they scrolled. That was one of the things that Serena had been really smart about when she started the business. Algorithms weren't great at making people fall in love, but they could be a tool in bringing clients to us. Increasingly, we heard from people who said that their friend, cousin, whatever, had found their partner after years of hopeless dating. *Get me what they have,* they said.

Once they enrolled, they took the intake questionnaire, which helped pair them with the appropriate matchmaker, and helped said matchmaker figure out the type of person they might be most suited for. During the intake meeting, we received the new client's profile, which included their picture, the results of their intake questionnaire, and basic biographical information.

After that, we set up an in-person meeting with the client. Serena always emphasized the importance of that step. Getting the facts about someone was different from really getting to know them. She wanted us to inhabit the same air, really get a vibe. That was something that apps couldn't do. They had no sense of vibes. All they could do was rely on the information that a user provided, and people were notoriously bad at assessing themselves.

From there, we began the matching process. Each client was given one option at a time, which they could either accept or reject. If they rejected, they were given new options as available until they found someone they liked. Typically, we encouraged them to give everyone a chance. *Remember, you're here because your own judgment wasn't serving you.* If they accepted, we arranged the first date. Clients didn't have to worry about where to go, what to do, or setting boundaries, because we did all that for them. Their only responsibility was getting to know the other person. After each date, they had a check-in with their matchmaker, which sometimes occurred over the phone and sometimes in person. We weren't therapists, but we weren't entirely dissimilar. I spent a lot of time unpacking clients' fears around dedicating themselves to other people. *I think I might love him, but is it possible to love someone after only two weeks?*

When things didn't work out after a date, we gave clients new matches until they did. We didn't have a 100 percent success rate, of course. There were people who were unwilling to engage fully, or found their matches lacking regardless of whom we presented them with. However, our percentage for long-term coupling was significantly higher than any dating app could claim. After a couple of months, clients graduated from the program with a request that they inform us if they got engaged or married. We didn't need to know about breakups unless they wanted us to match them again. That was a kindness to us both. No one wanted to make a phone call and say *I couldn't make it work. I got a professional matchmaker, and it still wasn't enough*, and we didn't need to hear about every circumstance in which we might've failed.

"Alexandra, you have someone new," Serena said, sliding a headshot and profile over to me. She disliked nicknames and insisted upon calling me by my given name, which I found slightly unsettling, since the sole people to do that previously had been my parents. When I changed my name, at eighteen, I'd altered only my last name. "Alexandra," I figured, was common enough that no one would make the connection to who I used to be.

"Great," I said. I was excited to have something to distract me from the situation with Noah and Molly.

The woman in the picture in front of me looked perfectly ordinary. *Rebecca Newsom*, read the text above the image. She wore a crop top that revealed a slice of her stomach above yoga pants. Like me, she had brown hair and eyes, traits that might've been banal on another woman if she didn't have a prettier-than-average face. Her profile said that she worked for a luxury car dealership. She listed her hobbies as *driving fast cars, exercising*, and most notably, *watching trashy reality television*.

She hadn't yet found a husband because none of the men she'd met lived up to her expectations, which she described as being *high, though not unreasonable.* She was looking for someone employed in a reputable profession, and she articulated that, though she didn't want to sound shallow, she had expensive tastes.

She confessed that in the past she'd cheated on a partner because she was bored with their relationship. They no longer had sex or did any of the activities that she enjoyed. She suspected that he was cheating on her as well, though she'd never gotten any proof. She regretted her infidelity, if only because of how it made her look in the eyes of others, and she assured us that she would never commit adultery if she were with someone she was truly committed to.

There was nothing in her profile that explicitly screamed *psychopath*, though I saw some subtle telltale signs. Driving fast cars, her inability to commit to a long-term relationship, cheating on partners. Her hotness. Sometimes I wondered if good-looking people were more likely to be psychopaths, or if it was their appearance that made them turn.

It was sweet, I thought, how much potential she still thought she had to love someone.

After I read through her profile out loud, we discussed some potential matches as a group.

"Maybe Paul? Or Tyler?" Serena suggested.

"Tyler was my first instinct," I agreed. "He drives that luxury car, which is right up her alley. I could see Paul working out too. I've been trying to find a match for him for a while, and she's a good fit for what he's looking for physically."

"Keep both in mind when you complete the next phase of intake. I trust your judgment here," Serena said.

She moved on to the next client, Hector, a gay man who was tired of the aesthetic pressures of the dating world and wanted someone who was happy staying home and playing video games.

"He should be easy to match," Oliver said.

It was a common thing we heard from clients in their thirties. Sometimes wanting love wasn't about a desire for romance. Sometimes wanting love was about being tired.

Another client was assigned to Nicole. The client was conventionally attractive, thin and blond haired. She worked as a surgical nurse, and taught aerobics classes on the side.

People frequently assumed that our clients were ugly or strange and that that was why they struggled to find love; often it was the opposite. Strange people found one another. They went to nerd conventions, lowered their physical expectations, and were kind to one another because of the bullying they experienced in their young lives. Alternatively, attractive people wanted partners who were as good-looking as they were and who worshipped them, not understanding that there was already too much ego in the equation. If they wanted to be treated like gods, they needed to date people willing to get on their knees and pray.

The client's problem was that she was getting older—already thirty-five—and her biological clock was ticking. She'd taken the step of freezing her eggs but was unwilling to undertake a parenting role on her own. The timeline meant that she wanted to get married sooner rather than later, and have children shortly after that. I understood why she was pressed. Life plans were a part of matchmaking. It was a common conundrum in romantic comedies: two people who were perfect for each other were made less so by their clocks' being out of sync. That was one of the ways in which Noah and I fit—our tracks aligned. Or they had until Molly ruined it all.

"I have a few ideas," Nicole said. "Maybe Brad? He comes from a big family, and he's older, so he might not mind her age. That's definitely going to be the biggest challenge here."

Though Nicole was twenty-nine, she often talked about people over the age of thirty like they were diseased. I enjoyed wondering how she would cope with her own aging body.

"At the end of the day, she's going to have to compromise. If she wants kids that quickly, she'll have to figure out what traits are most important to her in a partner," Serena said.

She passed out a couple clients to newer matchmakers, whom I didn't know particularly well. Matchmaking was a job that everyone thought they could do, but not everyone had what it took to be successful in the profession. Strangely, romantic comedies were the best kind of education, because they taught me that the pathway to love was rarely straight. I had, as Serena said, the guts to survive in the business.

———

I STARTED TO PACK UP MY THINGS, EAGER TO GET TO WORK ON Rebecca's case. She was the type of client I liked most—beautiful, and resistant to commitment. I enjoyed watching the change in a person when they found someone who was right for them. The perfect match meant that a night spent on the couch at home was better than a night getting drunk at a bar. It tamed a person. A feral cat domesticated.

I waited for Serena's usual monologue about the importance of love in the world, and I was thrown when she instead said, "I have a couple of announcements." The way she said it, that gleam on her face . . . Something was happening.

I'd heard women describe themselves as "empaths." I disliked the term. How could anyone truly know if they were more empathetic than other people? Everyone, inside themselves, believed that they experienced life more acutely than everyone else. In any case, I considered myself to be good at sensing others' emotional states. Serena was excited. The jewels in her necklace were especially sparkly, her teeth particularly white.

"I've been in talks with an investor. He loves what Better Love is doing, which is to say that he loves what all of you are doing, and he thinks there's a possibility of an expansion."

Across the table, Nicole took in a loud breath.

"We would start small. A couple of Midwestern cities to begin with, Chicago or St. Louis. If that goes well, then we'll expand into a national brand."

Oliver looked smug. He'd told me once that he thought this would happen.

"Serena likes to talk a big game about doing good for people. She's genuine in that, but in her core, she's a businesswoman. Her husband, her son—they would be nothing without her. I'm not sure they recognize that. She does though. She knows her power," he'd said.

Nicole was struggling to stay in her seat. She gripped the edge of the table like it was the only thing holding her down. An older matchmaker was frowning. I took another bite of doughnut. The sprinkles crunched satisfyingly between my teeth.

"You see," Serena continued, "people are increasingly starting to recognize loneliness as a crisis. Some have even called it an *epidemic*. Everyone is on their phones, watching television, ordering takeout, secluded within their homes."

I thought of all of my followers on social media. They knew what I ate, what I wore, the exercises that I did in the gym. They knew all my thoughts on *Love Island*, whose side I took in each season's drama. But they didn't know that, two days prior, my best friend had announced that she and my fiancé were in love and they were going to be together. Neither did they know about the things that my parents had done. On Saturday night I'd tried to think of someone, anyone, I could call, and had come up empty, choosing instead to spill my secrets to an attractive stranger. One thing about loneliness was that the people inside of it thought that they were the only ones. Everyone else, it seemed, was surrounded by friends and family. Serena's announcement revealed that my assumptions were incorrect. Lots of people were lonely—so lonely that investors were willing to stake money on their desperation to find someone. Things were worse than I'd thought.

"What's going to happen to this location?" Nicole interrupted, unable to contain herself.

"For the moment, things will stay the same. Sometime in the near future, however, I will be stepping down from the position of director in this location in order to help facilitate the opening of other branches. My hope is that I can train someone—one of you—to fill that role. Better Love has always been like a family, and I want to keep it that way."

I could sense the molecular shift inside myself as I transformed from a wallowing woman into someone with a mission. My position at Better Love was the first job that I'd ever had that had really engaged me, but unlike in my corporate roles, there was no room for growth here. I was jealous of the way that people looked at Noah when he told them that he was doing a medical residency. I wanted people to look at me the same way, though I had no interest in going to medical school. I admired Serena, with her sparkling jewelry and white, white teeth. This was it, my opportunity to become someone respectable.

I glanced around the room to see who else might be interested. Though Oliver had worked at Better Love longer than me, he had always claimed that he didn't want to be a matchmaker forever. His real dream was to be one of those famous people who somehow made their living doing podcasts. There were a couple of matchmakers who were older than me, but they hadn't been with the company as long, and they had lower success rates than I had. The job seemed like it was mine until my eyes met Nicole's. I could tell by the expression on her face that she wanted the position and knew that I did too.

A wave of possessiveness crashed through me. Over the weekend, Molly had stolen Noah from me, stupidly thinking that I would allow her to get away with it. *No*, I resolved. It was a new week. I'd win Noah back, get a promotion, and have the wedding of my dreams. All of the missteps, all of the drama, were just anecdotes that I was collecting on my pathway down the aisle.

"If you think that taking on a director role is something that might interest you," Serena continued, "please come see me. For the rest of you, know that the goal is to keep Better Love the thriving, pleasant workplace that it's always been. Now, go make some people fall in love."

6.

———

I WAS TAKEN ABACK BY Rebecca's physical presence.

Her first appointment was on Wednesday. I'd spent my time since the intake meeting on Monday morning strategizing how to win Noah back and how to convince Serena to give me the director position. I'd made little progress on either front. Neither Noah nor Molly had reached out since they'd revealed their infidelity on Saturday evening. Also worrisome was that I hadn't heard from Noah's mother, who typically texted me every couple of days to comment on the weather or on recent television she'd watched, or to ask my opinion about a new piece of clothing. Her silence made me think that Noah had already told her what happened. It burned that she would so easily cut ties with someone she'd once thought would be a kind of daughter to her. Mothers of all kinds were perpetually disappointing me.

I started typing texts to Noah, and then deleted them.

Bored of Molly yet?

Do your coworkers know what you did?

I can't believe you turned out to be such
a fuck boy.

Come back to me.

I love you.

Hey.

None of them seemed quite right, and as much as I wanted to
cry and scream, bang my fists on Noah's chest and ask him *why*, I
knew that it was important to tread carefully if I wanted to convince him to come back.

For Serena, I reformatted my résumé and ordered pink paper
to print it on, because I knew she liked little touches like that.
Connection, she'd once said, was as much about presentation as it
was about the soul. I couldn't tell my mother where I worked—it
was too risky—but as I purchased the paper, I thought about how
impressed she'd be if I was named director of the entire Twin
Cities branch. It seemed like the beginning of something greater.
I would be Serena's right-hand woman as she rose to the top. A
reality show about us could be made for Netflix, as with those real
estate moguls in California. If there was one thing that captivated
people more than expensive housing, it was love.

Rebecca was better-looking in person than she was in her photograph, which was saying something, as I had already found her
very attractive. What the picture hadn't captured was her height,

made possible by long legs, and her eyes, which had the sharpness of intelligence.

"Rebecca? I'm Alexandra. I'll be your matchmaker through this process."

I immediately noted how graceful she was. It would be impossible for her to catch a man the way that I had caught Noah, because she would never need to be helped off the ground.

"Nice to meet you," she said as we shook hands. She had one of those low voices like she'd been a smoker, though her intake paperwork said she didn't use tobacco products.

I led her to my office. Serena had eschewed the popular open office plan in favor of a building that provided discretion.

"Love requires privacy," she'd said as an explanation.

My office had a pink and gold desk with matching accessories. On the wall was a picture that I'd made during a paint-and-sip night that I'd attended with Molly. The painting was a poor rendering of the intertwined hearts of the Better Love logo. Next to my computer was a framed portrait of Noah and me, taken on the trip during which we'd gotten engaged. I'd been fighting the urge to scribble out his face so it became a hole.

I took a seat in my office chair and gestured for Rebecca to do the same in one of the velvet-upholstered seats across from my desk. The whole room was designed to prime my clients to fall for someone.

"Tell me, what brings you to Better Love?" I asked.

The first meeting was my favorite part of the process. It made me feel like a psychologist to have my clients seated across from me, spilling all the reasons why they were desperate for love. For a long time in my life I thought that I was going to become a therapist, until I realized the amount of schooling that it took. I liked to think of my job as counseling cosplay. *What is it about your mother that means you're unable to sustain a long-term relationship?* I never asked.

"I can't do the dating apps anymore," Rebecca started.

I nodded.

"That's something we hear a lot," I said.

"The thing that broke me was when I was talking to this guy. We'd been chatting for a couple of weeks. There were no red flags, which maybe was a flag in itself, because who has nothing wrong with them? Anyway, we started discussing meeting up, and I realized that I was totally uninterested. I knew without even going out with him that we weren't right for each other, and I was like, what's the point? I told him that and he got really dramatic about it, the way that men do. It was ridiculous. We'd never even met each other and there he was, acting like I'd destroyed this long-term thing. I might've put up with it a few years ago. It might've even been flattering then, but I'm too old for that now. I want to get married, buy a house. I don't want to deal with all the bullshit. Trying to date on apps is like having a second job where my co-workers want to have sex with me, and I already deal with enough of that in my paid position."

It was a monologue that I'd heard a million variations of, and I replied with a response that I'd uttered so many times that it felt like I was reading from a script.

"I'm sorry to hear about your bad experiences on dating apps. That's actually the reason why our founder opened Better Love to begin with. Her son used dating apps and grew similarly frustrated. We can help you here."

I smiled encouragingly. It was the expression of someone who was happily engaged, rather than someone who had been dumped by her fiancé for her best friend over the weekend. There was relief in zipping up my professional skin, in casting my personal problems to the side.

I continued. "You described, in your application, the kind of man you're looking for, but I want to hear about who you've gone for in the past. Tell me about your previous relationships and why they didn't work out."

"I've only been in love once. Or at least I thought I was in love at the time. Have you ever seen the show *Love on the Lake?* He was a lot like Pierce."

I sat up straighter in my chair. *Love on the Lake* was a reality television series that tracked a cast of young people who returned to the same Midwestern lake house to vacation each summer. It was less popular than many dating shows and the *Real Housewives* franchises, but it had all the romance and drama of both. Molly and I had a standing weekly date to watch new episodes of *Love on the Lake.* We were partway through the season, and I was despairing about the prospect of watching new episodes without her. Pierce was in the midst of what looked like a mental health breakdown. Against all odds, he'd maintained a relationship for a couple of seasons. His girlfriend ended up breaking up with him because he was unwilling to commit fully. He didn't believe in marriage. He wanted children, but only as an abstract concept. "I need to be strong and choose myself," his girlfriend had said.

"I'm *obsessed* with *Love on the Lake.* Pierce is such a dick. I was so glad when Callie broke up with him," I told her. The topic brought out a level of informality that I normally avoided while speaking with clients.

"Me too. She's way too good for him. He's also, like, what, fifteen years older than her? That was me and my ex. He was older. While we were together I thought he was hot, and now I look at him and cringe. When I broke up with him, he told me that he'd thought I would never do it. He'd assumed that I would stay with him forever, even if he never proposed. He assumed wrong."

"It's good that you stood up for yourself. We won't waste your time like that here. We'll only set you up with people who are serious about getting matched," I assured her.

Better Love didn't see a lot of people like Pierce. Men like that did everything possible to avoid any kind of commitment, until they got to their forties and woke up, single and alone, with a sudden desire for five children, and a wife in her early twenties. They were transparent to everyone other than themselves. I worked with psychopaths, but not psychopaths like that.

"Great." She smiled. Her bottom teeth were slightly crooked, which was charming on her otherwise flawless face. I struggled to imagine the man who assumed that Rebecca would lie down and take his shit.

"Tell me more about what kind of man you're looking for. Do you want a Sean or a Joel?" I named other cast members on *Love on the Lake*. Not everyone had enough star power to be asked back for multiple seasons. Some of the cast members were relegated to "friend" status, which, in the reality television universe, was understood to be an insult.

"Honestly, just avoid anyone who reminds you of someone from that show," she said. "All of those guys give me the *ick*."

"Even Landon?"

"Even him! Everyone talks about how he's reformed, but I can't trust it. His whole relationship seems like a business decision. I don't want intimacy that feels like a contract negotiation."

I laughed. I wished we were in a different setting. On the couch in my living room, maybe. That was one of the reasons why I enjoyed reality television. It was like a second group of friends to gossip about, ones who were especially messy and everyone knew. Unfortunately, Serena forbade any kind of fraternizing with clients outside the office. There was a power differential, she said, between the matchmaker and the client looking for love. To ask clients for anything would be to take advantage of them.

"So you want someone sincere?" I asked.

"Yeah, someone sincere. I like the sound of that. It wouldn't hurt if they were attractive too, but at this point I care more about personality. I'm sure everyone tells you that."

"No, you'd be surprised. We get a lot of clients who come in with very specific requests regarding height and appearance. I've had people say that they only want someone with blue eyes or that they hate red hair. That's not really what matchmaking is about though. They're not looking for love; they're looking for a poster on their wall."

"I like that," Rebecca said. "You know, I have such a good feeling about you, Alexandra. I was hesitant at first. What kind of person goes to see a matchmaker? Surely I'm too hot for that." She laughed at the acknowledgment of her own attractiveness. "But I told myself that if hot people can go on dating shows where the whole world is watching, then I can go to a matchmaker. Hopefully you have better taste in men than I do."

"Lots of good-looking people come to see us," I assured her. "There's nothing to be embarrassed about. And you can call me Lexie. That's what my friends call me."

There was something hollow in the statement. At the moment, my friends didn't call me anything, because I was friendless.

"Well, it was so nice to meet you, Lexie," Rebecca said.

I appreciated the sound of my name on her tongue—a confirmation that I still existed in the world.

"You too," I replied.

I walked her to the lobby. She smelled good—a perfume almost masculine with its caramel undertones.

"You should receive your first match in a couple of days," I told her.

I'd once heard the term "friend crush," which referred to a longing for someone you wanted to befriend. I hadn't totally bought the concept at the time. Could platonic feelings ever match the irrationality that overcame people when they desired romance? But as I watched Rebecca put on her coat and walk out the Better Love door, I recognized the phenomenon within myself. Talking with her about *Love on the Lake* had felt so good. She even looked like them, the women on TV. I could see her in a confessional, explaining which of the other cast members she liked and disliked and why she'd decided to throw wine in Pierce's face. Too bad we weren't allowed to be friends. The forbidden nature of becoming close with Rebecca made me want it more. I made a mental note to schedule extra time for our next appointment so that we could spend more time talking about TV.

I WAS WORKING ON FINALIZING REBECCA'S PROFILE SO THAT I could set up her first match when there was a knock on the door. I checked my calendar to make sure that I hadn't missed an appointment with a client, and I found it empty. The timing of Noah and Molly's announcement was frustrating. Why couldn't they have pulled their little stunt when Better Love wasn't on the verge of expansion? I didn't like feeling off-kilter in the workplace, where ordinarily I was so in control.

The door opened and Serena's face appeared. *She's here to name you director,* my brain said, before I saw who was behind her.

It was the handsome man.

The one from Saturday night, who I wasn't supposed to see ever again.

I vaguely remembered sitting on the bed in the hotel room. He'd taken off his sweater to reveal a tight T-shirt and an armful of tattoos. I'd told him about my parents, and he'd followed with *something*—a story of wounds, the specifics of which escaped me. What had I said after that? There was the truth that anyone could find if they knew my real name, and then there was the one hidden within myself. Whatever my confession, I hadn't expected it to come back to haunt me. I definitely hadn't anticipated that the handsome man would show up in my office, standing next to the boss I wanted to name me as her successor, something that would never happen if he told her what he knew.

I stood up in such a hurry that my hand knocked my empty water bottle off the desk. It made a clanging sound on the floor, which made me flinch.

"What's going on?" I asked.

"Alexandra, this is Aidan Lewis. He's a new client at Better Love."

Aidan Lewis. He'd told me his name during our night out, and I'd promptly forgotten it, because I assumed that I'd never see him again. What was he doing here? This wasn't how things were done. We always received new clients during the Monday intake meeting. I saw the way that Serena smiled at him as she led him into the office, and I realized that he'd charmed his way in. It was the kind of thing that my father used to be able to do. *I know these are the rules for everyone else, but can we alter them for me?* That I'd failed to see that ability within him spoke to my level of intoxication on Saturday night. Or maybe he'd charmed me the same way that he'd charmed Serena.

"Nice to meet you, Alexandra," he said, stepping forward to shake my hand.

He was just as handsome in sobriety. He wore a forest green sweater that covered his tattoos. I ran through the events of the night. Tequila shots and table dancing. A hot tub. I knew that I'd mentioned Better Love but wasn't certain whether I'd specified the nature of my clientele. Had I used the word "psychopath"? It hit me how much power I'd handed to a man whose name I'd learned only after the fact.

"I know that this is unorthodox," Serena explained from the doorway, "but I talked to Aidan, and, well, he's so eager to get matched that I thought it would be best to introduce the two of you immediately."

I narrowed my eyes. Serena *never* allowed exceptions, no matter how much a person begged. I'd seen crying women turned away at the door. *Please—I just want love,* they'd begged. *I can't take being alone anymore.* She'd shown them sympathy and then reminded them that we had a process, a *successful* process, that we couldn't rush. Apparently Aidan wasn't bound by such constraints.

"Did he complete the questionnaire?" I asked. I needed to know if he was actually a psychopath or if he'd simply requested me. It alarmed me that my judgment was so off.

"Of course," she replied. I could tell from her expression that she knew what I was asking. I didn't understand how such a shrewd woman had been taken in by Aidan's charm. Then again, hadn't I been taken in several days prior? We wanted good looks to equate to moral purity, and they never did.

"I'll leave the two of you alone," Serena said, and shut the door behind her.

"What are you doing here?" I asked as soon as I was confident that she was out of hearing range. Both of us were still standing.

"Looking for love," the handsome man—Aidan—said. His eyes were so wide, his face so innocent, that I almost believed him, and I would've if I hadn't been raised by people like him.

"Tell me the truth," I said.

"Are you going to invite me to sit down?" he asked, moving toward a chair. I was hesitant to follow his lead, but I did it anyway, as it seemed silly to continue to stand, my arms barricaded across my chest.

"You look good," he said.

"What are you doing here?" I asked again, though I couldn't help but appreciate the compliment. It had been strange getting dressed that morning without Noah's presence. I no longer knew how to evaluate my own appearance. I hadn't realized how dependent I was on an audience until I was alone.

"I wanted to see you again," Aidan admitted.

My fingers wrapped around an empty coffee mug on my desk. "Why?"

"Because we had a good time together," he said, and then amended: "More than a good time. There's something between us, Lexie."

I noted that he'd remembered my name when I'd forgotten his. What else had he remembered? Everything. Too much.

"No." I shook my head. "I have a fiancé. The other night was a mistake. I was upset. I shouldn't have gone with you." *I shouldn't have told you those things.*

"Did you get back together?" Aidan's eyebrows raised slightly, but he looked unperturbed. He was a man who had never had to fight to get a woman. Women fell into his lap like crumbs from a croissant.

"Not yet, but we will." My statement was firm. I could tell that Aidan doubted me, which made me want Noah more. There was some satisfaction in rejecting such a beautiful man. If only I hadn't confided in him, I could've marched him right out the door. As it was, I needed to tread carefully and keep him happy without allowing any boundaries to be crossed.

Aidan leaned forward in his chair. I leaned backward, straightening my spine. I couldn't allow the space between us to lessen.

"You know the best way to get someone back?" he asked.

"What?"

"Make them jealous. And I can't think of anything that would make him more jealous than if you were to go out with me."

He wasn't wrong. It happened all the time on TV and in movies. The guy refused to make it official with the girl until she started talking to someone hotter, taller; and then suddenly they were official. I knew that Noah was capable of such jealousy. I'd once drawn the attention of one of the other medical residents at a party we'd attended, thrown by one of his friends. Suddenly he couldn't stop touching me. It was a hunger so acute that we'd gone into the bathroom and Noah had eaten me out. Still, Aidan's argument wasn't enough.

"We can't date. It's against the Better Love rules for a matchmaker to date their client, and as of today, you're one of my clients," I told him.

"You didn't strike me as a rule follower, Lexie."

"I take my job seriously."

"Have you ever considered what would happen if you took a risk? Come on. I know you feel it. The universe is drawing us together, Lexie. You're denying a gravitational pull."

"It's not the universe; it's just your libido."

"Why can't it be both?"

"Because." *Because you're a psychopath and I'm engaged to a totally normal doctor. You're exactly the kind of person I've spent my entire life trying to get away from.* "Because it won't work, okay? Trust me. I know these things. I can match you if that's what you want. I'll find you someone amazing, a better fit than me."

Aidan picked up the framed picture of Noah and me from my desk. We were both in swimsuits. I got the urge to retroactively cover my body.

"Okay. You can match me."

He put the picture down.

I paused, waiting for him to continue. What was the catch? When he didn't say anything further, I cautiously said, "Great. I think you'll be very happy."

"I hope so. I've waited a long time for love."

I stopped myself from scoffing. It wasn't romance that emanated from his body, but something carnal.

I put on my professional voice.

"That's what we're here for. We've helped hundreds of people, and I know that we can help you as well. I do have something to ask of you though."

"What?"

"I would appreciate it if you didn't mention to anyone at Better Love what happened on Saturday night, the things that I told you."

I kept my reference vague. I didn't want him to know how little I remembered. He already had enough information that could be used against me.

Aidan studied my face. I did the same with him, but I struggled to parse what he was thinking. I'd made too many assumptions about him when we'd met. I'd seen his appearance, the people he spent time with, and I'd assumed that he was shallow. I could pour my secrets into him, because they would immediately come splashing out. I'd forgotten what my parents had taught me. *Trust no one.*

"I won't tell," he said.

All I could do was hope that it was true.

After that, I took him through our normal procedures. I treated him like he was any other client, an act so good that I deserved an award. I walked him to the door like he was ordinary, loosening my jaw only when he'd gotten into his car and driven away.

There was one thing that I didn't ask him, something that I couldn't get out of my head. He knew that I worked with people with psychopathic traits, and yet he'd assumed that if he signed up as a client I would be his matchmaker. That meant that Aidan knew he was a psychopath.

7.

DESPITE THE DRAMA OF Aidan's arrival, I was grateful to have new clients, as they were the only thing that stopped the situation with Molly and Noah from becoming all-consuming. Because neither of them had reached out since their big reveal, I was left scrolling their social media pages, searching for clues as to what they might be up to. It was a torturous practice. Rather than settling on the couch to relax after work, I put on my pajamas and stared at the faces of the people who'd broken my heart. It had to be done. Nicole followed Molly, so if Molly posted about her new relationship, then I would be exposed. Thus far, Molly had stuck to her usual memes, and Noah hadn't posted anything at all. Between his silence online and his lack of communication with me, he may as well have been dead.

Finding nothing interesting, I inputted *Aidan Lewis* into the search bar of the social media app. It was a common name, and I started systematically weeding through the results. There were short Aidans, tall Aidans, Black Aidans, white Aidans, but none of them was the man I was looking for. Could he be one of the rare people in contemporary society who didn't exist online? A search on my web browser didn't yield any further results. I logged on to the Better Love platform in pursuit of more information.

Here is what I learned:

He was thirty-seven years old and a private jet pilot. He'd been to every continent. His longest-ever relationship was two months. He had three siblings—two sisters and a brother—and wasn't currently close with his family. When asked to describe himself, he used the term "neat freak."

Looking at his profile, I understood why people became frustrated with dating apps. The facts were listed. I knew his birth date, where he was born, his favorite food and color, but none of that captured what it was like to be in a room with him. He was persuasive in a way that was dangerous. The kind of man women knew to stay away from but went home with anyway. An unexpected truth I'd learned from matchmaking was that there was such a thing as being *too* handsome and charming. Once that boundary was crossed, a person became untrustworthy.

Thankfully, Aidan and I were at no risk of becoming involved, despite his insistence that the two of us were compatible. Even if Noah hadn't been in the picture, I wasn't about to jeopardize my position at Better Love. I'd already built up the franchise in my head. First, Serena would open branches in every major city in the United States. Next, we would go global, become a leader in love across the world. The idea of moving to Europe appealed to me— to London or Paris—the safety of an ocean separating me from my mother.

It was going to be difficult to match Aidan. I'd seen that he persuaded Serena to let him into the building against protocol. He needed a woman who wouldn't cower before him, someone who would question his motives at every turn. Rebecca was the only current client I could think of who might satisfy that requirement, but as with Aidan, I didn't yet know her well enough to judge.

I'd enjoyed my conversation with Rebecca. I really had. It had been easy and natural in a way that most interactions with new clients were not. If I was grateful that Better Love's rules prevented me from pursuing anything romantic with Aidan, I was irritated that they kept me from forming a friendship with Rebecca. Ordinarily, I enjoyed sitting alone on the couch, wrapped in a blanket, but the loneliness of it was beginning to eat at me.

I did another social media search, this time for Rebecca's name. I was pleased that she popped up immediately. Like a lot of beautiful women, she had thousands of followers. People were willing to watch her do anything. Most of her posts were car-centric. She posed next to vehicles or took immaculate selfies behind the wheel. Based on the number of comments she got from men who called her "gorgeous," it was a successful sales tactic. Men weren't buying the car, but rather the woman who sold it to them, or so they thought. It never occurred to them that they were being manipulated. They couldn't see all the ways in which they were weak.

In addition to all the male commenters was a woman, Maureen, who commented on every single post in a platonic, motherly way. Were they friends? She was a glimmer of what Rebecca's life might be like beyond her external sheen. I clicked on Maureen's profile and found a series of poorly lit pictures of two sticky children. Sprinkled among them were older shots of a woman Maureen identified as "Mom." After a few minutes of scrolling, I determined that "Mom" was dead, and a few minutes after that, I came to the startling realization that "Mom" had been murdered, which explained the somber tone of everything Maureen said.

How did Maureen and Rebecca know each other? Aesthetically, they didn't belong in the same space. Attractive people flocked to attractive people. Could they be related? No, Rebecca said that her family lived in a different state, and when I checked Maureen's page it said that she also lived in the Twin Cities.

It was a group photo that allowed me to figure out the connection between Rebecca and Maureen. The group was an odd mixture of the young and old, attractive and ordinary, mostly women, and a couple of men, with their arms around one another.

I'm so grateful for the Children of Murdered Parents support group. They have literally saved my life, Maureen had written beneath the picture.

My brain latched on to the words, a hook through the eye of a fish. Had one of Rebecca's parents been murdered? She hadn't mentioned that in her intake paperwork. In my time as a matchmaker I'd heard about all sorts of ways that parents had fucked up their children so that it was difficult for them to have successful relationships: a dozen divorces, parents who stayed together but should've gotten divorced, second families, and affairs. I'd had clients with parents who had passed away due to age, heart disease, and cancer. Murder, however—that was something new.

I did a search for *Children of Murdered Parents support group* and discovered that they met on Thursday nights at a nearby library. Ordinarily on Thursdays, Molly came over with takeout and we watched *Love on the Lake*. It was a years-long pre-weekend ritual, with only occasional interruptions for travel or holidays. I was dreading having to spend the night alone. Though watching television was usually thought of as a solo activity, it was one of the ways that I formed connections with other people. Molly and I posted on social media about episodes as they aired. We shared memes with each other. We talked about the cast members like they were people we knew, and we basically did know them after watching them on-screen for so many years. Being a *Love on the Lake* fan meant a built-in friend group. Rebecca was proof of that. The two of us had bonded instantly over our shared viewing.

Reading about Children of Murdered Parents, I realized that there was more to my connection with Rebecca than I'd initially thought. We'd clicked instantly, and it wasn't solely because both of us watched *Love on the Lake*. We were drawn to each other because I had a murdered parent too.

8.

———

I HAD NO PLANS TO attend the Children of Murdered Parents
support group. That's what I told myself on Thursday morning,
as I sipped my coffee and sent Rebecca her first match.

When I was a teenager, my aunt repeatedly tried to get me to
attend therapy.

"Anyone who has gone through what you have needs some support," she'd insisted.

I wasn't opposed to therapy as a concept. After all, I had aspirations to become a therapist myself. The issue that I had was that
I felt therapy wouldn't work for me specifically—not because I was
special or some kind of unknowable being but because what I'd
gone through was so awful that the run-of-the-mill psychologist
wouldn't know what to do with me.

In an attempt to placate my aunt, I went to a few sessions, during which I'd sat in utter silence until the hour was up. In my
experience, nothing good could come from bringing up the past.

Eventually my aunt agreed that it was a waste of money and allowed me to stop going.

The thing that appealed to me about Children of Murdered Parents was that I would have something in common with the other attendees. To my knowledge, I'd never before interacted with anyone who also had a murdered parent—aside from my meeting with Rebecca. What would it be like to be in a whole roomful of such people? Too bad I wouldn't—couldn't—know.

The man I matched Rebecca with was named Paul. He'd been my client for a couple of months. He'd proved difficult to match, because I worried that if I matched him with the wrong woman he would destroy her life. The issue wasn't that he was violent or cruel. If anything, he was, similarly to Aidan, too charming. He came into our first meeting and described the trail of women he'd left heartbroken.

"I didn't want to hurt them," Paul told me. "I like making people happy, and sometimes that means telling them what they want to hear, even if it's not true."

A misconception that people had about psychopaths was that their lies were always vicious. Niceness, however, could also be cruel. Paul was the kind of man a woman went on a single date with and started imagining her first name combined with his last. He needed someone with a restrained heart—someone like Rebecca.

For a moment, I considered sending her Aidan instead, but his profile wasn't ready, and something in my gut told me that he and Rebecca were wrong for each other. Paul was everything that she'd asked for. It was better, I thought, to start with someone whose flaws were knowable to me, unlike Aidan, whose mysteries were contained to a drunken night that I couldn't remember.

While I waited for her response, I opened a Chinese takeout menu in my browser. I was still trying to convince myself that I could have a good time without Molly. I'd spent years of my life with no friends at all. While the other kids at my high school were at parties, at sleepovers, going to prom, I was watching movies in my room. That had been enough. When had I become so reliant upon another person? I vowed to reassert my independence.

My email dinged with a new message. It was from Rebecca.

I'm intrigued. Set up a date, she said.

Great! I replied.

Paul had already accepted. Of course he had. Rebecca was a catch.

I started making arrangements for their first date. I closed out of the Chinese takeout menu, deciding that I would order a pizza for dinner instead. The Children of Murdered Parents support group's website stared at me from the screen. I didn't even remember opening it that morning, but I must have. I closed out of that too. It didn't mean anything. I researched all sorts of things online.

I WAS FINALIZING THE DETAILS OF REBECCA'S DATE WITH PAUL when I heard Nicole's voice drift down the hallway. She was in Serena's office and had neglected to close the door. I quietly stood up from my desk chair and tiptoed down the hallway so that I could make out individual words. Oliver's office was next to Serena's, and he gave me a knowing glance as I passed by. I raised my pointer finger to my lips in a *shh* motion.

"I'm so excited about the expansion," Nicole said. "I've always told Ethan that I wished there were more Better Love locations. There are so many lonely people out there, and the work that we do really helps. It's basically charity! How many branches do you think there'll be?"

"We'll see how the couple of locations do. We'll open as many as we can sustain," Serena told her.

"Wow, that's amazing. Have I ever told you how much I look up to you? You're such a girlboss. It's so great to work for someone like you. You've shown me what it's possible to achieve. I tell everyone that you're basically like a second mom to me."

I rolled my eyes at that comment. Nicole didn't know the weight of the word "mom." She had one of those mothers who commented about how beautiful her daughter was on every social media post she made. She didn't know that a mom was someone who could break your world as well as make it whole. She didn't understand the sacrifice that came with loving a person like that.

"Thank you. I appreciate it," Serena replied. Typically, I was good at gauging tone, but I often struggled to read Serena, as she was kind to everyone—which was decidedly different from liking everyone. I struggled to parse whether she sincerely liked Nicole's company or she was just good at faking it.

"There could be no bigger honor in this lifetime than taking over the role of director at this location," Nicole continued. "I *love* love, and I *love* matchmaking. The way you've grown this company is so admirable, and I want to help further that growth."

"You've certainly helped us in that department," Serena told her.

Reluctantly, I had to admit that the compliment was accurate. Clients liked Nicole. They liked how she looked like the greeting card section of a store. Women appreciated how relatable she was—a true basic bitch—and men liked her conventional hotness.

In another industry, she might've been infantilized, but her sentimentality served her well in matchmaking. Despite all that, I didn't think she had what it took to be a leader. She hadn't totally shed her mean-girl persona from high school, and the little jabs she made in meetings led to her being a polarizing figure in the office. She wanted to serve only the clients who were like her. If she were put in charge, a lot of people would be left behind.

There were frequently characters like Nicole in romantic comedies. The rival woman was good-looking enough to be a threat, but never as charming as the main character. The viewer was supposed to root actively for her downfall; though, presented through a different lens, she probably had redeeming qualities. For instance, Nicole's cringeworthy style made me look fashionable in comparison.

Oliver agreed with my assessment.

"Nicole makes it impossible to respect her, with that little baby voice," Oliver had told me on more than one occasion.

I stopped myself from marching into Serena's office to declare *Me! It should be me!* as Nicole said, "Thank you so much. Everything I've achieved has been because of you."

What a suck-up.

"Your name is on my list of contenders," Serena said. "I hope to make an announcement soon."

I crept off before Nicole emerged from the office. Back at my desk, I seethed as I wrote clients emails like *I'm glad your date went well! Are you ready for round two?* and *I'm so pleased to present your next match! I just know the two of you will hit it off.* To anyone who was watching, I was the perfect representative of love. Inside, resentment ate away at me. I'd tried so hard to be the woman Noah had wanted, and still, he'd abandoned me for Molly. I'd worked so hard at Better Love, taking on challenging clients, and despite that, Serena was considering Nicole for the director position. Sometimes it felt like everything came easily to other people—friendship, love, stability—and I had to claw and scratch for even a scrap of what they had. What was the point of all my efforts? It was so tempting to break the rules.

———

PARKED OUTSIDE THE LIBRARY, I PRETENDED THAT I WASN'T there to attend the Children of Murdered Parents meeting. I told myself that I would go inside, maybe check out a book. I had a fondness for libraries, as I'd spent significant portions of my teenage years inside of one in order to get away from my aunt's house. Considering that I'd been getting most of my recent reads from Noah's mother, I probably needed a new source of books while I worked to win Noah back.

I walked inside, pretended to browse the new fiction titles, and eyed the meeting room's closed door, which had a sign that said COMP taped to the outside. Internally, I expanded the abbreviation to "Children of Murdered Parents." Though I was totally sober, entering the room didn't feel entirely different from Saturday night, when I'd gotten drunk, danced on a table, and spilled my deepest, darkest secrets to an attractive man I believed I'd never see again. Since Molly and Noah had told me about their affair, the world had taken on a dreamlike quality. I was making decisions that I wouldn't ordinarily make. I was jeopardizing my future with Better Love by attempting to see a client outside the office, and it wasn't even for sex. Was I really prepared to tell strangers about my murdered father in order to befriend a psychopath?

The shades were pulled down over the meeting room's windows, which meant that I was unable to see inside before entering. Was Rebecca in there? I took a breath and opened the door. Everyone inside turned to look at me. Eight women and two men sat in a circle of chairs. I guessed that the gender imbalance wasn't because women were more likely to have murdered parents, but rather because they were more likely to seek therapy in the aftermath. I'd seen the same thing at Better Love. Women were much more likely to acknowledge that they needed help finding romantic partners than men were. A not-insignificant number of our male clients told us that they'd signed up because their mothers had pressured them into it.

Rebecca wasn't among the people in the circle. I spotted Maureen, who frowned at me as though she knew I'd found my way there by looking at her social media accounts.

"Sorry," I said. I realized that I'd walked in on something intimate. In some ways, it would've been easier to intrude on two people making love.

"Are you joining us?" one of the women asked. I recognized her from Maureen's picture. It was evident from her body language that she was the facilitator of the group.

"Yes."

There were screeching sounds against the floor as the members scooted their chairs back and added one so that I could sit down. It was strange to consider that all of these people had murdered parents. Aside from Maureen, they all looked normal. Sometimes I wished that the real world were a little more like the internet, where everyone went around carrying words that indicated their traumas.

I took a seat next to Maureen. Her skin was spotty and wrinkled. I would've thought her to be fifty if I didn't know about her young kids.

"We were just doing introductions," the facilitator said. "Most of us already know each other, so why don't you start?"

Once again, everyone turned their gaze in my direction. It made me squirm. I hadn't expected to be put in such a spotlight. Coming to the meeting had been a stupid idea. Friendship was about more than liking the same TV show. Molly and Noah were making me act foolish. I thought about leaving. The people in the meeting didn't know who I was. I could disappear through that door without making a mark.

But something compelled me to stay. Maybe Rebecca had come into Better Love for a reason. Maybe the universe was telling me that it was time to talk about my father.

"I'm Lexie," I said.

The others continued to stare at me, as if they were waiting for me to speak. Did they want to know how it had happened? Was I supposed to name the weapon with which he'd been killed?

"Is there anything else you want to share?" the facilitator asked gently. "It's okay if there isn't. Each of us needs different things at different times."

I shook my head.

"I'd just like to listen for a bit, if that's okay," I said. I wasn't sure how to act, but I got the sense that no one did. One thing about experiencing horrific events was that afterward others judged you no matter how you behaved. If you were seemingly well-adjusted, then you were heartless. If you were so overcome by grief that you were unable to function, then you needed to get over it. Based on the appearances of the other people in the room, it seemed that the entire spectrum of coping was represented.

"In that case, I'm going to give Maureen a chance to speak, as I know today is a difficult day for her," said the facilitator.

Maureen was teary-eyed even before she began talking. She had on an oversized cotton shirt that had stains beneath her armpits. She was the kind of person who wore on the outside everything that had ever happened to her. If she'd ever been beautiful, her beauty had been destroyed by tragedy.

"Most of you know that it's the anniversary of my mother's death," Maureen said. "Five years ago today, she was killed by a monster."

She took some gulping breaths. I was glad that I'd never looked like that, not even in my worst moments. There were benefits to shoving everything down.

"People tell me that it gets easier. I want to know when that is, because it hasn't gotten easier yet. I still miss her all the time, and it's almost worse now, because my memories of her are starting to fade. Sometimes it feels like I miss someone who never existed. I can tell that everyone is ready for me to be over it. How can you still—"

Maureen was halfway through a sentence when the door opened again. It was Rebecca. The other faces lit up in recognition instead of displaying the iciness with which I'd been greeted. She was one of them. It amazed me how continuously life provided new opportunities to feel excluded.

We all scooted back, with another cacophony of screeching chair legs. Rebecca grabbed an empty seat and placed it between me and Maureen. She gave Maureen's hand a little squeeze before she sat down. I thought that she didn't recognize me in this new context, until she turned and gave me a sharp look that unsettled me enough that I worried that I'd made a mistake. Had I committed a friendship gaffe by showing up? I was so good at knowing exactly the right amount of effort to put in with men, withholding and providing with precision to maximize their desire. Friendship with other women was different, because no one wanted a friend who forgot to text back or purposefully acted distant. At the same time, neither did they want friends who were constantly needy. Both of those were errors I'd made in trying to meet people before Molly. There were also very few norms for establishing new friendships, especially in adulthood. Showing up at the Children of Murdered Parents support group was the most normal way I could think of to develop my connection with Rebecca, and yet it was possible that I'd gone too far.

"I'm so sorry, Maureen. I got caught up at work," Rebecca said. The two women were at opposite ends of the grief spectrum. Rebecca was polished everywhere that Maureen was rough. I could tell that Maureen, like me, relished proximity to Rebecca.

"It's okay. I appreciate you so much, Becky. You've done more for me than almost anyone else in my life," Maureen said, the tears now dripping fat down her wet cheeks.

I knew from Rebecca's file that being called "Becky" was a pet peeve of hers. Either Maureen and Rebecca were close enough that Maureen was allowed to cross those boundaries, or Maureen thought they were better friends than they were.

"What was I saying? I can't remember." Maureen's face had become a waterfall. It wasn't a flattering look on her. I wondered who she'd be if her mother were still alive. I noticed that she didn't wear a wedding ring. An irony was that it was almost always easiest to love those who needed it the least.

"I need a minute," she gulped.

"Take as much time as you need," the facilitator said kindly. I suspected this wasn't the first time that Maureen had had such a meltdown.

The facilitator started to speak, but Rebecca's voice broke

through. She had a command that overrode any established hierarchies in the room.

"Did our newcomer introduce herself yet?" she asked, referring to me. "I'm sorry to have missed what she said."

I noticed that she didn't mention that the two of us had a prior relationship. It was possible that she wanted to obscure the fact that she was seeing a matchmaker. People often did, especially people as attractive as Rebecca. They were embarrassed that they needed the help. I'd even attended clients' weddings at which they talked around the fact that they'd met through Better Love. However, I got the sense that something more was at play here. The two of us were speaking a language that no one else could understand.

I realized that I needed to give Rebecca something to show that I was trustworthy. I needed to show her that we were cut from the same kind of cloth, even though it had a different pattern, that the connection between us went further than a shared interest in reality television.

"I'm Lexie," I said, though she already knew. If she wanted to keep the details of our prior relationship a secret, then so did I. Ostensibly, I was speaking to the whole room. Really, I was speaking only to her. "I haven't shared yet. It's hard for me to talk about it."

"It's hard for all of us," a woman across the circle said. It was intended as a show of solidarity, but I resented the interruption.

I made eye contact with Rebecca before I spoke. I wanted her to know that what I was about to share was an admission of goodwill. I wasn't there to hurt her. I was there because I wanted us to be friends.

"My father was murdered," I told them. They were words that I'd rarely spoken out loud. I let my voice crack the same way that Maureen's had. She was a veteran when it came to talking about her parent's death, whereas I'd spent years doing the opposite. It was uncomfortable to open a box whose hinges were rusted shut.

"He was stabbed to death. His head was cut off. His organs were removed. I don't think I've ever totally processed it. He wasn't a good dad. He left me alone a lot, forgot about my birthday, things like that. There were times when I wished he would die. Then, when he did—well, sometimes I worry it was my fault, like I ushered it into the world."

A hush fell over the room. Normally I resented things like that. I didn't like being treated differently because of who my parents were. I wanted to be taken as I appeared to be: a happy, smart, pretty woman who was worthy of marrying a doctor.

"You didn't, honey. It's not your fault," she said.

There was pleasure in the confession. For the very first time in my life, I'd been accepted by a group because of who I was, rather than ostracized. Of course, I hadn't told them the full story. Almost no one knew that. Molly knew most of it, and Aidan—well, he knew an amount that I wished I could remember. When I told her, Molly did her best to put on a mask of empathy, but I could see her squirming in her seat. Stories like that were all good and fun when they were embedded within a movie or a true crime podcast. No one wanted to actually be close to the by-products of horror, because they worried that it was contagious. All I could hope was that Molly hadn't told Noah what I'd told her, or that if she had, he didn't believe it. That was the kind of childhood I'd had—the kind that was so uncomfortable that people needed to believe it was fiction.

Rebecca's eyes met mine. I saw no sign of revulsion or fear. Instead, it almost looked like she was smiling.

9.

—

I HAVE TO ADMIT," REBECCA said, over a heaping plate of pad thai, "I was shocked when I walked in and saw you there. I thought . . . well, I don't know what I thought."

I laughed.

"It was a weird coincidence," I agreed. "You showed up at Better Love, and then a couple days later, there I am in your support group. It's like when you hear a word for the first time and then suddenly it's everywhere. There's a name for it. The Baader-Meinhof phenomenon? We're Baader-Meinhoffing each other."

There were, of course, no real coincidences. In romantic comedies, protagonists were always bumping into their soulmates and enemies. The whole premise of the movie *Serendipity* was that the love interests would find their way back together if they were meant to be. In real life, I had stalked Rebecca on social media until I figured out where she'd be, and my entrance had been met with appropriate suspicion. It was so much easier to make friends and fall in love in a fictional world.

"I couldn't believe it when you said that your father was killed," she said. "I've never actually met someone else whose father was murdered—you know, outside of COMP. I'm sorry if I forced you into talking about it. I think I was feeling territorial."

"No, it was good, actually," I assured her. "Like I said, it's hard to talk about. I needed the push."

Everyone in the group was very supportive after I told them how my father died. I was in a safe space, they said. They understood what I was going through, and they hoped I would come back. Afterward, Rebecca invited me out to dinner at a nearby Thai restaurant while Maureen watched enviously. I knew how that felt, longing for friendship. I was grateful that Rebecca had chosen me. I saw the invitation as an olive branch after the way she'd looked at me when she saw me sitting in the meeting. She was accepting me as one of them, the child of a murdered parent— a member of a club that no one wanted to be in.

I still wasn't certain how or when her father had died. Everyone in the group already knew, which made me jealous. I wanted to suck the information out with my teeth.

"I don't like to talk about my father either," she told me at dinner. "I joined COMP after a couple of outbursts at work. My boss said it wasn't mandatory, but it was basically mandatory. I ended up liking it. It's nice to not feel alone for a few minutes every week."

She paused and took a bite of her food. I'd noted that she ordered it "Thai spicy," a level of heat that came with a warning in the menu.

"Should I be telling you this? Are you going to hold it against me as my matchmaker?" she asked after she swallowed. There was no sign that she was affected by the heat. I was the same way—I took the warning as a dare. It made me respect her all the more.

I shook my head.

"No. We're not talking as matchmaker and client. We're talking as friends," I told her.

At the word "friend" a small smile flashed across Rebecca's face. She could sense the connection between us too. There was something about us written in the stars.

"Okay, I'll tell you what happened as friends, then," she said. "I had this coworker, another salesperson. He was the kind of slimy guy that people think of when they think of someone who sells cars."

"So the opposite of you?"

"Exactly. The opposite of me. Anyway, he kept asking me out on dates and I kept saying no. There is no universe in which I would've gone out with him. I tried to stay polite, because you know how men are when you reject them."

I did.

"Then we were at the company holiday party and he got drunk. Really, really drunk. He followed me into the bathroom and tried to kiss me. Thankfully, I've been taking boxing lessons for years. He didn't know what hit him."

"What the fuck? That's so messed up."

"I know. The worst part was that he's married, and his wife was at the party."

"Oh my god."

"Yeah. I reported him to HR, and they told me that they couldn't fire him because it was a case of 'he said, she said,' and that he claimed that *I* came on to *him*. Let's just say that my reaction was . . . well, not cute."

"Obviously! How did they think you would react? You should've punched the HR person too."

"Somehow nothing happened to him, and I was required to go to therapy. I tried a more traditional therapist at first, but he came on to me and I was like *Fuck that*. COMP has been a lifesaver. I didn't know that I needed to talk about my dad until I did."

"What happened to the guy you worked with?"

"Oh, he died."

"What?"

"Yeah, it was crazy. I guess he got drunk, went into work, and ended up taking one of the cars for a test drive. He drove off a bridge and drowned."

"Wow. That's wild."

The restaurant was crowded. It was the kind of late-January evening that begged for comfort food. Around us, people spooned steaming curry into their mouths. I barely noticed them. I was a horse wearing blinders, and all I could see was Rebecca sitting in front of me. Our lives weren't identical, not exactly, but she was more akin to me than anyone else I'd ever met. She was the kind of friend I'd been looking for my whole life, what I'd thought I'd found in Molly.

"Tell me more about this Paul guy," she said, changing the topic. "Will he be the love of my life?"

"He might be. You'll like him. He's attractive, a good conversationalist."

I was mildly uncomfortable talking about work in that setting. However, the line of impropriety was so far behind me that I could no longer see it when I turned back to look. I struggled to consider the director position when Rebecca's face glowed across the table.

"If he's so great, why hasn't he found someone?" she asked.

"I think it's a struggle of abundance. Too many women have fallen in love with him, and now he doesn't know how to commit. You could be the person to change that."

"Is that a challenge?" she teased.

"If you want it to be."

"Did you meet your fiancé through Better Love?" she asked.

The question startled me. How did she know about Noah? Had I mentioned him? Had she spied on my social media the same way that I'd spied on hers? Then I remembered the ring on my finger, the framed picture on my desk at work. There were so many ways in which I gave myself away for free.

I almost told the truth, admitted to her what Noah and Molly had done. I had, after all, told her about my father's passing, which I almost never mentioned. After that, talking about my breakup was like telling her about my favorite color or how I liked my eggs cooked in the morning. But my father's death wasn't the recent, raw thing that the breakup was. More important, it didn't make me look pathetic. I couldn't admit to Rebecca that my fiancé had left me for my best friend, because I wanted her to think that I was worthy of love. If I told her the truth, she might wonder what was wrong with me. I would be reduced to the status of Maureen from the support group, someone desperately longing for attention from a woman who gave it only incrementally. So I created a world in which Noah and I were still together.

In other words, I lied.

"No. We met in a bar," I told her.

"Ah. The old-fashioned way of meeting. I didn't know that people did that anymore."

"It was very cute. Also, painful. I fell down in front of him, and he helped me up. It turned out that my ankle was broken, and he had to take me to the hospital."

"Oh my god. It sucks that your ankle broke, but that's so precious. What does he do?"

"He's a doctor. Or he will be. He's in the last year of his residency."

"Wow, what a meet-cute. I can't believe you fell into the arms of a doctor. I only seem to meet finance bros and lawyers," Rebecca lamented.

Both of us had finished all the food on our plates. We were voracious eaters. It was nice to share a meal with someone who wasn't constantly talking about dieting, the way that Molly did.

"I'm familiar with that type from the corporate jobs I had before I started at Better Love. They were awful," I said.

"How did you end up working as a matchmaker anyway? It's not exactly a conventional career. Did you major in love in college?"

I laughed.

"No, I majored in psychology. I thought I was going to be a therapist. I guess I've always been interested in people and what makes them the way that they are, why they do what they do. Matchmaking is an extension of that. My mom and I used to watch romantic comedies together, and I still love dating shows. I think who we choose to love or not love reveals a lot about us as people. So many of my clients tell me that everyone they've dated in the past showed up waving giant red flags. They think that it's coincidental or, like, it's separate from who they are, but it's not. It's my job to figure out how they can develop a healthy relationship despite their impulses."

Rebecca clasped the charm on her necklace, dragging it back and forth across the chain while I spoke, her eyes on my face.

"You make matchmaking sound so noble," she said when I'd finished. "Meanwhile, I just sell cars to horny married dudes."

"Hey, we all have a role to play," I told her.

We split the bill, because that was what friends did. It also gave me plausible deniability with Serena. Yes, I'd met up with a client outside the office. Yes, we'd had dinner together. But it was an equal exchange of goods and services. We were becoming friends. What could be harmful about that?

"I had a wonderful time getting to know you tonight, Lexie," Rebecca said in the parking lot.

The two of us lingered. Had she been a romantic interest, I would've wanted her to kiss me. As it was, I wished that she would come home with me so that we could sit on the couch and watch television.

"We should exchange numbers," I blurted out before we parted.

Technically, I already had access to her number, but it didn't look good to text clients from my personal phone.

"Oh, yeah, of course."

Rebecca handed me her phone so that I could input my contact information.

There was nothing that could rectify what Molly had done to me. I couldn't think about her face without wanting to smash something. Meeting Rebecca felt predestined. We'd known each other for only a few days, and already I could tell that she would be the friend to me that Molly never was.

I was so excited by the possibilities of our burgeoning friendship—nights spent drinking wine, girls' trips to the beach like cast members always took on reality television—that I completely forgot about the results of the Better Love intake questionnaire. The one that had labeled Rebecca a psychopath.

10.

I'D SET UP THE date for Rebecca and Paul for Saturday night. In addition to our matching services, Better Love had connections with local restaurants that allowed us to get reservations at places that were booked months in advance. I got Rebecca and Paul a table at one of my favorite restaurants. I wasn't going on the date, but with my level of excitement as I made the plans, I might as well have been.

My own social calendar remained achingly blank. I hadn't heard from Noah since the night that he'd ended things—"paused," not "ended." I told myself that nothing was truly over with him, not yet.

I was less perturbed by the absence of his physical presence than by the cessation of his messages. Because he spent so much time at the hospital, a lot of our relationship had consisted of notes that he wrote on Post-its like he was filling out a prescription pad with pills for love.

Have a great day, beautiful, he left on my bedside table.

I left something sweet for you in the fridge, said one stuck to the counter.

I wish I could spend the day with you, said one on the door to the garage.

During his breaks from work, he would send me texts that reinforced what the notes said. Because of the constant reminders of adoration, I never had to question whether he loved me. It was written—literally—all over the home that we shared together. Such correspondence had continued all the way up until the day that he left me, and the sudden termination came as a shock to the system.

I thought of a date with Aidan as a way of making Noah jealous, and then pushed the idea aside. Jealousy worked only when the person I wanted to feel it was looking at me, and Noah, it seemed, had forgotten me completely.

Are you going to come get your things? I messaged him on Friday.

I carefully considered my strategy before I pressed SEND. Men were very sensitive when they perceived that women close to them were experiencing emotion. The most important thing was to avoid coming off as hysterical. All women, regardless of how cool, calm, and collected they felt internally, were at risk of falling into the trap of hysteria. Get dumped and feel bad about it? Hysterical. Expect your romantic partner to care about your feelings? Absolutely insane. "Hysteria" was another word for "feelings," except that it applied specifically to feelings that men disliked. It created an impossible bind. Women weren't allowed to express displeasure or heartbreak, or to suggest that any men had wronged them. It meant that the only way to get Noah back was to pretend that I was unaffected by the things that he'd done.

Dots immediately popped up on the screen, indicating that

Noah was typing something, and then disappeared. Each time my phone buzzed during the rest of the day, I hurriedly picked it up thinking that there was a message from him, only for it to be from Rebecca. She was the only thing in my life that wasn't consistently proving to be a disappointment. The two of us had been chatting nonstop, recapping all of our favorite shows. It was like bingeing on friendship, catching up on the years when we hadn't known each other.

> Did you watch the season where
> Lulu released her album?

> > Yes!!! Secretly, I kind of loved it.

> Oh, I know. She's a terrible singer,
> which makes it better in my opinion.

It wasn't until I was in the shower the following morning that Noah finally got back to me. I got out, naked and shivering, grateful that Noah was unable to witness my eagerness to hear from him. Nothing killed a relationship faster than wanting to be in contact with someone.

> Can I come by tonight?

Yes. Noah in the town house. It was a more promising response than I'd expected. I saw a vision of the two of us standing at the altar, our eyes meeting as he slipped onto my finger the ring that signified *forever*. I didn't let any of that come through the phone. As far as Noah knew, I was the ice queen.

I have plans at 8, so it has to be fast.

There were no plans at eight. Rebecca would still be on her date, my mother in prison, and I had no one else to call, but pretending I was busy seemed a surefire way of protecting myself from charges of hysteria. He couldn't know how much I wanted to see him, how certain I was that he was going to come back.

———

I DEDICATED THE DAY TO GETTING READY FOR NOAH'S ARRIVAL. It was a twisted version of my birthday—rather than being about *me* it would be about *us*. I couldn't help but wonder if that's where I'd gone wrong to begin with. Had I spent too much time focused on my own needs? Maybe I should've been the one planning surprise parties during the long hours that Noah was at work.

My first stop was the flower shop.

I didn't used to understand the appeal of flowers.

"Flowers die," my mother had told me, before extolling all the virtues of diamonds.

Though my mother's statement was melodramatic, she wasn't totally wrong. I couldn't figure out the purpose of spending money on something that would wither within a few days. At least a bottle of champagne or a nice cut of fish would provide me some physical pleasure.

Then Noah had bought me flowers for our first Valentine's Day. I'd come home from work exhausted. We always got a rush of new clients in February. People were trying to make good on their New Year's resolutions; they were cold, and the holiday reminded them of how alone they were. Even psychopaths weren't immune to that kind of pressure. On top of the new clients, my existing clients needed assistance with making reservations, and figuring out the right gestures to cement their relationships. It was my responsibility to make sure that none of my newly matched couples fell apart because they'd gifted each other too much too soon or nothing at all.

I hadn't expected Noah to do anything for Valentine's Day. He'd left me a note in the morning.

I love you.

After that, he'd disappeared into the abyss of the hospital. I figured that neither of us had the capacity to plan anything, and that was fine. I'd spent the holiday alone for the majority of my life, and there was no reason that I couldn't continue the pattern.

The flowers were waiting outside the door. A bouquet of a dozen roses in a vase. The card: *You're my match.*

"You must be freezing," I'd said to the flowers, and brought them inside. I coveted them like a new pet. I trimmed the stems, gave them food, kept them alive for as long as possible. Noah wasn't able to make it home in time for dinner, and it didn't matter. I ordered a heart-shaped pizza and ate it on the couch, with my bouquet sitting next to me. Suddenly I understood that flowers were special *because* they died. They served no purpose. They weren't nourishing or healing. They were the ultimate extravagance, an ephemeral kind of beauty. My mother couldn't appreciate that. Then again, my mother was a murderer. As much as she thought otherwise, her tastes were rarely indicative of objective truth.

I went to the florist because I wanted to remind Noah of that night. He'd seen how much I liked the bouquet and he'd set up an order for a weekly delivery, a recurring gift that had stopped after he revealed his infidelity. I hoped that when he saw the bouquet he would assume that I had a suitor. I couldn't use Aidan to make him jealous, but that didn't mean that I couldn't use jealousy as a strategy. I would fabricate a man out of air if I needed to.

When I saw the broad shoulders, the gray hat, and the jacket in front of me in line, a ding of recognition sounded in my brain.

Noah. It's Noah. He's here and he's buying me flowers.

I reached my arm forward and tapped him on the shoulder. The man turned.

"Lexie."

It wasn't Noah at all, but Aidan. I was horrified at my mistake. I'd heard of clients making similar gaffes. *We were making love and I accidentally called him my ex's name. He's so mad at me, but I didn't mean it. I don't think about my ex anymore, not consciously. I don't know where that came from. Can you perform an exorcism? Erase him from my brain?* I was grateful that at least I hadn't spoken Noah's name out loud. I was the only one who knew what my psyche had done, switching out one man for another. I could imagine the smug look on Aidan's face if he knew.

"Aidan."

"It seems like we can't avoid each other," he said.

There were two people in front of him in line. The woman ordering asked questions as though she'd never seen a flower before in her life. I needed to go. I had food to put in the oven. I was uncomfortable with the way Aidan was looking at me. I wished that I'd put on makeup before leaving the house.

"Yes, it's weird, isn't it?" I replied. "Do you have a hot date tonight?"

He was holding a prearranged bouquet. He glanced down at the flowers like he'd forgotten they were in his hands.

"No. I'm still waiting for you to find the love of my life—remember? These are for me. Men can buy themselves flowers too, you know. What about you? Did your fiancé come crawling back, as you predicted?"

"Yes, actually. We're seeing each other tonight. He's coming over."

The line hadn't moved. I shifted impatiently. I'd never been good at waiting.

"Well, I hope that it works out for the two of you."

Aidan's tone indicated the opposite of his stated sentiment. He leaned in closer. He was always doing that, the kind of psychopath who didn't understand boundaries.

"Does he know?" he asked.

"Know what?"

"About your parents?"

I jerked backward, in an attempt to put distance between us, and bumped into an irritated-looking bald man. Usually I was capable of playing it cool in the most stressful of situations, but Aidan had brought up a topic that activated me. It confirmed what I already knew—I'd told Aidan about my parents. But what else? Secrets were boxes that held smaller boxes within. Just when it seemed the most deeply embedded package was reached, there was something new to unveil.

"He knows what he needs to," I replied.

What went unsaid: that I hadn't told him because men like Noah didn't marry women with families like mine. He came from the kind of people who pretended to be accepting, until they were presented with someone who defied their understanding of the world.

"I've heard that good relationships are built on trust," Aidan said pointedly. He knew that I hadn't told Noah. *I never tell anyone this*, I'd said to him that night in the hotel room.

"We do trust each other," I said.

Finally, the line began to move, and Aidan and I each took a step forward.

"What about you? Are you going to tell me how you figured out that you're a psychopath?" I asked him.

Until that moment, I'd never seen Aidan look uncomfortable. The paradox of the psychopath was how they fit in everywhere, and nowhere at all. He was so smooth that he could talk his way into any room, no matter how tightly the door was locked. I'd figured out his trigger the same way that he'd figured out mine.

"I told you," he said, "the night we met. Don't you remember?"

No. I searched through the parts of the night that had turned black, and found nothing. The steak, the table, the hot tub, the car, the bed . . . What had he said, and when had he said it? I hadn't thought any of it important. He was supposed to be a blip.

"Sir," the cashier called out to him.

Aidan turned away. There was a kind of energy buzzing off of him that I hadn't felt before.

"Have a nice night, Lexie," he said after he paid.

I ignored the urge to reach out and grab him. *Tell me what you did*. Aidan was a distraction from the pathway. I couldn't let myself get interrupted again.

After the florist, I went to the grocery store to purchase dinner ingredients. I walked through the aisles with a new wariness, worried that I might somehow bump into Aidan again. As I gathered my items, I told myself that it wasn't the universe or serendipity pushing Aidan and me together. It was coincidence, just as it had been a coincidence when I'd shown up at the COMP meeting Rebecca attended each week. I ignored the fact that my presence at the meeting had been a planned thing.

Grocery shopping was a comforting routine.

Noah had never explicitly voiced that he expected a female partner to make dinner, but he acted in such a way that implied it. Everything clicked together when I met his parents and realized that he understood their relationship to be emblematic of "normal."

"I love my children more than anything," his mother had confided in me once, "but sometimes I worry that I spoiled them."

There was evidence of said spoiling in the way that Noah inhabited spaces. He left dirty dishes sitting on the table, a sink full of hair after shaving, and he dumped his clothes on the floor at the end of the night.

"What's for dinner?" he asked when he came home from a shift, regardless of what time it was.

It used to drive me crazy, before he left me for Molly. We would get into fights about it during which he would attribute his household laziness to the number of hours he worked in the hospital. I knew that it went deeper than that. He had the demeanor of someone who had always been cared for, which was something I'd never experienced, not even before the murder. In addition to being bad at cleaning, my parents didn't know how to cook, and nearly all our meals came from restaurants. Sometimes we went without eating completely. I was six the first time I snuck into my dad's wallet to steal cash in order to buy something for dinner from the convenience store down the street. Hours spent in front of the television taught me that the way that we lived was abnormal.

Everyone on-screen had family dinners, clean houses, wholesome parents. Though I couldn't totally define it, I knew something was wrong in our house. None of the places where we lived were the kinds of places where I could have my classmates over, which intensified my loneliness. I deeply wanted to live somewhere like the homes on television, a spotless abode that was worthy of backyard barbecues and kids' birthday parties. The town house wasn't exactly that, but it was a start. When he left me, Noah and I had been months away from upgrading to something bigger. I wanted a bathroom with two sinks. A room reserved for "entertaining," even though I rarely had people over. The kind of place people strolled past when walking their dogs and wondered who was lucky enough to be inside.

Molly couldn't provide any of the things that I had provided. She lived in an apartment that cost a disproportionate percentage of her salary, especially considering its small size. Because of her online-shopping habit, the apartment was overflowing with her belongings. She kept saying that she was going to donate stuff or move to a bigger spot, but I knew neither would ever happen. Also, Molly hated to cook. She lived off protein shakes and the salads from a place near her work. I was certain that, after a week of staying with her, Noah was starving.

Back at home, I started in the kitchen, chopping onions, potatoes, and garlic on a cutting board. Noah always raved about his mother's casseroles, and I'd witnessed the way that he'd devoured her food when we'd gone to visit. His mother, in contrast, picked, birdlike, at her plate. No one aside from me seemed to notice that her eating habits looked suspiciously similar to an eating disorder.

What do you think of my outfit? Rebecca texted a photo featuring an emerald green dress over tights, the combination of which was both fashionable and perfect for the winter weather.

You look amazing!!! I replied. Paul is going to love it!!!

I longed to tell her about my current predicament as I pulled on sheer black tights and a low-cut, backless dress, an outfit that I hoped suggested a date later in the evening. One thing that people rarely mentioned about lying was how lonely it was. I was reliant on a future in which my falsehoods had become the truth. I imagined Rebecca and Paul on a double date with Noah and me. How cute the four of us would be! People around us would be envious of our good looks. *How do I become one of them?* they would wonder.

Thirty minutes before Noah was set to arrive, I stuck the casserole in the oven, arranged the bouquet that I'd purchased after my run-in with Aidan in a vase, and poured myself a glass of wine. I left some clutter on the dining room table. The scene needed to be enticing but not appear planned. Never mind that I never made casseroles. Never mind that I never lounged around the house alone, in a sexy dress, with a glass of wine poised between my fingers. Never mind that I was possibly closer to hysteria than I'd ever been.

11.

—

HOUGH HE STILL HAD a key, Noah rang the doorbell. The formality of it was painful. I hated the acknowledgment of what he'd done, that the town house had so instantly reverted to being solely mine. He had moved in with me quickly. Molly pushed me in front of him; he pulled me up, tended to my wounds, and a month later he was spending seven nights a week in my bed. I hadn't considered that the easiness of his moving in with me was an indicator of the easiness of his leaving. I couldn't let it happen again. I would invite him in and make sure that he stayed.

I took a minute to answer the door, pretending that I was busy doing other things. *I wasn't waiting for you. I haven't spent the day preparing for your arrival.*

"Hi," I said when I'd opened the door. I turned my face to stone, expressing neither joy nor sorrow. Only hysterical women glared and grimaced at the men who had hurt them.

He stood there, the same as he'd ever been. He wore my favorite blue sweater, the one that matched his eyes. I wondered when he'd taken it, and I realized with a sudden epiphany that he must've spent weeks preparing for his departure with Molly. His hands were in his pockets, his shoulders hunched with apprehension.

"Hey, Lexie."

He paused awkwardly in the doorway, like a vampire waiting for permission to enter.

"Are you cold?" I asked, noting his lack of a jacket.

He shrugged. I took it to mean that he was using the chilliness as some kind of self-flagellation for his sins.

"You can come in, you know," I said after a moment.

"Okay. Thanks," he replied, stepping across the threshold.

I shut the door, wishing that I had handcuffs and a chain so I could keep him inside forever. I pushed the thought away. Only hysterical women kept their ex-fiancés hostage in the houses they'd once shared together.

"Where's my stuff?" he asked.

"Where you left it."

In the kitchen, the oven timer went off with a beep. Perfect timing.

"Hold on," I told him. "I need to get dinner out of the oven."

Noah followed me into the kitchen. I did my best to bend over sexily as I reached for the pan, my hands covered by thick oven mitts.

"That smells good," he said.

If I knew anything, I knew what my man liked to eat.

"Do you want some? There's plenty."

After a pause, he replied, "Okay. Just a little."

I turned my back on him, smiled to myself, and poured more wine.

"Want a glass?" I asked, gesturing to the bottle.

"Why not?" he said.

No pause this time. I'd forgotten how pliable he was. It was one of the things I'd initially liked about him. As long as it didn't interfere with his job, he was happy to go along with whatever I wanted to do. No wonder Molly had been able to break him between her fingers.

I cut us each a thick rectangle of casserole. The cheese stuck to the spatula. I knew what my mother would've said about the dish: *so pedestrian*. She was the type of woman who preferred to eat a luxurious meal or nothing at all. That meant that I was hungry a lot as a child, and hungry people will consume all kinds of stuff.

We sat at the dining room table. It was a place where we'd sat a million times before, but it felt like new now. He glanced at the flowers, and I did my best to read jealousy into his expression.

"How have you been, Lexie?" he asked after a moment of silence.

The question was a test rather than a true inquiry. *Are you going to turn hysterical on me, Lexie?* he might as well have asked. He sounded like Dr. Noah, the man in charge of the exam room, instead of the person who'd had sex with me a thousand different ways. He was assessing me, trying to determine whether I was ill.

"I've been okay," I said, giving away nothing.

He nodded. I'd passed.

"Me too," he said. "Okay."

I took a bite of the casserole. Fuck. It was good. It tasted wholesome, like his family. If Noah hadn't been there, I might've eaten the whole thing in a single sitting.

"How's your mom?" I asked. *Does she still love me? Does she miss me, her once and future daughter?*

Some hurt came through on his face. Noah disliked disappointing his mother more than he disliked doing the same to me.

"She's sad."

And what about you? Are you sad too?

"It's okay, you know, if she wants to text me. I miss her," I said. He nodded.

"I'll let her know."

Noah didn't ask about my mother. We'd established early on in our relationship that I didn't like to talk about my family, with the implication that they were abusive. I appreciated how uncurious he was. Other women wanted men who asked them questions, but I wanted someone who accepted what I was willing to give.

"I'm sorry that you didn't have a good relationship with your parents," he'd said. "My parents can be that for you, the mom and dad that you never had."

When he told me, that was probably the first moment I really knew I was in love.

I changed the topic, because it was difficult thinking about his mom. I didn't want my relationship with her to be altered. People on television were constantly saying things like *You're like a brother/sister/mother/father to me* to people they'd known for only a few weeks. I'd wanted his mother to be that adoptive parent for me. I'd wanted to be a daughter to her, even though she'd already birthed one of her own. The previous week had shown how easy it was to sever the closeness we'd established. The expression "like a mother," it turned out, was just a simile after all.

"Work has been interesting. Better Love is going to expand

into other cities soon, become a national brand. Serena is going to promote someone to take over her role at the original office."

Noah's face brightened.

"It's yours," he said.

"I hope so. Nicole wants it too."

"Fuck Nicole." A rare swear word out of his mouth. "You deserve it."

I smiled. Noah liked that I was a matchmaker. Though he hadn't voiced as much, he seemed to believe that it was an appropriate profession for a woman. I was responsible for the metaphorical heart while he was in charge of the literal organ. Secretly, each of us believed that we held the more important position. Despite the patronizing tone that he sometimes used to describe my role, I appreciated Noah's belief in my abilities, as it was further proof that we were supposed to be together. He believed in me as a matchmaker; ergo, he believed me when I told him that the two of us were a perfect fit.

"Thanks, Noah."

"Do you mind if I have more?" he asked, gesturing toward his empty plate.

"Go for it," I told him.

He went into the kitchen. I quickly checked my reflection in my phone screen, to make sure my lipstick was intact, and I saw that I had a text from Rebecca.

Paul is cute, but our conversation isn't
going great. Seems a little full of himself?

Give it a little more time! I responded, then put my phone down as Noah returned.

"You're such a good cook," he said. He wiped his mouth with

a napkin after taking too big of a bite. He was a messy eater, which was incongruous with the rest of his persona. Most of his food consumption occurred in the hospital, where he hurriedly stuffed whatever he could into his mouth.

"Thanks. I'm trying something new tonight." I didn't tell him that I'd used one of his mother's recipes, that I knew what he wanted because what he wanted was a replica of his own mom.

"It's great. You should definitely make this again."

His compliments were followed by several beats of silence. *Say the word, and we can go back to normal. It doesn't have to be like this.* I hated how palpable the shift between us was. I could feel Molly in the room even though she wasn't there.

"There are new episodes of that show you like," I said when Noah was almost finished with his food.

"Which one?"

"The one about the detective."

"Oh yeah. I haven't had much time to watch television lately."

The implication was that he was busy at the hospital, but I couldn't help considering what he and Molly had been doing together. I thought of all the stories that Molly had told me about her sexual escapades and her various boyfriends, including the time she'd actually vomited while giving someone a blow job. Now Noah was part of that lore.

"We could watch an episode if you want. Oliver gave me an apple pie. I guess someone he's dating gave it to him, but he's on one of his crazy diets where he's off sugar, so he passed it along to me."

Noah looked down at his smartwatch. I saw the numbers flash: six forty-five. Still plenty of time before my fictional plans at eight o'clock.

"You know I love pie," he said.

I did.

"I'll go cut us each a slice."

Though Oliver *was* on a sugar-free diet—one that involved a conspicuous number of doughnuts during our weekly intake meeting—he hadn't given me the pie. I'd picked it up while at the store, shopping for dinner ingredients. If nothing else worked—the casserole, the decorations, the dress, my body—I knew that the pie would hook him. Outside of the hospital, where he was brilliant, Noah really was a simple man.

I refilled our wine glasses while he took a seat on the couch. I was on my third glass, and drunker than I'd intended to be. I told myself that I needed the alcohol to help me be brave. I didn't. I was brave enough on my own. I wanted to be drunk because it helped me block out thoughts of Molly and Noah, their bodies moving together as one.

I checked my phone and found another update from Rebecca.

He invited me back to his place.
Should I go?

No! That's against the rules, I replied.

While Better Love couldn't fully control what clients did, we highly recommended that people wait until the third date before they saw each other's living spaces or engaged in sexual intimacy. The suggestion wasn't related to any kind of moral purity but because sex complicated things. One of the reasons why people struggled to find someone compatible out in the world was because they confused lust and love, and our guidelines were set in place to help them avoid such confusion.

Knowing that it's against the rules makes me want to do it more, Rebecca texted.

I knew what I should say as a matchmaker, and I knew what I should say as a friend. Maybe Serena hadn't been totally off the mark in trying to establish separation between those roles.

You do you, I said. I wasn't about to cockblock my new friend.

I cut big slices of apple pie and scooped vanilla ice cream on top—the fancy kind, embedded with dark spots of vanilla bean. I decided that when we got back together, I'd make sure to do nice things for him more often. A lack of pie wasn't the reason why Noah left, but maybe pie would be enough to make him stay.

When I walked into the living room and saw Noah sitting there, it was as though he'd never left. I'd always wondered how people could forgive their cheating partners, but I got it now. It was like he'd spent a weekend in Aruba or Hawaii, had his little adventures, and come back home. Once again, I longed for a rope to tie him to the couch. It didn't have to be unpleasant. There were a lot of people who got off on being bound.

"Wow, that looks amazing," Noah said.

I put on the detective show. Compared with reality television, this show's colors were muted, the sound dulled. Oftentimes, things that were labeled "prestige" were simply difficult to comprehend.

I took a bite of pie, then another. I looked down and realized that the whole piece was gone. Noah and I were mere inches apart. I wanted to devour him. One of the questions on the Better Love intake form asked clients to give three adjectives to describe themselves. Sometimes I considered what I would write, and the only thing that I could think of was "hungry."

Noah leaned forward to set his empty plate on the table. Our fingers brushed as I put my plate on top of his.

On television, the detective raced after a suspect.

"Don't let him get away!" the detective screamed. The uniformed police officers were ineffectual, as usual. That was part of the premise of the show. The detective could depend only on himself to solve crimes. Luckily, he'd run cross-country in high school. The suspect was fast, but the detective was faster. After all that effort, the cops let the suspect go a mere three hours later.

"Goddamn it!" the detective yelled.

My hand crept closer to Noah's leg. Ironically, I wanted him more now than I ever had when we were together. I liked having sex with him, but sometimes it was perfunctory. I was accustomed to putting on a show for men, making them want me by being who they wanted me to be.

Jump my bones, I mentally hissed at him.

Strangely, he'd never been able to read my mind.

It was the detective who guided Noah into my arms. He had a female acolyte, young and attractive. There had been hints that they were going to get together since the first episode of the show. They'd almost done it in a prior episode, when someone had shot at the acolyte and the detective had tackled her to the ground to protect her from the bullets that flew through the air. Once the gunfire had ceased, the two became aware of the closeness of their bodies, how the detective rested between the acolyte's hips. They didn't kiss then, but only because an officer interrupted them to ask if they were okay. The audience lamented the interruption. Inherently, they understood the connection between sex and danger.

In the episode we were watching, the acolyte went to the detective's house to comfort him after the suspect was released. People frequently went to one another's houses on television shows. In real life, I rarely had guests. Only Molly and Noah had routinely breached the border of my front door, and of the two, one had been permanently banned.

Like Noah and me, the detective and the acolyte started drinking. Like Noah and me, they grew closer and closer. The acolyte made the first move. She had to. He was her superior, old and experienced. If he pursued her, he would be accused of taking advantage of his position.

She climbed on top of him. I climbed on top of Noah. He continued watching television, over my shoulder, while I kissed his neck. It was an immersive experience. He became the detective and I the acolyte, the same way that earlier he'd been the son and I'd been the mother, feeding him casserole. It was only when I pulled my dress over my head, revealing my bare body, that he dragged his eyes from the screen. I wanted him to worship me.

Noah didn't bother taking his clothes off; he merely unzipped his pants.

"Lexie," he murmured, "you feel so good."

I was surprised to feel a spark of anger within my chest at the sound of his pleasure. The hysterical woman never would've allowed Noah to feel good again. She would've taken the opportunity to castrate her former lover or, worse, end him completely. I shut out the thought. I let him fill me. I wished that I wasn't on birth control, so that there was potential for a pregnancy.

The episode ended. I climbed off of Noah, wrapping around my naked body the blanket I kept on the couch.

My phone buzzed, causing an outsized tremor in the couch cushions. I picked it up. I had a text message from Rebecca.

His dick is disappointing, she wrote.

The movement disrupted the spell. Noah's expression returned to the blank doctor's gaze.

"I should go," he said, looking back down at his watch. "You have plans."

Oh yes. My fictitious plans. I'd nearly forgotten.

"Okay."

I held up my phone, pretended that I was texting, and snapped a picture of Noah on the couch before he stood up. It wasn't a flattering shot. His face was a postcoital red, and angled in such a way that it gave him a double chin. His underwear was wrapped around his knees and his penis was deflated. Noah would've hated it if he'd seen it. He wanted to view himself only in the most flattering of lights. He struggled when he received criticism at work, and on numerous occasions I'd consoled him about the critiques, regardless of how valid they seemed. It didn't matter. The picture wasn't for him.

Noah restored his pants to their rightful position before making his way to the door. He looked at me. He leaned forward as though to give me a kiss, and then backed away. He was uncomfortable in all situations in which there wasn't a prescribed script.

"Bye, Lexie."

I fought off the impulse to beg him to stay. *This could all be over right now.* Neither of us brought up his belongings. I viewed that as a purposeful omission. The longer his things were in my closet, the more of a reason he had to come back. The sound of the door closing was painful. I almost immediately regretted letting him leave. I wanted the universe to deliver me an award for my ability to act like a normal, stable woman. I gave myself a minute to breathe. I put on my comfiest pair of pajamas. I opened a second bottle of wine. Then I set the next part of my plan into motion.

———

I WASN'T SO NAÏVE AS TO THINK A SINGLE PLUNGE INTO MY VA-gina was enough to get Noah to reverse course. He wasn't alone in what he'd done. Molly was the true ringleader of their affair, something that I doubted Noah recognized. He was good at memorization, at regurgitating bits of information he'd been told, but he wasn't a great critical thinker. Often I'd mention current events to him and he'd reply, "Oh, yeah, I haven't really been paying attention." It felt a little like he'd sleepwalked his way into an affair.

I knew that if I prodded Molly enough, she would become the hysterical woman. She was, after all, quite an emotional person—much more so than me. I'd even seen her cry while watching episodes of reality television.

"I really thought they would end up together," she said, her eyes wet and red, about two people who worked on a superyacht who'd split up after a three-week fling.

Feelings like that were not Noah's forte. He was used to caring for the tangible—bones, blood, and skin. Emotions were trickier. Despite attempts from the pharmaceutical companies, there was no prescription he could write that rid a person of their tears. His inability to provide a fix made him uncomfortable.

"I like you because you don't get upset about stupid things," he'd told me once. "I always know how to make you happy."

It was one of the highest compliments that a man could give. *You're not like those other women, who scream and cry and whine.* If I revealed that side of Molly to him—the crying woman—then maybe he'd leave her. If I showed her what he'd done, then maybe she would be the one to kick him out.

I opened up my text thread with Molly, which extended back for years and years. All those stupid little intimacies. There were times when we'd even texted each other about pooping. In some ways, it was easier to tell her things than to tell Noah. I wasn't worried about embarrassing myself in front of her. I didn't need her to find me sexy. I wasn't trying to be promoted to the next step in the relationship hierarchy, because we'd already reached the pinnacle of friendship. Everyone needed a place where they weren't trying to prove themselves, and they could just be. It stung to think of how mistaken I'd been about the nature of our bond.

The last message she'd sent said Happy Birthday Queen!!! The words were recontextualized by the fact that they were sent mere hours before she told me that she was sleeping with my fiancé.

I couldn't—wouldn't—allow her to have the final say in our friendship. At the conclusion of each season of *Love on the Lake*, there was a reunion episode in which, after viewing the season, all the cast members got together to air their grievances. They wore ball gowns that were suitable for the Met Gala and screamed in one another's faces.

"I wish there were reunion episodes in real life," I told Molly once—a kind of fantasy to be able to tell everyone exactly what you thought of them after viewing all their bad behavior.

I didn't have a soundstage on which to share my grievances with the world. I was sitting in my pajamas on the couch, drinking my second bottle of wine, my underwear wet from Noah's semen leaking out of me. I had no microphone through which to convey my anger, no platform for revenge. All I had was a picture, which I uploaded into the thread.

Do you know where your boyfriend is tonight? I wrote beneath it.

I imagined all the ways it would make her crazy, which wasn't particularly difficult, as I'd inhabited my own forms of crazy in the week since Molly and Noah had told me about the affair. I hoped that she would scream and cry, pound her fists against Noah's chest until he realized the error of his ways and came running back to me.

You were right. You were right all along, he would say.

I was so certain of the outcome that I felt smug as I poured myself another glass of wine. It felt like everything was back in my grasp. I was a matchmaker. I was in control of love.

Things got fuzzy after that. More wine. Somewhere, I found a bottle of vodka. I remembered eating cold casserole with my hands. Rebecca texting I cannot WAIT to tell you about my night. At some point I went outside. My fingers got so cold that they ached.

12.

HOW IS MY DAUGHTER tonight?" my mother asked during our weekly phone call.

I was hungover, a state that was becoming habitual for Sundays. That was the kind of drinker that I was. I either abstained or consumed until I was sick.

"I'm good," I told her.

"And your fiancé?"

"He's good too."

I hadn't heard from Noah or Molly. I expected her rage. I expected him to come knocking on the door, begging for forgiveness. I wasn't sure what to do with the silence. Had my plan failed?

"I hear it's cold there," my mother said next, a comment that made me sit up straight on the couch.

It *was* cold, but how did she know? I purposefully hadn't told her which state I lived in, never mind which city. Was it possible that she'd found me? The weather was one of the reasons I'd initially settled in Minnesota, as my mother didn't tolerate freezing weather, because heavy coats obscured her beauty. Apparently I hadn't gone far enough. I ran through a list of countries where I could hide—Wales, Thailand, New Zealand . . .

"What did you say?"

"I said it's cold here," my mother replied, and I slowly relaxed back into the couch.

"I remember being young and in love," my mother reminisced, reverting to our previous topic of conversation like she'd never mentioned the weather at all.

She took in a breath that was loud enough to hear through the phone. Sometimes I tried to imagine her surroundings while she talked to me. I'd never visited her in prison, so I had no reference outside of the facilities I saw depicted on television. On a show that Molly and I watched, a cast member was arrested while cameras were rolling. While she was cuffed, the rest of the cast was on a party bus, getting drunk and discussing the possibility of her guilt. *She can't have done what they said she did*, they concluded, with the caveat that maybe she had. Maybe she was hiding a criminal self for the length of their friendship. When she was found guilty and sentenced to a decade in prison, they changed their tune. *I knew it. I was in denial about the truth. She lied! We were never really friends.*

Though I knew that my mother was in a maximum security prison and the cast member somewhere more casual, in my mind they were locked up together. I imagined a line of pay phones, a row of jumpsuited women with receivers pressed to their ears. My mother still looked just as she had when I was young—beautiful and terrifying.

"Your father knew he loved me immediately," she continued. "I was with someone else when we met. I bet you didn't know that."

I did know that. I knew all about their love story. My mother frequently talked about my father, leaving out the inconvenience of his death. She repeated the same anecdotes again and again, as if describing it enough might make it one of the romantic comedies that we'd watched together, instead of a horror show.

Here was how it went:

My mother was with a boyfriend in a restaurant. They were having a nice meal when my father walked up to the table and said, "Excuse me, but you're the most striking woman I've ever seen in my life. I think I'm in love with you."

If it had been anyone else, it wouldn't have worked. My father could do and say things that other people couldn't get away with. He could take another man's girlfriend while she was on a date with him. That was why I burned his manifesto. No one should be that convincing.

"Thank you," my mother had said. It was common for people to compliment her, because she was an attractive woman. I understood from a young age that I would never be as alluring as her, and that maybe that wasn't a bad thing. My father was too charismatic, my mother too beautiful, and the combination was disastrous.

Her date thought things had ended there, but my parents met up in the bathroom and had sex. They didn't need a conversation to establish what was happening; they just knew. Physically, my mother returned to the table, to her date, but mentally, she was gone.

"What happened to your boyfriend?" I asked my mother once.

"Who?" she'd replied, as though she didn't understand the question.

My mother remembered only the things that she wanted to remember. When I told her how I'd starved as a child, about the hours that I was left alone, she acted like I was making it all up.

"Stop telling lies," she told me.

"Why would I make any of that up?" I asked.

"Because," she said, "you're determined to hate me."

What I didn't say was that she'd already given me more than enough ammunition to despise her. The thing that stopped me from saying it was that, despite everything, I still loved my mother. There were depths of cruelty that I was unwilling to explore because I was worried what might come out of my mouth if I allowed it to open.

"I hope that you're making your fiancé work for it," she told me. "I made your father do all kinds of things before I would marry him—nice meals, fancy jewelry, you name it. 'What can you do for me that no one else can?' I asked him, and he showed me. That's what love is."

"What *exactly* did he do?" I asked, not sure that I wanted to know the answer.

"That woman died," she said.

"What woman?" I asked before I realized she had changed the topic on me. She did that whenever I asked something that she didn't want to answer. She was referring to the woman from the week before, the one who had been stabbed in the prison.

"Her family is suing," she continued. "They're claiming that it was negligence. Someone needs to tell them that no one liked her. Not everyone has a right to life."

—

MY MOTHER WAS STILL TALKING—DESCRIBING THE BEST DATES my father had ever taken her on—when the doorbell rang.

Noah.

"I have to go," I said.

My mother started to protest, her words changing from sweet soliloquies about the years spent with my father to a curse-laden rant about what a terrible daughter I was. I pressed the END button. It was nothing that I hadn't heard before. Besides, part of my motivation for getting back together with Noah was *her*. A stupid, stubborn part of me forever wanted to please my mother, regardless of what she did or said, and she wanted me to be with Noah. Above all else, she was fixated on a rom-com ending.

I flung open the door, expecting to find Noah standing there. I pictured all the ways that I was going to make him beg. Instead, I found a heart.

The heart was a pink helium-filled balloon that floated at eye level. We put something similar in the Better Love office on Valentine's Day. The end of the balloon's string was attached to a box wrapped in red paper. Whatever it was, the gift was clearly romantic.

It was from Noah. It had to be. It was exactly the kind of sweet gesture that he would make. He didn't have a lot of time, but he'd mastered the art of romantic delivery.

I was giddy when I picked up the box and brought it inside. I returned to the couch and examined the outside of the box for a card, and found none. The wrapping was so neat that I suspected that it had been done professionally, as Noah had always been hopeless with gift wrap. It was touching that he'd put in so much effort to get me back. I hoped that this was the first of many gifts to come.

I peeled back the tape, doing my best to avoid tearing the paper. The box beneath was of a shiny, high-quality cardboard. My fingers trembled as I took the top off and looked inside. What could it be? Diamonds? Keys to a new car? There was no limit to what Noah owed me after what he'd done.

It was immediately clear that whatever was inside wasn't any of those things, though exactly what it was proved difficult to process. It lay on a pile of tissue paper that had once been pink and flecked with gold and was now stained the reddish brown of what I soon realized was blood. The thing itself was of a meaty purple hue and about the size of a fist, which was one of the reasons that I didn't instantly recognize it; I would have thought it would be bigger.

Not wanting to touch it with my bare hands, I put on a spare pair of gloves that I used for cleaning, and delicately removed it from the box. As I examined the shape, its identity suddenly became clear.

"It's a heart," I said. The silent air around me gave no response.

A funny thing about working as a matchmaker was that I was surrounded by hearts at all times. They were in the company logo, and they adorned every piece of clothing that Nicole owned. They were so prevalent that it was easy to forget that, in addition to being a symbol of love, the heart was an organ that beat within our chests. Rather than having a cute shape, the thing in front of me was ugly, lumpy and asymmetrical. If I looked closely enough, I could identify the ventricles sticking out of the sides.

The giddy feeling remained, though it had become the inverse of itself, the excitement of something awful. My initial, irrational, impulse was to feel my own chest, as though someone might have broken in and removed the thing from between my ribs. I was relieved when I found my heart beating away, as steady as ever.

The questions came as a barrage.

Who had sent it, and why? Noah worked at a hospital. Though he didn't work in surgery or on corpses, he could probably access a disembodied organ if he really tried. However, it seemed out of character. His standard gift-giving strategy was going to a jewelry store, naming his price range, and selecting the piece of jewelry he thought I would like the most, a practice he'd picked up from his father. On top of that, he had no reason to send such a vicious gift. We'd slept together the night before!

I tried to think of who else might do such a thing. Molly certainly had motive, and she knew all the ways in which I was linked to death. However, she was squeamish. She was one of those people who threw up when they saw someone else vomiting, fainted when their blood was drawn at the doctor's office. She also worked in tech, a profession notorious for its lack of tangible human elements. Personality wise, Aidan seemed more likely. He had no reason to send me such an object, except that I had turned down his suggestion of a date, which really was one of the more dangerous things that a woman could do. He hadn't *seemed* angry. If anything, he'd seemed amused, as if Noah and I being together was a funny joke. Maybe I'd misinterpreted things. Maybe I'd gotten too comfortable working with my clients, like a snake charmer who'd forgotten that the reptiles could bite. After all, he'd done *something* that had informed him of his psychopathy.

An intrusion: Could it have been my mother? She had a proven track record of dismantling bodies. I reassured myself that she was in prison and that she didn't know where I lived or what I'd changed my name to. Next to her, Aidan was a comforting possibility.

The next question: Who or what had the heart belonged to? Could it be human? I delicately placed it back in the box, peeled the gloves off my fingers, and washed my hands with scalding water. I fetched my laptop and opened an incognito browser window. I knew better than to search for things like *what does a human heart look like?* out in the open.

I compared the image results with the thing in front of me. The coloring on mine was off—grayer than the deep red hues of the ones that were pictured, probably due to the fact that mine was dead and disembodied—but otherwise it matched. I hadn't done well in biology class in college, mostly because it required levels of effort that I wasn't accustomed to. Now I was getting a crash course.

If the object was indeed a human heart, that meant that somewhere out there was a human body that was missing its heart. The knowledge overwhelmed me. I shoved my laptop aside and ran to the bathroom as my stomach emptied its contents. This was bad. This was very, very bad.

I knelt on the bathroom floor, noting a dust accumulation along the floorboards that I'd failed to clean, and considered what kind of message the heart was intended to send. Even if my mother had nothing to do with the gift, it was undoubtedly related to her. Everything went back to my parents. The cruelty of life: no matter what I did, how I altered myself or changed my name, I would always be their child.

I know who you are, the heart said from the other room.

I know what you've done, it hissed.

I got up from the floor. I was dizzy. Anyone else would've

called the police. That was the right thing to do. I had an organ of mysterious origins in a box in my living room. However, I didn't trust the police. If I were capable of diagnosis, I might have identified my distrust as a symptom of PTSD. Sirens made my skin itch and flashing lights made me want to hide.

Besides, how would I explain the heart? It seemed possible that the delivery was a setup designed to destroy me. Once I'd called the police, I would have ceded control to them, and I was unwilling to do that.

I had a plan before I'd even thought about making a plan.

My parents hadn't taught me much. They didn't know how to cook or clean. I'd taught myself how to read out of spite when I was four and another little girl had taunted me for my illiteracy on the playground. My second-grade teacher was flummoxed when I, her smartest pupil, didn't know how to tie her own shoes. The one thing my parents had taught me, the single thing that I knew thanks to them, was how to dispose of body parts.

13.

___

HERE WAS WHAT MY brain allowed me to remember—what *I* allowed myself to remember. Was there a distinction there? I'd always struggled with the distinction between the conscious and unconscious selves, the things that I told myself that I wanted versus what I actually wanted.

"My dad was murdered," I told Aidan in the hotel room on the night that Noah and Molly admitted their affair.

"Oh," he responded. What else was there to say?

"In prison," I continued. "He was murdered in prison. I hadn't spoken to him in ten years when it happened. I don't think I've ever processed it. Apparently talking helps, but who am I supposed to talk to? People look at me differently when they find out what happened. It's like I'm diseased. No one would willingly mark themselves like that."

Aidan held my hand. He had neatly trimmed nails, and I wondered if he got professional manicures. He wanted to ask; I knew he did. *What did your father do?* Most people, especially those who claimed otherwise, loved to hear about disgusting things.

"It was both of them—my mother and my father. They killed people. You've probably heard of them. Their names are Peter and Lydia Schwartz."

"Yeah," he replied. With his other hand, he produced a bottle of tequila. Where had it come from? I lost track of the words as they came out of my mouth. What had he just told me? My brain had stopped processing things correctly. It did that sometimes, when I felt too much pleasure or too much pain.

"They're the serial killers, right? The ones who picked up women in bars? I know all about them," he said.

If only I could transmute notoriety into gold.

WE WERE LIVING IN MY FAVORITE HOUSE THE FIRST TIME IT happened. It was a remodeled historic building located in the downtown of a small Southern city. Somehow my parents had negotiated with the owner to allow us to stay there for free while a buyer was sought. That was the only way we would be able to live in a place like that, as my parents wouldn't have passed a credit check or been able to afford a deposit.

The ceilings were tall, and sound carried easily throughout the structure. I knew when my father was in the kitchen, eating a late-night bowl of cereal to feed his perpetual hunger. I had memorized the sound of my mother's makeup bottles clinking against one another as she got ready for the day. I took comfort in such things, though neither of my parents were particularly nurturing.

They liked to go out at night. By the time I was six, they'd decided that I was old enough to stay home on my own. I thought it was a compliment to my maturity. I didn't consider the possibility that it was neglect until I enrolled in psychology classes in college. When they'd left, I liked to raid the pantry for sweets. Each of my parents had a sweet tooth, so although the refrigerator was frequently empty, I could usually find a package of cookies or a carton of ice cream to indulge in. I would take my loot and scroll through channels on the television, looking for a movie. That was before streaming networks existed, so I caught small portions of a lot of films. Because my parents never mentioned my junk food consumption or television viewing, I thought my endeavors were subtle, sneaky. I buried deep in the trash can the remnants of whatever container I'd eaten out of so they wouldn't see it, and I was sure to be in bed before they came home, which wasn't difficult, as they often came back late in the night. Eventually, I developed an understanding that they probably knew what I was doing but they didn't care as long as they were able to go out and do what they wanted to do.

They'd been bringing women home for a while. It never occurred to me that there was anything weird about that. My parents were always making friends wherever we went. When we were kicked out of one housing situation, or they lost their jobs, they talked their way into another one. I assumed that was how the world worked. The women, at first, were just more friends who my parents had brought home. The initial few were the lucky ones, because they were the ones who lived.

One of the features of my favorite home was a second-floor balcony that overlooked the living room. When my parents brought the women home, I'd sneak out of my room to watch them. They would put a CD on the stereo, make drinks. Everyone was having fun! The women were always exceptionally beautiful, exuding a kind of sexuality that was obvious to me even as a child.

I understood why my parents had picked them. They'd always had good taste.

Later, what they did became a meme.

Hey, we saw you across the bar and we really dig your vibe. Can we buy you a drink?

None of the shared images captured the kind of people my parents were, because photographs were incapable of capturing that. They were good-looking, of course, but their appearance was the least of their charms. They could get anyone to do anything, at least up to a point. Their spells had expiration dates, at which time they were fired, or we were kicked out of our house, or they were expelled from yet another social circle. People frequently judged the women whom my parents picked up for choosing to go home with them—strangers—to engage in group sex acts. Surely, people said, they'd known it would end badly, and that decision was indicative of who the women were.

I doubted, however, that the women they brought home with them ordinarily made decisions like that. Probably, they'd gone to the bar to have a fun night out, and when my parents approached them they thought it was an innocent encounter, because what could two married people want with them? By the time they were dancing in my living room, they were fully bewitched.

Because sound carried so easily in the house, I'd heard numerous types of moaning before I ever heard screams of pain. I asked my mother about the noises once and she'd told me that the sounds were part of what grown-ups did when they felt especially good. I knew she was referring to sex. My parents didn't believe in parental guidance on movies, and I'd seen a number of R-rated films. However, the details were murky. The moans were common enough that I often slept through the noise, the way that people who grew up near train tracks got used to the horns.

The screams woke me up.

My initial thought was that the monster had finally arrived. See, I was convinced that a vicious beast was residing somewhere in the remodeled house, a leftover from a previous era of the home's existence. The primary thing that the monster wanted was to kill and eat us, and as I fell asleep I debated whether I wanted him—because he was certainly male—to eat my parents first, giving me a chance to escape, or I wanted to be consumed quickly, so that I wouldn't have to witness the carnage.

When I heard the screams, I thought my mother was being consumed by the monster. It never occurred to me that the monster might *be* her. I was so frightened that I failed to enact any of my previously thought-up plans. I didn't run away, or hide in the closet. Neither did I try to save my parents. I just lay there, paralyzed by fear. Whatever was happening, I knew the screams were the sounds of someone dying, even though I'd never heard anyone die before. There were some types of knowledge that were passed down through the blood.

Eventually the noise stopped, and I waited for the monster to come after me. I was awake for the rest of the night, my heart pounding. I was tempted to check in on my parents, but worried that the monster was hiding out in their room. I wasn't totally wrong. Had I opened the door, I would've found them attempting to dismember the body for easier disposal. It wasn't going well, as they didn't have the right tools. During their trial, I'd learn that my father went to the hardware store to buy a saw the next day.

It wasn't until my mother came into my room in the morning,

to tell me that I was going to miss the bus if I didn't get up soon, that I finally moved.

"You're alive," I gasped.

She laughed airily.

"Of course I'm alive. I'm never going to die," she told me.

Eventually I made the connection between the women and the screams. Rather than eating my parents, the monster was eating the women they brought home. I started to think of them as a kind of sacrifice, and while I felt bad for them, I was happy to remain intact myself. I didn't yet understand that there were ways to be dismembered that weren't physical.

At some point after that I realized that the monster didn't exist, or at least not as I'd imagined it. Still, I tried to rationalize things as I struggled to consider the possibility that my parents were bad people. They were my parents, which meant that they were good. If they weren't, what did that say about me?

Even then, at the start, I knew that I couldn't tell anyone what was happening. I worried that my parents would go to jail, yes, but more than that, I worried that it would reflect poorly upon me. I was a good girl, a smart girl. Everyone said so. I didn't want to see the looks on people's faces when they realized that I lived with two monsters.

I wasn't wrong. It was such judgment that caused me to change my name and move across the country when I was eighteen, so that no one would be able to connect me with them and what they'd done. The mean girls in high school were one thing—by the time I graduated I'd learned to tolerate them well enough—but the groupies were something else. My father, in particular, grew a large following of men who were convinced that he was a kind of god. Both types of people—the obsessed and the condemning—were something I wanted to avoid.

My parents buried the women in the woods. Forensic analysts were able to determine the order in which the women were killed, based on the skill involved in the dismemberments. Murder was like anything else—most people were bad at it, because most people had little to no experience. Both of my parents struggled to hold on to hobbies. They'd start something new—knitting, or exercise—only to abandon it out of boredom within a couple of weeks. Apparently, killing never got boring. There were always new things to try and ways to improve. Outside of moral wrongness, the primary reason why most people didn't murder anyone was fear of getting caught. What they didn't realize was that, depending on the state, only around 50 to 70 percent of such crimes were solved, and the majority of the solved cases were committed by someone connected to the victim. My parents and the women had no connections. Their interactions were supposed to be limited to a one-night fling. Even when cameras caught glimpses of my parents' faces in the crowded bars where they met their victims, it was difficult to identify who they were, never mind connect them to multiple deaths.

They tore the first body apart. What choice did they have? They had no power tools, and it was too difficult to lug an entire corpse to the car for disposal. My father had the ability to make everything my parents did sound rational. I had no doubt that, if he'd been allowed to speak to the jury members one-on-one, he would've been released. The first dismemberment was a bloody affair. Remnants of their work stuck around for weeks, like glitter after an art project.

"Did someone get hurt?" I asked.

My mother gave me a confused expression.

"Now, why would you ask that?" she replied.

Because my parents buried the bodies in the woods, hiking became a kind of inside joke to them.

"We love to hike," my mother told servers at restaurants, while wearing stilettos and a dress with a revealing cut, and she and my father would laugh. I would laugh too. It was funny! My parents were so obviously not outdoorsy people. They were constantly tricking me into thinking that I was having a good time, when I was their unwitting accomplice in murder.

There was nothing special that they did to hide the bodies, no secret lair or unknown cavern. People theorized that their carelessness was because they wanted to be caught. Once they got over the initial shock of the arrest, my parents delighted in the attention. My mother strutted in front of the cameras, and my father adopted a pseudo-intellectual persona. They were loved and reviled, which was their favorite combination of affection. However, I knew that they didn't need murder to draw that kind of attention. People looked at them everywhere they went. My father was at the center of every picture that he'd ever been in. No, the reason why they took little care in hiding the bodies was hubris. My father thought he was smarter than everyone else, and my mother was convinced of her main-character status. Main characters didn't get caught. They didn't age or go to prison. My mother's plan was to be a young, beautiful killer for the rest of her life.

Irritatingly, they weren't totally wrong. In the end, it wasn't the bodies in the woods that brought them down. To this day there were victims the police hadn't found.

"You probably think I'm disgusting," I told Aidan when I'd finished my story.

That was when things went dark. I'd thought it had been nothing, the result of the tequila that we'd drunk. I couldn't remember what else I'd said or what he'd told me.

Unlike a lot of women my age, I didn't watch true crime documentaries. I told people that was because of a moral objection to the way that they tended to center on the killers rather than on the victims. *All those forgotten women.* The real reason was because I understood that they never captured the whole story. There were always screams that went unheard, bloodstains unwashed.

I wanted a world that was palatable. I wanted the social media version of myself—the matchmaker engaged to the doctor—to be the full truth of who I was, someone who didn't know what it sounded like when people were dying.

EARLY IN OUR COURTSHIP, AFTER MY BROKEN ANKLE HEALED, Noah took me hiking. I'd expressed reticence, disguising it as a squeamishness about bugs rather than admitting the truth, that it reminded me of what my parents had done.

"Please?" he said, and I went because I wanted him to love me.

It had been a beautiful fall day, the woods a phantasmagoric blend of red and orange hues.

"I see why you like this," I said, leaves crunching beneath my feet.

Things were different at night during the beginning of February. Living in Minneapolis made it easy to forget what true darkness looked like outside the city. I used my phone as a flashlight as I ventured deeper into the woods. In my other hand, I carried a plastic bag that contained the heart.

I'd heard people describe how they regressed when they

went home and visited their families. I couldn't relate, because my father was dead and my mother in prison. My parents left me alone so often that I'd been forced to grow up fast. I could barely remember my small self, what it had been like to be young. But walking through the woods, I became her again. I wanted my parents to be there to hold my hand. I worried that I was somehow responsible for the heart, though I knew that I hadn't committed the killing. I thought about whom I could tell. No one. I could tell no one.

I paused at the unusually shaped tree that Noah had pointed out to me.

"It's the kissing tree," he'd said, and then shown me where other couples had carved their initials into the trunk.

We did the same, with the tip of a ballpoint pen that I'd dug out of the bottom of my bag. Our initials were still there, NR + AS. I thought of the look on his face after we fucked on Saturday night, a mixture of guilt and satisfaction. It occurred to me that maybe Noah had liked having an affair because he was a person who had followed the rules his entire life. For him, it was probably enjoyable to break from his cookie-cutter mold. I was the opposite, constantly trying to squeeze myself into confines that didn't know how to hold me. How nice it must be to commit a wrong for pleasure rather than necessity. I learned to steal because I was hungry rather than because of a desire for any kind of rush. I was hiding an organ in the woods because someone had delivered it to my house.

I ventured off the marked trail and into the night. Most people, I knew, stuck to the paths that were laid out before them. I just needed to go far enough away that no one would be able to identify the heart from a distance.

When I reached a suitable place, I knelt and tried to dig into the earth, but the ground was frozen. Even if I'd had a shovel, penetrating the dirt would've proved impossible. In the end, I had to settle for covering the heart with a pile of leaves. I wasn't so stupid as to do an internet search for how long it took organs to decompose, but I assumed it would be quicker than for a whole body, due to the absence of bones. There were small things to be grateful for.

I hoped that it was over, that the heart was an end rather than a beginning, though I knew death wasn't really like that. My parents' actions had *escalated*. That was the term often used in crime procedurals on television. They'd gone from bringing women home to bringing women home to kill. That went from once or twice a year to every couple of months to being a regular occurrence. Killing was a ball rolling down a hill—until it reached an obstacle.

14.

RETURNING TO WORK ON Monday morning was like walking onto a film set. I was pretending to be the same Lexie that I'd been before. I had a fiancé; we were planning a wedding; we were going to buy a house. No, I hadn't spent my night burying an organ in the woods. That wasn't dirt beneath my fingernails. Yes, I was ready to help people fall in love. First, though, I needed a doughnut.

"What are these?" I asked.

Instead of our usual pastries with sprinkles, the box in the middle of the table contained heart-shaped monstrosities that leaked some kind of dark red filling. They were the kind of food that looked good in photos posted online, but wasn't actually edible.

Oliver helped himself to one.

"Whatever they are, they're beautiful," he said, snapping a picture and posting it online.

I watched as he took a bite. He appeared unperturbed. I cringed as the red jam smeared across his lips.

"I see you're enjoying the doughnuts I brought," Nicole said. She beamed as she walked into the room. "They're from my favorite place."

I let myself relax a little, though this revelation was upsetting in a new way. The doughnuts were a sign that Nicole was trying to insert herself into the director position. *See? I can do it all, even bring the pastries.* It upset me that I hadn't thought of the idea first.

The lights of the office were too bright. I felt like I had a hangover, though I hadn't drunk a thing.

"Are you all right?" Nicole asked. Someone who didn't know her as well as I did might've taken the question as expressing genuine concern.

"Yeah, I'm fine. Noah and I had a late night—that's all," I told her.

Something that I'd learned at a young age was that the worse things were at home, the more important it was to act normal in public. That was especially true when it came to things of dubious legality. *She doesn't* seem *like someone who would bury a potentially human heart in the woods,* I needed people to say.

Serena cleared her throat to let us know that the meeting was starting.

"Thank you, Nicole, for volunteering to bring the doughnuts this week."

A chorus of "thank you" rang out around the table. I kept my mouth shut. Of course Nicole had time and brain space to think about things like doughnuts. She wasn't spending her evenings attending meetings for children of murdered parents, trying to win her fiancé back, or hiding organs in the woods. Women like Nicole were always given advantages in life.

Nicole glowed under the spotlight. It wasn't difficult to imagine her in her high school cheerleading uniform—because she frequently posted photos of such on social media—doing flips through the air, while the bigger girls, the ones who supported her, were overlooked by the crowd.

"Are there any updates on the timeline for the expansion?" Nicole asked after the new clients were handed out.

I nibbled at a doughnut. The frosting was too sweet, and the dough was chewy. It was the pastry equivalent of a person who knew how to make themselves look good on a dating app and then turned out to be unappealing in real life.

"Things are coming along," Serena said. "And before you ask a follow-up, I still haven't made my decision about the director role."

Nicole looked disappointed. That was the problem with being someone who got whatever she wanted—she didn't know how to fight. She'd never been hungry the way that I had.

REBECCA ARRIVED MIDMORNING, TO DEBRIEF ABOUT HER DATE with Paul. There was something illicit about bringing her back to my office, even though we weren't sexually intimate. Could my coworkers tell that we were more than matchmaker and client? Could they see from the way that we walked that we were *friends*?

"So, his dick is small," I said after I shut the door.

"Metaphorically and literally," she complained.

"Oh no. I'm sorry. Other clients haven't given me such . . . explicit feedback." Truth be told, the two other women I'd set Paul up with had begged for a second date that never came, because he'd turned them down. One of them cried when I broke the news to her. Rebecca had seen things in him—or on him—that others hadn't.

"He spent the whole night talking about himself. On and on! I don't think that he asked me a single question the entire evening. I can see how that might be read as confidence, but I think it indicates a deep insecurity."

"If you disliked him so much, why did you sleep with him?" I asked.

She shrugged.

"I thought he was hot. I wanted to see what he was like in bed, and the answer was disappointing."

I laughed. The conversation felt so normal, like something Molly and I might've shared. Rebecca, though, had more swagger than Molly ever did.

"You know," I told her, "there's a reason why we advise clients to wait a few dates before engaging in intimacy."

"If I'd waited, I wouldn't know how much of a bore he is in bed. I saved all of us time. Besides, it's not like anyone got hurt. I'm fine; he's fine. We're all fine. Now we can both go out with people we really like. Who do you have for me next?"

Aidan's picture flashed through my mind. No, I couldn't match them. On top of the things I'd told Aidan, the two of us had kissed. I was tired of sharing romantic partners with my friends.

"What do you think of him?" I passed her Tyler's picture. He wasn't as conventionally attractive as Paul, but he drove a nice car, which I thought might appeal to her.

"He's okay. I'll give him a chance, I guess. Who knows? He might surprise me," she said.

"Great. I'll send your profile his way, and if he says yes, then I'll set up a date."

Rebecca leaned forward conspiratorially. I recognized the position as one that people took when they were about to share juicy pieces of gossip. My nail beds suddenly hurt with the memory of trying to dig through frozen dirt. What was it that she knew? I hated how my secrets ruined such a delightful rite of womanhood.

"Have you watched the most recent episode of *Love on the Lake?*" she asked, and I relaxed.

"Not yet. I've been really busy."

"Oh my god, you have to watch it. I'm pretty sure that Kiley and Tim are going to get divorced."

"Really? They were doing so much better."

"I know, but I don't think that Tim ever really loved her. He's so mean all the time. I couldn't believe it when they got married. I was sure that one of them was going to get cold feet."

"I hoped that, beneath it all, they really cared for each other. They've been together so long."

"Hopefully she'll find someone who really appreciates her now," Rebecca said.

"As long as she doesn't end up with Pierce. He flirts with her sometimes."

"Oh god. That would be jumping from one psychopath to another. I guess some people have a type."

"Yeah," I said, meeting her gaze. "Some people do."

Rebecca stood up to leave.

"We're still on for Thursday, right?" she said. "The COMP meeting and dinner?"

I nodded. I ran my thumb over my fingernails and realized that one of them had broken, probably from clawing at frozen earth.

"You didn't deliver something to my house, did you?" I asked as Rebecca zipped up her coat.

She pulled a hat down over her forehead. Her long eyelashes peeked out from underneath.

"I don't know where you live," she said. "Why? Did someone send you a gift?"

"Something like that. Never mind—it's not important."

I walked Rebecca to the door. I felt bad for even considering her as a suspect. That was Molly's fault. It was my mother's fault. They'd made it difficult for me to trust anyone at all.

I SENT A MESSAGE TO PAUL, LETTING HIM KNOW THAT REBECCA wouldn't be moving forward with a second date. People thought that matchmaking was all hearts and roses, but rejection was part of the process.

> Unfortunately, we cannot set you
> up with a second date at this time.
> However, I'm pleased to announce
> a new potential match.

I included a photograph of Laura, whom I was almost certain he would reject on the basis of appearance. Paul was a shallow man who recognized his shallowness. That was one of the hardest things to overcome in a client. Some clients refused to understand that looks could take a relationship only so far. Real chemistry went deeper than that.

After sending the message, I finished updating my résumé and printed it on the pink paper that I'd specially ordered. I put a little heart on either side of my name at the top of the page—♥ Alexandra Smith ♥—because I knew that Serena liked touches like that. After Nicole's doughnuts, I knew I needed to do something to impress her. I'd let emotionality take over my priorities, and Nicole had capitalized on that weakness, with her little meeting and her box of doughnuts.

I checked my face in the mirror, to make sure I'd properly concealed my exhaustion, and knocked on Serena's door.

"Come in," she called.

I was careful to close it behind me after I entered. I didn't want Nicole to spy on me the same way that I'd spied on her. Nicole's lack of decorum was one of many reasons why she wasn't suitable for the position of director. Unlike at a doctor's office, there were no laws governing privacy here, but Better Love assured clients of discretion. Oftentimes, the difference between a literal heart and a metaphorical one seemed to be a matter of mere semantics.

I passed her my résumé, and Serena nodded approvingly at the paper. She sat in the red wing-backed chair that Oliver and I had once looked up online and discovered that it retailed for more than two thousand dollars. There was nothing in Serena's life that wasn't imbued with luxury. Even my mother, the pickiest woman on earth, would've approved.

"I'm here to tell you how interested I am in the director position," I told her. I pushed all the noise aside—Noah, the heart, Aidan . . . It wasn't especially difficult. I'd lived a life of compartmentalization. One moment, I was Alexandra, whose life was forever marked by murder. The next, I was Lexie, normal girl in the world. We all did what we needed to do in order to pass as ordinary.

I thought about what I'd overheard Nicole saying in her conversation with Serena. *You're basically like a second mom to me.* Motherhood was used both to compliment and to demean women. It implied the deepest of bonds, but it was also used to justify excluding women from the upper echelons of the workforce. Serena looked nothing like the snarling, screaming woman the police had taken away in handcuffs; she sounded completely different from the person who berated me over the phone from the prison where she'd lived for twenty years. Nevertheless, I couldn't let Nicole win.

"You're a mom to me," I forced through my lips. I removed the "like" and the "second." I invented a world where Serena *was* my mom. A person who had never committed murder. A person who wouldn't leave her small children hungry and alone for days on end. *Despite all her care, her son is still a psychopath*, the voice in my brain reminded me. *Yes, but he's one of the good psychopaths*, I replied, and pushed the voice away.

I continued.

"In my time here, I've worked with difficult clients. I've successfully matched people who were uncertain that they could ever hold a committed relationship. Those same people have gone on to get married, have babies. Through our work, we've fundamentally altered the courses of their lives, and I'm so glad that these services will not just be offered here, but all over the country."

A small part of me hoped that I would deliver my speech and Serena would pass over the keys. *Of course you're my pick for the next director. It's always been you. I just didn't have the heart to break it to Nicole yet.* That wasn't what she did.

"I appreciate your application, Lexie. I know how dedicated you are to your clients. You're definitely one of the names that I'm considering for the director role."

I put a smile on my face. If I were on *Love on the Lake*, the scene would've cut to a confessional in which I wore a dress with a million straps and had perfect makeup.

Yeah, I'm disappointed, I would've said. *Don't get me wrong. I love Serena, but sometimes she's bad at reading people. She didn't know her own son was a psychopath, after all!*

The audience would've eaten it up. *#hirelexie* would be trending. Competing matchmaking companies would've offered me jobs. As it was, I had no audience. I could only advocate for myself.

"Thank you so much," I said.

I stood up. The room spun a little. I felt so incredibly alone.

I STOPPED TO PICK UP TAKEOUT ON MY WAY HOME. I WAS TIRED in a way that didn't equate to sleepiness. I braced myself as the town house came into view. Would something else be waiting for me? A liver or, worse, a brain? I didn't have the energy to return to the woods.

Unexpectedly, there was an entire body at my door. Unlike the delivery the day before, this one was living and identifiable. It was Molly.

I parked my car in the driveway. What was she doing here? The Molly I'd originally met had been nonconfrontational. She had a prettiness that she struggled to acknowledge, and though she was outgoing, she backed down at any sign of a struggle. Until she'd stolen my fiancé, I'd considered myself the dominant one in our friendship. I typically picked what we did, where we ate, and what we watched, and not in a mean-girl sense but because I knew what I wanted when she didn't. Slowly, over the course of years, Molly gained confidence. There were women, like Nicole, who would never be better-looking than they were in high school. Someone like Molly got hotter as she aged, largely because she was away from the stringent rules that dictated beauty for teenagers. Without my realizing, she'd gone from deferential to being someone with the capacity to steal my man. And now she blocked my entrance to my home.

I got out of the car with my food, aware of how every minute spent outside made it colder. I recognized the look on Molly's face. It was the expression she wore when she'd had to deal with a coworker she hated or when her Starbucks order was wrong. She was angry, and that anger was pointed at me. I couldn't totally blame her. I'd elicited the emotion by sending her that text message after Noah and I hooked up, but I'd assumed that she'd point the rage at him. Women were so eager to claim that they were "girls' girls," until men got in the way.

"Is he here?" she demanded as I approached her.

"Who?" I asked, playing dumb.

"You *know* who," she said. The words were enough to provoke tears. It seemed unfair that she was crying when *she* was the one who stole *my* fiancé. She'd sacrificed the right to empathy the first time they slept together.

"Do you mean you lost him already?" I was jubilant and puzzled at the same time. It had been a mere week and a half, and already the two of them had disintegrated. My instincts had been right—Noah and Molly were no match in love. They should've listened to the person who knew better.

"It's all your fault," she said. She took a step toward me. I'd never known Molly to be a violent person—she refused to watch movies in which children or animals got hurt—but there was something new in her stance: a threat.

"You couldn't let me have this one thing. Everything has to be about you. You can't accept when you're not the center of attention. Guess what, Lexie. It's not 'main-character energy.' It's just being a bitch."

Molly was confused. I'd fought to get where I was. The biggest struggle she'd faced in life was thinking that she was ugly, when she was actually relatively attractive. Sure, she'd faced depression, and her parents were divorced—run-of-the-mill sorts of things—but my parents were killers. Nothing had ever been normal for me. For me, just getting up in the morning and going to work was breaking a kind of generational curse.

"He's my fiancé," I said softly. "We love each other."

Molly got an incredulous look on her face.

"You want to believe that you love each other. You've painted this picture in your head of what your life is, and Noah matches that image. It's not real though. He doesn't know who your parents are, Lexie. He doesn't know who *you* are. How can you keep something like that a secret?"

"Did you tell him?" I dropped any pretense of friendliness.

Molly was an obstacle. Revealing my parents' identity was a brick wall. There were people, maybe, who could get over something like that. There were even those who got off on it. Noah wasn't in either of those categories. He looked cookie-cutter because that was what he was. He didn't know what to do with people who didn't fit a preordained shape.

She shook her head.

"No. No, but I will if you don't leave him alone."

"He's never going to marry you, you know," I told her. "He might fuck you, say that he loves you, but you're not what he wants. He wants me. I think that what we did on Saturday night is proof enough of that."

Her hand met my cheek before I realized what was happening. Molly's eyes widened in surprise as I touched my stinging skin. I doubted that she'd ever hit anyone before. She didn't live the kind of life in which she had to fight.

"Is he here?" she asked again. "I tried knocking, and no one answered."

"No," I admitted. "He's not here. I last saw him on Saturday night."

Molly crumpled at that.

"Where is he? We got into an argument on Saturday, after you sent that text. He said that he 'needed time,' and left my apartment. I haven't heard from him since then."

Beneath the anger, I sensed her humiliation. She'd put everything on the line for Noah, had betrayed her best friend, and he'd given her so little in return, a single week of togetherness. Men just wanted to know that women were willing to do such a thing, and hated it when they actually went through with it. It put too much pressure on the situation. Nothing thrived in an environment like that.

"I haven't seen him either. He's not here." How I wished that I could say otherwise. It burned that Noah had left Molly and hadn't immediately come running to me. Maybe she and I had both been wrong. Maybe he didn't belong with either of us.

"I don't know what to do," she cried. Her tears begged for comfort, and I refused to give it. That kind of relationship was over between us, regardless of what was happening with Noah. I didn't need her anymore, not when I had Rebecca. In retrospect, it seemed like Molly had been a placeholder while I was waiting for something real.

"Should I call the police?" she asked.

The suggestion was alarming. One night, Noah had been at my house, and the next, I'd received what looked like a human heart.

I'd buried it in the woods, done my best to scrub surfaces clean of the evidence, but it was impossible to cover any trail completely. Wherever Noah was, I didn't want the police to come sniffing around the town house.

"I think that's a little bit dramatic. It's not like he's *missing*. I'm sure that he's just at a friend's house or something. He can sleep anywhere."

That was a required skill for a medical resident. Their hours were so precious that they needed to be able to conk out wherever they lay down to rest. It was why it'd been so easy for Noah to make the transition to Molly's house from mine. I was confident that Noah was sleeping on a couch somewhere. Well, mostly confident.

"You didn't send me something, did you?" I asked Molly. She stood there, uncertain of what to do with her body.

"Why would I send you something?" she asked. "What are you talking about?"

The anger had returned. I could've said anything and she would've hated me. It occurred to me then that the resentment had started long before my birthday and I'd missed it. I didn't know the exact timeline of her affair with Noah, but they'd implied that it had been going on for months. I thought of all the evenings that we'd spent watching reality television together during that time frame, the way that she'd questioned me about my relationship, going so far as to say "Are you sure you want to get married? It's a lot easier to call off a wedding than it is to get divorced" when I'd complained about how much time Noah needed to be at work. The clarity of hindsight was painful. She wanted me to end things so she could have him for herself. Our friendship had meant nothing to her.

"I need to go inside. I don't think that I owe you this, but I'll let you know if I hear from Noah. I'm sure that he's fine. If you're really worried, you can call the hospital. He'd rather die than miss a shift at work."

Molly accepted none of my graciousness. She narrowed her eyes at me.

"You better not have done something to him," she said. "Don't forget, I know all about you, Lexie. Stuff like that can be genetic, you know."

I glared at her.

"I can't believe I ever thought you were my best friend. I'm going inside, and I expect you to leave."

I stepped through the door and shut it before she could say anything else. I didn't want her to see that her comments had rattled me. I hadn't done anything to Noah, but I *had* received a human heart, delivered to my house a day after the last time either of us had seen him, and it was starting to settle in that those two events might somehow be related.

15.

THE WHOLE TIME THAT my parents were killing people, I continued to go to school. I learned long division, and how to spell words like "neighbor" and "disappear." I was strange, but strange in an ordinary way. I kept my hair longer than that of the other girls, dressed more formally, because my mom liked that type of clothing. My classmates were nice enough, and my teachers lauded my intelligence. No one knew that things at home had escalated, and I didn't tell anyone, because even at the age of nine, I understood the value of keeping secrets. If the other children knew about the monster in my house, they would ridicule me for it. If the monster—my parents—knew I'd told, it might turn its murderous tendencies in my direction.

I liked school. It was pleasurable to learn things, to prove to others just how smart I was. There was always food in the cafeteria, and even when my classmates were mean, they were mean in a predictable manner. Getting on the school bus was like entering a portal to a world where things were normal. I lived two different lives—one in the night, during which I heard the sounds of people dying, and the other in the classroom, where my teacher told me what a good reader I was.

Entering the Better Love building now evoked a similar feeling of duality. I put on professional clothing like a costume. In the office, I was the same Lexie I'd been a couple of weeks prior, engaged and free of dismembered organs. No one knew that my fiancé was missing, or that he'd left me for my best friend a week before he'd gone, and I wasn't about to tell them. I knew how quickly safe spaces could sour when people found out the truth.

After closing the door on Molly, I'd spent the night frantically looking for evidence of Noah's well-being. I scoured his social media pages, as though I hadn't been checking them multiple times a day since he'd ended things. He'd posted nothing new, and when I sent him a message—Just checking in. Molly said that the two of you had a fight, are you okay?—it remained on SENT rather than shifting to READ. I did a Google search for his name, and found his headshot in the list of medical residents at the hospital where he worked. There were no news articles, or alarms raised about his absence.

Still, a sense of foreboding settled into my bones. I ate my takeout, a gyro and fries, and went to the kitchen to scrounge for dessert. I was ravenous, like I was back in my parents' house and hadn't eaten for a couple of days. One thing about being hungry was that it was a sensation that never really left. It didn't matter how full my stomach was or how much food was in the cupboards. When stressful things happened, my body immediately became convinced that I was starving to death.

Could the heart belong to Noah? On the one hand, it had to belong to *somebody*. On the other hand, I was convinced that if it was his, I would know. I thought of the tree on the path, the one scarred with our initials. A part of me was certain that his insides would bear the same marks.

When my father died, I didn't let myself feel it. I told myself that there was little difference between death and prison when he didn't speak to me anyway. Like lying to other people, lying to myself wasn't effective. I started drinking a lot, slacking on my homework. I couldn't sleep.

"What's going on with you?" my roommate asked.

"Nothing. I'm fine," I insisted.

In retrospect, it was likely that my irresponsible behavior was a manifestation of my grief. I thought I'd matured in the decade since my father passed, but that was one of the things about death—no one ever really got used to it.

I couldn't accept the possibility that the heart belonged to Noah. I assured myself that he would show up at any moment. *Molly and I got into a fight. I needed to spend a few days with the boys. I'm ready to marry you now. Let's go buy that house.* I couldn't think about the other possibility, that he had disappeared and been murdered mere hours after coming by and having sex with me.

———

I HAD A LOAD OF EMAILS WAITING FOR ME AT MY DESK. ORDI-narily I would've been annoyed, but I was grateful for the distraction. Compared with disposing of body parts, emptying my inbox was easy.

Tyler accepted the date with Rebecca.

Finally, a woman with a real car.

Aidan rejected Mary, a woman whose profile I'd sent him knowing it was futile. Was that because I was waiting for the perfect person to match him with, or because I didn't want him to match with anyone at all?

> Not quite my type. I'm looking for someone a little bit more like you. How was your date with your fiancé?

A couple I'd set up the year prior informed me that they were engaged, and they wanted to know where to send a save-the-date card.

> The Better Love offices are fine. Congratulations on your engagement!

I ignored the thump in my chest, the one that said *Noah is missing.* And then, a beat later, *What if he's dead?*

I paused midmorning to refill my coffee and use the bathroom. I almost felt ordinary. On *Love on the Lake*, cast members would get into near brawls with one another on a drunken night out, and then spend the following day playing games on the beach. It was an odd contrast, but all of us did things like that. We walked around with the knowledge of the worst things that had ever happened to us, and drank our cups of coffee and answered our little emails like doing so might heal something. The cognitive dissonance was mind-boggling. I supposed that it was necessary for survival.

I ran into Nicole outside the restroom. She wore a frilly fuchsia dress that hurt my eyes.

"Hey, Lexie," she said.

Like most pretty girls, Nicole was adept at pretending to be friendly with people she loathed, mostly because she couldn't bear the thought of someone disliking her. When we'd first started working together, I'd taken her greetings as olive branches, before realizing that they were covered in thorns.

"I've been meaning to pull you for a chat," she told me, like we were on an episode of a reality dating show.

"I actually need to pee really badly," I replied. I tried to move past her, but her body blocked the door. I was envious that such a small person could be so good at taking up space.

"It's only going to take a minute," she said. She placed her hand on my arm, and I resisted the urge to pull away. Her long nails, painted pink for Valentine's Day, pressed into my skin. I suddenly got the sense that she knew more than she said. She and Molly followed each other on social media. Was it possible that she knew about the breakup? Or, worse, could she somehow know about the heart? I wouldn't put it past her to somehow have discovered secrets about my life. Nicole was the kind of woman who understood how to weaponize gossip.

"Both of us are in the running for the director position," Nicole continued, relaxing her grip. "It's important that we remain civil. I'll be happy for you if you get it, and in return, I expect you to be happy for me."

Her words said one thing and her tone another. It was clear that she thought the job was already hers. She was relishing the idea of being in a position in which she would have power over me.

In response, I gave her a genuine smile, relieved that she didn't know anything aside from the obvious. Why had I overestimated her like that? The news of Noah's disappearance had put me on edge.

"Of course," I replied. "I know that we both just want what's best for Better Love."

"Yeah, what's best for Better Love," Nicole echoed. She seemed pleased with herself, like something had been resolved. It was clear that she had never been desperate for something.

———

WHEN I GOT BACK TO MY DESK THERE WAS A BOUQUET OF ROSES waiting for me, with a small white envelope tucked among them.

Noah! My heart leapt.

He was alive after all. I'd been so stupid to think that the heart could be his. He was so young, so alive, so destined to be mine. It was impossible that he would be murdered and delivered to my door in pieces. I'd read online that pig hearts resembled those of humans. That was probably what it was—a silly prank that I'd mistaken for a capital crime.

I pressed my nose to the petals and breathed in that quintessential scent. It was relatively common for us to receive thank-you bouquets at Better Love, but they were platonic things. Roses were unmistakably romantic, too expensive to indicate anything other than love. As I pulled the card from the prongs that held it in place, Aidan's presence at the florist passed through my brain. Could the roses be from him?

The outside of the envelope was blank.

Noah—please be Noah.

I took out my letter opener. One year, Noah had gotten me a basket full of pink office supplies as an anniversary gift. It was romantic in a way that he knew how to be; for him, everything was about work.

The letter opener had a pink handle; it was a cute little weapon.

I ran it underneath the seal, wondering whether Noah's tongue had licked that flap, and I slid the card out of the envelope. I flipped it open.

Written in all caps, with red pen, were the words: *I KNOW WHO YOUR PARENTS ARE.*

As though it had transformed into a centipede between my fingers, I dropped the card and it landed on the desk. Rather than being a message of love from Noah or Aidan, it was a secret third thing. I could feel dread creeping up my throat, wrapping itself tightly around my airways until I could hardly breathe.

I'd gone through a lot since my birthday dinner, when my best friend and my fiancé announced that they were sleeping together, and seeing this card was like spilling an expensive latte when I was already having a bad day. While it might have been manageable during ordinary times, it was a death blow to me in my vulnerable state. It brought me back to my teenage years, when I'd been isolated and alone, separate from my parents and ostracized by my peers. I'd done everything I could to escape, but somehow I hadn't gotten anywhere.

I experienced all kinds of torment after my parents were arrested.

My father was long estranged from his family, and my mother's parents had died in a house fire when she was in her twenties, which left only my aunt to care for me.

My aunt worked for the DMV, and she had the demeanor of someone who dealt with angry, impatient people all day long and had no patience reserved for the rest of her life. She owned a modest house that she'd once shared with her ex-husband and then resided in alone until I moved in with her. To establish my bedroom, we had to move all her junk into the garage.

At the time, I didn't see the way that my aunt suffered. She'd deliberately decided not to have children, and she enjoyed a mundane existence of going to work, returning home, and eating dinner in front of the television. Though we'd lived in the same area my entire life, I'd seen her on only a couple of occasions, as she and my mother weren't close. My aunt rarely spoke of her sister, except to make vague references to how difficult it had been growing up together.

"You look just like her," she told me the day that I arrived.

Though adults usually had a better sense of decorum than children, she likely suffered some of the same kinds of nosy glances that I did from people who knew who her sister was. However, my aunt had the advantage of having a different last name than my parents, as my mother had changed her name after getting married, which meant that strangers couldn't make the connection. I wasn't so lucky.

Everyone at school knew immediately. People might assume that fifth graders were too young to know about serial killers, and they would be wrong. In my experience, people of all ages were obsessed with what my parents had done. The story had it all! Love! Sex! Murder! Beautiful victims! They were exhilarated by it.

Meanwhile, I was trying to adjust to the smell of my aunt's laundry detergent. My parents had never made me do homework or go to bed at a particular hour, and my aunt was insistent on both. This was the first time I'd had a parental figure suggest that I might not be a beautiful genius, and that I needed to follow the rules.

The girls I had longed to befriend were suddenly paying attention to me, in the worst of ways.

"My mom said I'm not allowed to talk to you," they told me.

They placed "kick me" signs on my back, wrote about me in their burn books, and dared boys to ask me to dance. In middle school someone vandalized my locker with red handprints, and in lieu of finding the culprit, the principal gave me a suspension.

I didn't tattle on the bullies, not to my aunt, my teachers—who certainly knew about some of what was happening—or the principal, because I wasn't a weenie. I figured out how to be happy on my own. I started stealing my bullies' wallets when they left their purses unattended, and I used the funds to buy a television and DVD player for my bedroom. I bought all the movies that my mother and I used to watch together. I became involved in the lives of fictional characters, who were better friends than anyone in real life could ever be.

In high school, I got a fake ID and began wooing men in bars. They affirmed what I already knew to be true: I was beautiful, smart, and funny. The sole reason that my peers didn't like me was what my parents had done.

My junior year, other students tried to *Carrie* me by nominating me for prom queen. When the names were announced, I watched their heads swivel in my direction as though they were expecting some kind of joyful reaction. *These fucking idiots*, I'd thought. *Don't they know that I spend all my time watching movies?* Needless to say, I didn't show up for the prom. Later, I heard that I'd lost the title to Katie Franzen, one of my primary tormentors.

Things became really dire when I started dating Josh, a man fifteen years my senior. He gave me all the usual lines: *You're so mature for your age*, blah, blah, blah. I bought them because I knew I *was* mature for my age. I'd heard people die, seen body parts scattered about the house. I hadn't seen my parents in six years.

I'd gone through worse than most people experienced in their entire lives.

I figured out that Josh was obsessed with my parents when he started trying to choke me when we were having sex. I played it cool for a couple of minutes, because that was what girls were supposed to do. We were supposed to go along with whatever men wanted, lest we be viewed as hysterical. Then my airways started to feel seriously constricted, and I was grateful that Josh was one of those thin, malnourished men, because it meant I managed to push him off of me and gasp, "What the fuck!" Josh's response was to ask if there was a way he could meet my father.

That was when I realized that, in addition to being a social outcast, I was in physical danger due to my link with my parents. When it came time to apply to colleges, I applied only to schools in other regions of the country, and on my eighteenth birthday I promptly changed my last name. I left for school thinking that I was finally safe.

Unbeknownst to me, Josh had published a picture of me online. It was of poor quality, grainy and dark, but it was good enough that people—men—occasionally recognized me. For several years I dyed my hair blond and did everything I could to distance myself from my former appearance. When I was in my twenties I figured I looked different enough from the image that Josh had circulated to let my hair grow out to its natural brown.

It was so freeing to become an autonomous adult. There were still nights when I woke up and thought that I heard the sounds of death in another room. When Noah lived with me I'd snuggle up next to him and listen to his breathing.

"I like it when you do that," he told me. "It's a reminder of how much you love me."

I didn't say that for me it was a reminder that I was away from my serial killer parents, the girls who had tormented me in high school, and the men who wanted to have sex with me because they idolized a murderer. I'd crafted an entire life for myself, one in which I had a normal fiancé, a monthly mortgage payment, and a steady job. Now all of it was falling apart. My fiancé was missing, an organ had been delivered to my door, and I'd received threats at my workplace. All of that combined seemed like a plot to destabilize me completely.

I was still trying to process what the card said when the door to my office burst open and a man rushed in. I flipped through my mental Rolodex of men and tried to put together what was happening—*Noah? No. Aidan?*

Wait a minute.

"Paul?"

It had been a couple of months since I'd seen Paul in person, as we did most of our communicating over email. He looked bad. His breath reeked of liquor, and he wore a T-shirt that was streaked with stains that were just as likely blood as ketchup. It had been only a few days since his date with Rebecca, during which she'd commented on his handsomeness. What had happened in the meantime?

The receptionist hurried after him.

"I'm so sorry. I tried to stop him. He said that it's important to talk with you right away."

Paul was gasping like he'd sprinted to the office. I glanced at his feet and noticed he wasn't wearing shoes. His toes were a deathly kind of white, probably due to the chill outside. Dirt marred the floor behind him. I grabbed the letter opener off my desk and held it in my hand as a weak form of protection. It wasn't optimal, but I would do what I needed to in order to survive.

"You have to set me up on another date with Rebecca," he said.

I stifled a laugh. That's what this was about? I'd gotten so deep in paranoia that I was convinced that he was there to kill me. It didn't make sense, but it didn't have to. My parents didn't kill women because they were vigilantes or they followed a creed. They did it because they wanted to. That was all the reason they needed. Paul wasn't that kind of crazy though. He was a more common kind of crazy—he was in love.

"Why don't you sit down, Paul?" I suggested calmly.

"I don't want to sit down," he replied. "I need to see her again. I can't stop thinking about her. She won't reply to my calls or texts. Can you give me her address?"

It wasn't the first time that a client had made such a request after being denied a second date. In fact, one of the women I'd set Paul up with had done something similar. The difference was that she'd sent a polite email. When I'd told her no, she ended up canceling her Better Love membership because she was convinced that I wouldn't be able to find anyone more suitable than Paul had been. That was the power of romantic possibility. It made people behave in all sorts of ways that they ordinarily wouldn't.

"I'm sorry, Paul, but I can't set you up with a second date at this time. How about some water? I could make you a cup of tea? Get you something to eat?"

One of the mistakes that Rebecca had made was that she'd given Paul her phone number. That was something that we asked clients to reserve until the second date. Before then, all communication was supposed to go through us. I wasn't surprised that she'd done it. After all, she had slept with him. What was a phone number compared with that? As stressful as the situation was, I looked forward to telling her about it. *Paul came into the office demanding to see you. I think he loves you. Look at how powerful you are.*

"No, no water. Why won't you set up a second date? Why don't you want us to be together?"

His face was stricken. I realized that he'd probably never been in that position before. He was the kind of man women became desperate for. He didn't know what to do now that the tables were turned. He couldn't fathom that Rebecca didn't want to see him again. I almost felt bad for him.

The receptionist fetched Serena.

"Paul, I need you to calm down," she said, coming up behind him.

He turned to her.

"I *am* calm," he insisted, though he looked anything but.

He wasn't used to being treated like that. It was women who were hysterical, not him. Everything that he did was right and just. It wasn't his fault that women were always falling in love with him. Honestly, it was an inconvenience, because it made him look like a bad guy when he wasn't one! He had been so convinced that if the situation were reversed he would behave rationally. He would take rejection gracefully, insist upon remaining friends. He hadn't anticipated becoming the person who stood before me now, a man so desperate for love that he'd lost his shoes.

"Just give me her address."

Paul lurched toward me. I clenched the letter opener more tightly; I was prepared to use it, when two police officers entered the room. The letter opener clattered to the floor when they told us to put our hands in the air.

"Nobody move!"

I froze. Had someone found the heart? Were the police there to arrest me? When they grabbed Paul's arms and secured them in cuffs behind his back, I realized that they were there for him. Serena must've called them before coming in. The bros at my corporate jobs made fun of the word "triggered." They said it was a term for "snowflakes" who couldn't make it in "the real world." I never joined in, because I knew what it meant to be triggered. The presence of police did it for me. Just the sight of the uniform brought me back to the day that my parents were arrested.

"I'm going to fucking kill whoever is responsible for this," my mother screamed, and I buried my face into the legs of the female police officer who stood next to me.

"It's okay," she said. "It's all okay now."

I'd never been able to figure out why she would tell me such a blatant lie; clearly nothing would ever be okay again.

Luckily, no one seemed to notice my discomfort, as everyone's attention was focused on Paul, who was yelling, "Let me go! You're making a big mistake. You don't understand. Rebecca *loves* me!"

I sank into my chair as the police pulled him out of the room. The firmness of the chair was reassuring. Serena escorted them out of the building, and then came back to find me. She took a seat across from me, in the chair ordinarily reserved for clients, a kind of role reversal.

"Are you okay?" Her face didn't move much because of all the Botox she'd gotten, but I could tell that she was concerned.

"Yes." It took more effort than it ordinarily did to work my tone into something convincing.

"Walk me through what happened."

I told her about the date with Rebecca—leaving out key details, such as all the time that the two of us had spent together, and how she'd confessed that they'd had sex. *I understand how she could make a person behave that way. There's something about her.*

"Paul isn't used to rejection," I concluded. "He expects women to become obsessed with him. He doesn't know what to do when the opposite occurs."

Serena sighed. It was the kind of sigh that mothers let out when their children make bad decisions. *I created you, and this is how you thank me?*

"The investors aren't going to like this," she said.

"Isn't the deal closed?" I asked.

"Not yet. Fundraising takes a long time. We need to get more people on board to ensure that we have enough startup capital. It's critical that we show our best face, so that the investors don't get spooked. I've seen deals fall through over smaller problems."

I realized then that there were things she hadn't told them. She'd packaged matchmaking up in a cute little box with a bow on top. She hadn't told them about all the psychopaths. They didn't know about her son.

"She thinks it's her fault that he turned out the way that he did," Oliver had confided in me once.

"Why? What did she do?"

"She spoiled him. She couldn't resist giving him everything that he wanted."

"Is that enough to turn a person into a psychopath?" I asked.

He shrugged. "I don't know. Why? How do you think it happens?"

I swallowed. "I don't know. Genetics?"

Serena presented herself publicly as a woman who was in control of all facets of her life. She had a marriage of forty years, an adult child with a thriving career. She gave large sums of money to charity and spent her weekends going to galas. I'd seen her as an aspirational figure. Even her toenails were spotless. She had nothing to hide.

Something that I hadn't understood, something that was so easy to miss, particularly during this era of social media, was that everyone had skeletons in their closet. Her son wasn't perfect. When she talked about how she'd started Better Love because he'd had such a tough time dating, she made it sound like it was the dating apps' fault, but maybe it was his fault. Maybe the women he contacted could sense that something was off and they protected themselves. No one could see clearly when it came to their offspring. No one could believe that anyone would reject the person who was the most beloved to them.

While I was trying to prove to Serena that I was capable of taking on the director position, she was engaged in a performance of her own, trying to show that Better Love was a viable business. My psychopaths were getting in the way of that. My psychopaths turned love into a dangerous venture.

"Do we have to tell them?" I asked her.

I expected her to say something like *We have to.* She was the good and moral mother. Instead, she looked away.

"We'll see," she replied.

Serena stood up, her eyes following the trail of dirt that Paul had dragged in. She turned back to me.

"You'll tell me if you need anything?" she said. "I'm sure that was quite a shock."

Serena reached out and touched one of the flowers in the bouquet. I wanted to slap her hand away.

"These are nice roses. Did Noah get them for you? He's such a good boy."

"Yeah, Noah got them for me," I replied weakly. I'd almost forgotten about the flowers during the uproar, but there they still were, staring at me from my desk. I grabbed the card off the desk as though Serena had X-ray vision and could see the text through the flap.

Again, that refrain—*Noah is missing. What if he's dead?*

"What's going to happen to Paul?" I asked before she left. In my experience, when the police took someone away, they were gone forever. Paul, however, hadn't committed a crime, as far as I could tell. He was drunk and belligerent, but so were many men in bars.

"They'll stick him in the drunk tank for a few hours, let him sober up. I informed him that he's no longer a Better Love client, effective immediately, and that if I ever see him again, action will be swift. Don't worry. He's not going to hurt you."

I wasn't worried about Paul. He'd humiliated himself in front of a woman, the thing that men hated the most. I doubted he would come back even if Serena hadn't banned him. He wanted Rebecca to love him—he didn't want to hurt me. The problem was that someone else out there did.

16.

———

I MET AIDAN AT A coffee shop the following day. Between the flower delivery and Paul's intrusion, the office, which had consistently felt like a safe space, had become something dangerous.

Aidan showed up wearing his pilot's uniform. It made him look like a different person, a mask of professionalism covering his rougher edges. I understood how wealthy people could look at him and trust him enough to pay him to take them into the sky.

The uniform must've had some effect on me as well, because we hugged in greeting. I hadn't realized that I needed comfort until I had it. He smelled good, like a man who considered how others perceived him. I leaned in too long, and then remembered the identity of the man whose arms were wrapped around me and started to pull away. As I did, my head turned in such a way that my lips accidentally brushed against Aidan's, and I realized that he'd been about to kiss my cheek when I moved. I hurried to create distance between us, my brain unhelpfully reminding me of how we'd kissed the night that we met. *What can it hurt? He likes you. It'll make Noah jealous. You've had a tough week—you deserve a little sugar,* said my worst impulses.

I sat down at the nearest table.

"Something to drink?" Aidan asked, still standing. I could tell he was pleased, which irritated me.

"A latte would be great," I told him.

Ordinarily I would never let a client purchase a beverage for me, but my life had stopped being ordinary when a human heart arrived at my door—or, perhaps more accurately, when my parents had murdered all of those women. I had insisted upon being a stickler for the rules because I knew the kinds of things that happened to people who resided outside the confines of morality.

I collected myself while Aidan waited in line. I calmed the thumping in my chest, and picked at a hangnail. When my life calmed down, I would need a manicure. I was doing my best to hold myself together under stressful circumstances, but the body always revealed the truth.

"Is this a date?" Aidan asked when he sat down. He had a mug of black coffee. I wondered if he sincerely enjoyed the taste or if he drank it to prove some kind of manliness. If women had won any war, it was that drinks that tasted good—iced lattes, blended cocktails—were identified as feminine, with the power of emasculating male drinkers. It seemed unlikely that Aidan was self-conscious about what he drank, but I knew better than to doubt a man's ego.

"No," I said firmly. "I wanted to talk to you more about what you're looking for in a romantic partner, and I thought it might be nice to get out of the office."

"I think I've been very clear about what I'm looking for," Aidan said. He picked up his mug, took a sip, and set it down again without breaking eye contact.

If I were prone to blushing, I would've been bright red. Though I knew that the two of us could never be involved—that I didn't *want* to be involved, because I still, however futilely, hoped that Noah would return and be mine—the continued pursuit was flattering. I was attractive, but not the same way that Aidan was. I'd seen how the barista grew flustered when he ordered his drink. Aidan's appeal was more than just looks. There was something about the way he carried himself—a swagger to his walk, a confidence in his posture.

Admittedly, I didn't look my best. After the encounter with Paul, Serena had let me go home early, which felt like a punishment. My mind had jumped from the flowers to the heart to my missing fiancé, and back again. I'd tried to watch a Netflix rom-com and ended up scrolling social media, looking for signs of Noah.

Noah is missing. What if he's dead?

Alarmingly, some of his coworkers had tagged him in posts asking whether anyone knew his whereabouts. He hadn't shown up to work since the previous week, and they were concerned. I was concerned too. Noah never missed work. It took precedence over everything else. He'd decided at a young age that he was going to be a doctor, and every major decision he'd made since had centered around that choice. When we'd first started dating, he told me that it was good that we'd met when we had, because he wanted to get married after he finished his residency. There was no way that he would put that at risk, not when he was so close to being done.

I mentally listed the possibilities from most palatable to least:

- Someone had kidnapped Noah and was holding him against his will. Doctors, like matchmakers, inspired all kinds of negative emotions when they didn't give the kinds of results that their patients wanted. As a strong man who routinely went to the gym, he would fight his way free and seek help.

- Noah had gotten into some kind of accident that rendered him unable to get help. Eventually someone would find him, and I could help him heal the same way that he'd done with me.

- Noah was dead.

- Noah was dead and it somehow related to me.

- Noah was dead and his heart had been delivered to my doorstep, wrapped in a bow.

I didn't know how to comprehend any of the options. Noah's coworkers remained hopeful that he would be found. That was human nature. Even when my parents were slaughtering women, their victims maintained an optimism that they might change their minds.

"Please, you don't have to do this. It's not too late to stop. I won't tell anyone what you've done if you just let me live."

My response was more realistic—I got blackout drunk and hoped that no more body parts showed up at my doorstep.

I woke up in the morning and found evidence of the previous night's activities on my phone.

I'd texted Rebecca about the situation with Paul.

Paul showed up at my office today. He
was upset that you didn't want a second
date. What did you do to him?

OMG. Are you okay? He kept texting
and calling so I blocked his number. I
didn't think that he would bother you.

I'm okay. A little shaken up. They took
him to the drunk tank to cool off.

He was drunk??? Yikes.
What a psycho.

Right? Good thing that you didn't
go out with him again. Do you still
want to go out with Tyler? I wouldn't
blame you for saying no.

Yeah. I'll meet Tyler. I'm just sorry
that you had to go through that.

It's on me. I should've known that the two
of you weren't a match from the jump.

Another thing I'd done was text Aidan. I wasn't even aware
that I'd saved his number in my phone, but apparently I had, under
"Handsome Man." Oh no. What had I said? Why couldn't I stay
away from him? There was something that drew me to Aidan
when my defenses were down. It was like food that made my
stomach hurt but that I couldn't stop eating.

We need to meet.

The time stamps showed that he responded quickly, like he'd been waiting for me to reach out.

> You name it.

> Coffee tomorrow? 9am?

I named a local place. It was unclear whether I understood the implications of what I was writing. Aidan hadn't been wrong—it *had* sounded like a date.

> Looking forward to it.

I tried to guess my own motivations. Had I texted Aidan because there was some small part of me that was attracted to him? Or had I done it because I suspected that he had something to do with the heart delivered to my house, the flowers to my office? Unfortunately, I was prone to using the phrase "two birds, one stone."

With Aidan seated across from me, I attempted to regain my footing. One of the reasons that I enjoyed being a matchmaker was because it made me feel like I could control destiny, my own included.

"Why did you turn Mary down?" I asked.

"She's not the kind of person I'm looking for."

"How do you know? You haven't even met her."

"I can tell. You understand that, don't you? Looking at a person and knowing that you're meant to be. By the way, how are things with that fiancé of yours?"

He delighted in the question like he knew things weren't right. Could Aidan have done something to him? Was Aidan the one who delivered a heart to my house? I didn't know how to answer. I was like a basketball player who'd forgotten how to put up a shot. An intrusion: *Noah is missing. What if he's dead?*

"That's not why we're here," I said.

"Then why are we here? There's something on your mind, Lexie. I can tell. This isn't about Mary."

There was concern on his face, and I struggled to ascertain his sincerity. The skepticism was something that my parents had given me. I'd watched them lie and lie and lie, their expressions conveying utter honesty and then, as soon as they were out of hearing range, they'd burst into laughter over how gullible people were. I'd learned to assume that no one really meant anything that they said. Aidan might've looked like he cared, but Aidan was also a psychopath.

"Some strange things have been happening," I said. "I've been getting . . . gifts."

"Gifts? You make it sound like a bad thing. Normally women love getting presents."

"They're anonymous."

"So a secret admirer?"

"They're not nice gifts."

"Cheap?"

"No, threatening."

Aidan took a sip of his coffee. He stared intently at a picture on the wall, an amateur painting of a local landmark.

"You think that I sent them." His voice was quiet. If I didn't know better, I would've guessed that he was sad.

"No." The lie was an impulse. I wished that I could remember what he'd told me the night we first met. I'd told him who my parents were, but why? What could he have said to make me trust him like that? It wasn't like me. I'd done everything in my power to escape their shadow. I'd revealed myself to Molly, and clearly that had been a mistake. Instead of bringing us closer together, my secrets became a weapon for her to wield against me. "I mean, maybe. Whoever is sending them knows things about me. There might even be multiple people—I don't know. That's what I'm trying to figure out."

"What did they give you?"

"I can't say."

"Why don't you trust me, Lexie?"

"I barely know you."

"That's not true. What about the night that we spent together?"

"I thought I would never see you again. I just needed someone to vent to."

Aidan shook his head.

"No. It was more than that and you know it, Lexie. I think that you're scared of getting close to someone. That's why you want your fiancé back, because he'll always be at a distance. You can't be with me because I know who you are. I know about your parents."

The invocation of my parents in the coffee shop felt like a bullet. I looked around to see if anyone had noticed the comment or my distress, but they continued to move about their lives like Aidan and I were normal people discussing normal things. Aidan's phrasing was also alarmingly similar to the wording used in the card I'd received at work.

"You sent me the flowers, didn't you?" I said.

Aidan let out a painful laugh.

"You're in denial," he said. "You're scared to let yourself have what you really want. You're making me the villain because it's easy."

"I'm making you the villain because that's what you are. Did you send the heart too? Did you do something to Noah?"

"Whoa, wait a minute. What happened to Noah?"

He sounded so sincere in his surprise, like he hadn't known that Noah was missing. I disliked the popularization of the term "gaslighting," because most of the time people used it incorrectly. They didn't know what it was like to grow up with chronic liars. *This is the world,* my parents had told me, and I believed them until the paint started to peel. Aidan had the same effect. I started to doubt myself. What if it hadn't been him? What if Noah was fine? Was that really a human heart that I'd held in my hands, or was it something else entirely?

"Never mind," I said. "Forget that I mentioned it. I shouldn't even be talking to you about this. I'll match you with someone else, but you have to give them a chance, okay? You're never going to find the love of your life if you continue to judge people based on first impressions."

"Okay, I'll give them a chance. But I think that you've gotten too deep into matchmaking, Lexie. Sometimes people just know that they're meant for each other."

"Sometimes people are wrong," I told him.

I left the coffee shop more rattled than when I'd arrived. It was possible that Aidan was feigning his shock at the news of Noah's disappearance. Psychopaths, after all, were known for their acting abilities. But what if he'd been sincere? That meant either that Noah was alive and Aidan was delivering me parts of someone else's body or that Aidan hadn't done it at all.

Molly, my brain hissed, followed by *Mom.*

17.

———

I WANTED TO TEXT REBECCA after work, but she was on a date with Tyler. No doubt she was casting her spell over him the way that she'd done with Paul. I hoped that their relationship wouldn't end with a man storming into my office.

With no one to call, I went home and tried to forget. That was the key to surviving something horrific. It wasn't like I walked around thinking about how my parents were murderers all the time. Over the years since their arrest, I'd found ways to dissociate. Drugs and alcohol were an obvious way, but drinking too much was what led to divulging my secrets to Aidan, and I was wary of a repeat performance.

After their arrest, there were rumors that my parents had committed their murders in a drug-fueled craze. People liked the theory because there was logic to it. If they could pinpoint why my parents did what they did, then maybe they could prevent something similar from happening to themselves or their loved ones. My parents did, on occasion, use drugs. I didn't realize that until I was older. I thought my parents acted strangely from time to time because they were strange people. They weren't addicts though. It could even be argued that they were less likely to kill while they were drunk or high, as they already had the rush that they needed. I tended to stay away from harder substances, because losing control like that scared me. Drinking, at least, was an acceptable form of recklessness.

My real method of escape was watching reality television. That was something Molly and I had done together, but the hobby both predated and outlasted her presence in my life. I got into my comfiest clothes—pajama shorts, thick socks, and an oversized sweatshirt that Noah had left behind—lit a candle, made a bowl of popcorn, settled beneath a fleece blanket on the couch, and let the dulcet sounds of women arguing wash over me. It was like having a lobotomy. Within minutes, I was no longer concerned about my missing ex-fiancé, the psychopath who was threatening me, or the organ that had shown up at my house. I was worried about the two housewives who were fighting because one had implied that the other wasn't as rich as she claimed she was. I fretted about the couple that had gotten engaged without ever having seen each other. I developed anxiety for the two friends who were opening a restaurant together without any actual restaurant experience. I noted, as did others online, when a cast member was looking very thin, and wondered whether that was an indicator that she had an eating disorder.

On the episode of *Love on the Lake* that I was watching now, the cast members decided that they needed to get away from their vacation home and visit a winery.

"I didn't even know there were wineries around here," one of them said.

"That's because they're not very good," replied another.

They piled into a party bus together. I suspected that, legally, the show had an obligation to make sure that no one drove drunk. Since the show's premiere, several years prior, everyone had aged significantly, and they were desperately trying to stop it through a variety of fillers, which in many cases served only to make them look older. Two of the women had children, who were occasionally shown on camera but otherwise spent their time with nannies. As in most episodes of the show, in this episode the cast members were drunk in a beautiful locale, and absolutely furious with one another.

"I can't believe you said that my party was tacky," one woman hissed at another.

"I didn't say it was tacky. Who told you that? I swear, I can't trust anyone in this group," the other woman responded.

It was possible that, at some point, the cast members' friendships had been authentic. I knew from social media that some of them spent time together when the show wasn't filming, while others were excluded until the cameras picked up again. Though I had little desire to be on television, to have my personal affairs aired in a space where everyone could see, I was envious of the forced friendships. I longed to go on vacation with a group of women, all of us dressed in silly costumes. Molly had never been willing to indulge in my fantasy.

"I've already used up my vacation days," she said when I'd suggested that we go somewhere together. She didn't need me, because she had her family. Molly's mother planned family trips to Europe, where they took cute pictures in front of historic structures. On one of the few trips that I took with my parents before their arrest, we'd had to abscond from our hotel in the middle of the night because they'd scammed their way into our room and had been caught. If we had gone to Pisa, my mother never would've deigned to pretend to hold up the Leaning Tower with her finger.

Because I had no group of friends, and no family, to go on a trip with, I watched reality television. I watched people fight, fall in love, cheat on one another. I yelled, "Girl, break up with him!" more times than I could count. I learned about fertility struggles, addiction, and trauma, intermixed with silly parties and nights at the club.

The cast members on television provided friendship without being friends. Kinship without being kin. They allowed me to function even as my life fell apart.

I'd dragged myself to bed after staying up too late and felt like I'd been asleep for only a couple of minutes when a noise woke me up. That was a benefit of having a significant other or a pet—they gave middle-of-the-night sounds an explanation. Noah frequently came home late, climbed into bed when I was sleeping. Occasionally I stirred, but more often than not, I stayed asleep, because my body was confident in its safety. I hadn't realized how much of my attachment to being in a relationship with a man wasn't about the man at all.

My eyes shot open. I tensed into stillness, listening for any additional sounds. *There, a clink, two objects knocking together. Footsteps.* In my grogginess, my first thought was that I was hearing my parents—my father, a zombie, accompanying my mother, a prisoner, to commit more murders. I didn't doubt that my father was capable of wooing women even in death. I became a child again, too afraid to move or breathe. I regretted making fun of the neighborhood busybody who was convinced that there were strange figures wandering the streets, breaking into cars and homes. "I saw them," she insisted. "They were trying car doors to see if they were unlocked. Criminals!" I'd chalked it up to paranoia or racism or both, and now the thieves had come for me.

I had no weapons. Surprisingly, my father disdained guns. He said that they were the tools of weak, frightened people. He thought that if people wanted to kill something, they should do it with their whole chest. That was one of the few things that we agreed upon. Guns made it too easy to kill. Firearm owners with the best of intentions could end up killing their loved ones or themselves before they realized what was happening. I didn't want to be one of those people. I didn't want to kill. I just wanted the monsters to leave me alone.

I forced myself out of bed, pulling on a pair of shorts over my underwear. I wasn't a kid anymore. I couldn't lie there waiting for a monster to come eat me. *What's the worst that could happen?* The problem was that I knew. The worst was that I could be cut into pieces and scattered throughout the woods.

A small, stupid part of me hoped that whoever—*whatever*— was downstairs was Noah, even though the sounds were different from the ones that he usually made. Perhaps he'd been altered in our time apart, like when people were brought back to life in movies and they were unable to rid themselves of the touch of darkness. I couldn't let my hopefulness interfere with the feeling in my gut, the feeling that there was an intruder who wished me ill.

Cautiously, I opened the bedroom door and tiptoed down the hallway toward the stairs. I cringed as the floor creaked beneath my feet. There was a slamming sound that I recognized as that of the front door shutting. Whoever was in the house must've heard me.

No longer tiptoeing, I ran down the stairs. There was one kind of fear, elicited by confronting an intruder, and another, from knowing that someone had been inside the house but not knowing who they were. Neither was a fear I wanted to live with, but I needed answers. I beelined to the door, and was met with a blast of cold air as I pushed it open and stepped into the night. My bare feet sank into fresh snow, an unpleasant sensation. The world was still around me—too still?—with no sign of anything amiss, aside from a trail of footprints snaking away from my front door.

A detective might've been able to do something with that, but I didn't trust the police. I took another step in the snow. The cold burned. I needed to put on boots. I thought of the footprints that Paul had dragged into the office, dirt mixed with blood. I hadn't understood how such a thing could happen, until my own desperation made me venture into the freezing weather in only a T-shirt and shorts. I knelt to examine the prints. They were almost certainly made by boots, but there were no clear brand markings. I put my own foot inside one print to gauge its size. I had large feet for a woman, and the prints were bigger than mine, which could be an indication that the intruder was a man. Aidan? He'd been so insistent that he didn't want to hurt me, and a mere fifteen hours after our meeting, someone had broken into my home. I thought of Paul again, his face close to mine. *I need to see Rebecca again.* Had he somehow found my home address, his love transformed into rage? It wouldn't be the first time that such a thing had happened. All extreme emotions were related.

Unable to tolerate the cold any longer, I turned to go inside. Being in my house felt the same way that talking to my mother in prison did—simultaneously familiar and dangerous. Even if Noah and I didn't get back together, it might be time to move.

The intruder's handiwork was immediately apparent, and it made me wish they were a mere thief. On top of the mantel, they'd arranged a village of tiny pink and red houses. I'd seen a similar display at Noah's parents' house during Christmastime. It'd been cute and unsettling, a perfect little village without any people. In our own ways, we were all trying to create the worlds in which we wanted to live.

On my mantel there were a post office with a sign that said LOVE LETTERS, a pink bakery shaped like a cupcake, and a house with a glowing cutout heart in the middle. It would've been nice if not for all the body parts scattered between them. At first glance, I counted three fingers, a couple of toes, and several un-identified organs. A string of pink lights cast a pale, eerie glow over it all. I'd been awake for only a few minutes, but it was clear that whoever had done this had been there for a while.

It was the fingers that did it.

Molly was right when she said that I hadn't let Noah in, not entirely, but there were ways in which we knew each other implic-itly. I recognized the sounds he made as he moved around the house, what it felt like when he climbed into bed next to me. I was familiar with his exclamations of delight when he ate food that he enjoyed, and I could predict what kinds of shows he'd like to watch. And, apparently, I knew his fingers, the specific way that his nails met their beds, and I recognized him in the body parts in front of me, in a way that I'd failed to recognize him in the heart.

It was Noah.

It had always been Noah.

And I'd buried his heart in the woods.

18.

———

THERE WAS A SEASON of *Love on the Lake* during which it was discovered that Pierce had been cheating on his long-term girlfriend for several months. She'd responded to the discovery in a normal way, which was to say that she was absolutely hysterical. In that hysteria, she confessed that sometimes she thought about killing Pierce.

"I mean, not literally kill him, but, like, I want him dead. Metaphorically," she'd said.

We all knew what she meant, because everyone had people like that in their lives, whether they were significant others, friends, parents, or coworkers. Wanting someone to die didn't mean we wanted them to die. Rather, we wanted some kind of finality in our interactions, and we wanted them to suffer a little bit for whatever they'd done.

Had I wanted Noah to die? I recounted our last night together, how he'd come over, eaten my food, slipped inside me, and left. Afterward I'd gotten drunk. Had I been so drunk that I could've forgotten killing my fiancé? Or maybe the drinking was a mere excuse. In my college psychology classes I'd learned about repressed memories. They were a defense mechanism of the mind, a kind of protection enacted when we experienced things that were too terrible to comprehend. The concept was complicated. It meant that sometimes people weren't able to come forth with accusations until years after the fact, not because they hadn't wanted to before but because they didn't know until they did. On the flip side, the concept had been used to accuse people of crimes they hadn't committed. Remembering and forgetting were equally fallible.

I didn't remember hurting Noah. I wanted to believe that I wouldn't do such a thing to a person I loved. I certainly hadn't been responsible for the heart at my door or the display laid out in front of me. It had to be someone else who had killed him, someone who wanted to implicate me in what they'd done.

I checked social media. That was how my brain processed things. I had a free moment at work? Time to look at my phone. There was a catastrophic weather event? Better look online and see what people were doing. Parts of my murdered fiancé's body were arranged as a kind of grotesque Valentine's display in my house? I should check and see if his disembodied limbs had posted anything.

It was lucky that my parents had gone to prison before social media became the beast that it was now. My mother was the kind of person who would've disdained the concept until suddenly she had a camera roll filled with selfies. She wouldn't have been able to resist posting pictures of herself with her victims—they were very beautiful women, after all. I knew from watching crime shows that serial killers liked to collect trophies. My mother's fetish was to keep pieces of jewelry. Social media turned everything into a trophy. A good brunch was counted as a win, as was an outfit or a face full of makeup. People ran marathons solely to post pictures online. There were multiple reasons why the scene in front of me was difficult to cope with. The man I thought I was going to marry was dead, my whole future obliterated. Someone had broken into my house in the middle of the night to arrange his body parts. That someone was likely a killer, which meant that I was fundamentally unsafe in my own home. All of that, and I couldn't even talk about it online. I was left to process everything by myself.

When I checked Noah's accounts, I discovered that, while he hadn't posted in a while—for obvious reasons—one of the other medical residents had reported his disappearance to the police and had tagged him in the post, which meant that everyone who followed that resident could see what they'd said.

"Fuck," I said.

I was wary about police involvement when I thought that Noah might still be alive. Now it threatened my very existence. It was only a matter of time before they showed up on my doorstep. I couldn't let any piece of Noah still be here when they did.

I wasn't allowed to grieve.

I got extra-strength garbage bags out of a closet as well as a pair of rubber gloves, and packed up the whole display. I'd once thought that I'd be a woman like Noah's mother, who decorated her suburban home for all the holidays, and instead I'd become a woman cleaning up a corpse. Well, parts of a corpse. A lot of it was still missing. The head, for instance.

In some ways, having a task was nice. What would I have done if given space? It wasn't like me to sob. I probably would've sat on the couch and watched old episodes of *Love on the Lake* until my eyes bled. That was one annoying thing about death—there were no good ways to react to it. I could go to therapy, or I could get drunk, but at the end of the day Noah would still be gone.

The absence was greater than him. It was the absence of my whole future. As I wiped my mantel clean, I said goodbye to the house, to the wedding and the kids that we never got to have. The weight of Noah's body getting into bed when he'd come home after a shift. The anniversary dinners, the little gifts, the notes left around the house. All of it was gone.

I hadn't totally processed it. Our love was a phantom limb that would continue to ache.

I loaded the garbage bags that contained the dismantled display into the trunk of my car and drove back to the hiking trail, putting my phone in airplane mode and hoping that was enough to prevent the police from tracing my whereabouts.

It struck me that a murdered Noah wasn't entirely different from Noah when he was alive. Our relationship had been good because it was convenient. I didn't mind that he spent so much time at work, and he didn't mind that I never entirely let him in. Or at least I thought he hadn't minded. It turned out that there were a lot of things that we hadn't told each other.

I made my way down the dark trail like a map of it was ingrained in my veins. There were, I reasoned, more destructive things I could've done in the hours after finding out that my fiancé was dead. Due to the cold, the heart was still where I'd left it beneath a loosely arranged pile of leaves. I'd read about cryopreservation, when rich people had their corpses frozen with the idea that they would be reanimated when science caught up to their dreams. It didn't seem totally impossible that, if I hadn't been missing his head, I could Frankenstein Noah back together. But I wasn't the doctor; he was. I was a matchmaker, and somehow I'd gotten our love wrong.

I looked down at the body parts in front of me. They looked like Noah and they didn't. A person was more than the form in which they resided. That was why people could fall in love through letters, through DMs on social media, and by seeing someone on a television screen. Whatever Noah was, whatever he had been, it was clear that he'd vacated the body parts that were now on the forest floor.

I had a confessional in the woods. The trees were my viewership. They'd dressed for the occasion, branches stark and empty.

What would you have said if you could have had one final conversation with him?

My brain, the producer.

"I would've told him that I really thought the two of us were going to end up together. I would've told him about my parents, explained why I held him at such a distance. I would've painted a portrait of the world that I wanted us to live in before it all started to crumble. I would've told him that I loved him. I would've explained the pain of his absence in terms that would've made him cringe because they wouldn't have been medically accurate. I would've warned him that someone was about to kill him."

The words failed me. I talked and talked, and nothing I said brought him back to life. I began to shiver. The cold was a punishment made especially for me.

I remembered talking to my mother after my father died.

"What are you talking about?" she asked when I tried to broach the topic of his passing. "Why would you say such a thing?"

I'd taken her denial for indifference. I hadn't realized that grieving was standing on the edge of a cliff on a windy day and doing everything in your power to prevent yourself from being knocked over the edge. Noah was dead, a truth that I would have to grapple with forever and ever, but I was still alive and I needed to keep moving forward, regardless of the feeling of glass in my spine.

It wasn't until I was back in the car that I returned to the question of who was responsible for killing Noah and setting up that night's spooky display. Aidan was the obvious answer. There was something comforting in the easiness of it. Of course it was the psychopath I'd turned down for a date.

The other possibilities were more unsettling. Paul, somehow having discovered my address. Molly, suddenly a killer. Then there was my mother to consider. She didn't know where I lived, what I did, or what my last name was, but was it possible that she'd somehow engineered Noah's murder? Maybe her obsession with Noah wasn't rooted in a love of romance as I'd thought. Maybe she'd wanted to kill him.

19.

D O YOU EVER FEEL like your parents are like a wound that won't close?" I asked at COMP the following day. "And you're just walking around bleeding and everyone is staring at you and you're like, 'Why are you staring?' because you're so used to it that you've forgotten about the blood, but everyone else thinks you're a freak."

I expected the other members to look at me like I was crazy. I wasn't ordinarily so frank with my speech, but yet again, I'd gotten little sleep, which made me prone to verbosity. I showed up at the Better Love office with bags beneath my eyes, so tired that I might've fallen asleep at my desk if I hadn't been filled with adrenaline. My brain spun in circles.

Noah was dead.

I'd hidden his body parts in the woods.

Someone I knew had killed him. But why?

Should I confront Aidan? If he was the killer, that might be a dangerous action. And if it wasn't him, confronting him would give him even more leverage to use against me. I couldn't figure out another solution. It was annoying how he and I were pushed together again and again.

The only relief was in the prospect of seeing Rebecca again. Having plans, in and of itself, was a balm amid the chaos of my thoughts. COMP helped people by giving them an outlet to discuss their feelings, but more than that, it helped by giving them a place to go. Sometimes that was all a person needed to survive another day.

Rather than looking at me like I had two heads, the other members of the support group were nodding as I finished my rant.

"Yeah. I joked to my husband that I should just get a 'my mom was murdered' tattoo, because that might make things less awkward," one woman said.

"I *did* get a tattoo for my mom," one of the two men said, gesturing toward his bicep.

One thing that I'd noticed was that most of the murdered parents in the group were women. Rebecca and I were alone in having fathers who were killed. Even in a group of people marked by tragedy, my tragedy was exceptional.

"I want to go back to what you said about feeling wounded," the facilitator said. "Is there any kind of bandage that we can put on the wound to make things easier?"

I shook my head.

"I don't know. Every time that I think I'm better, or wearing a perfect disguise, something happens to remind me that I'll never be like other people."

"Grief isn't linear." Maureen nodded sagely, and then launched into her own speech about how she'd had a panic attack in a grocery store because a brand of flour made her think of her murdered mom.

Maureen, I knew, would never survive the things that I had survived. She thought that she understood other people's pain because of how she hurt, but her attempts to relate served only to reveal how fundamentally she misunderstood what I was saying.

"Are you okay?" Rebecca asked when we met up in the library parking lot after the meeting. She'd been quiet, listening to others' stories rather than sharing her own. I enjoyed being ingrained in a group, but more than that, I liked sitting next to her. In my puffy coat, I looked like a marshmallow compared with Rebecca's tight black pants and leather jacket. She could've played an assassin in an action film.

"Yeah. Yeah." I repeated the word like doing so might make it true. "I had a weird week, and I guess it rattled me."

"Rattled" wasn't exactly right. I was feeling something that I hadn't felt in a long time, not since I'd become a fully functional adult. Suddenly I was a child in her room, listening to people die.

"You poor thing." Rebecca threw her arms around me. The touch made me flinch. She didn't seem to notice. She pulled back.

"I know we're supposed to go to dinner, but I think we should go for a drive. That always helps me when I'm feeling a certain way," she said.

I recognized the proposition, as it was a frequent trope in movies. *Fuck it. Let's drive.* Such a proposition was less common in real life, because people had jobs, families, gas tanks that needed filling, and bodies that needed sleep. I hadn't slept well in two weeks. I'd gone from being brokenhearted, to worrying about body parts delivered to my door, to discovering that said body parts belonged to my ex-fiancé. Every action served as a reminder of Noah's death. I walked into the town house and remembered that he'd never come home again. I brushed my teeth and wondered who was keeping his as a grotesque kind of trophy. I got into the bed that had transformed into a vast gulf without Noah's form taking up half of it. I got dressed and wondered who I was trying to look good for. I pondered who was trying to frame me, and then wondered if prison was really all that bad, which was how I knew that things had gotten dire. For my whole life, staying out of prison had been one of my top priorities, the way that other people aspired to get into good colleges.

"Fuck it. Let's go," I said.

I knew which car belonged to Rebecca before she unlocked its doors, because it looked like her, sleek and sexy.

"This is my baby," she said as she unlocked the doors.

I sank into the passenger seat. It was my preferred place in the car. Noah had viewed driving as a man's responsibility, and I'd been happy to let him take the wheel. Now that he was gone, I was responsible for getting myself wherever I wanted to go.

Rebecca started to drive without putting an address into the GPS, which contrasted with my own habit of putting in my destination even when it was somewhere I'd been a million times.

"You like to drive, don't you?" I asked.

"I love to drive," she said, as she shifted the manual transmission.

Rebecca put on a playlist titled *Be Here*, and an angsty female voice came on over the speakers. She turned the volume up to a level at which I could feel the bass through the seats. In another car, with another person, silence might've felt uncomfortable, but in that moment it was necessary for processing. I looked out the window as the city gave way to suburbs and the suburbs gave way to fields, interspersed with woods. Thoughts spun in my head—*Noah is dead; I hid his body parts in the woods; someone is out to get me*—but as I sat next to Rebecca, things felt more manageable. No one was supposed to go through the death of a fiancé—*ex-fiancé*—alone. That I'd survived the imprisonment of both my parents when I was a child seemed miraculous in retrospect.

I glanced behind us like someone might be tagging along. No one was there. In truth, some part of me was always paranoid, feeling that I was being trailed by the police or one of my father's followers, and the events of the past week had only increased said paranoia. A theory of my father's was that everything we had the capacity for was already inside us, and no one could make anyone else do or feel something that they wouldn't do or feel on their own. I didn't buy into that. How could I? I was constantly being forced to do things I didn't want to do.

As we left the city, shedding the lights and the noise, I wished that I could rid myself of my emotional baggage with the same ease. Instead, I carried Noah with me, his body parts a weight even though I'd deposited them in the woods.

Why didn't you save me? he asked.

Why didn't you stay? I questioned in return.

WE WERE IN THE COUNTRY. IN THE SUMMER, THE FIELDS WERE tall with corn. Now they were barren. Life and death existed in the same spaces.

"Can I ask what happened?" Rebecca asked. She glanced at me. She continued to look beautiful in the dark.

I wanted so badly to tell her. Gossip was considered malicious, but I understood that people told one another things because holding on to information alone was lonely. *I'm alone, I'm alone, I'm alone* was a constant refrain.

There was also the possibility that if I told her the truth she'd immediately call the police and have me arrested. *I'm really, truly heartbroken about his death* wasn't a good defense.

"I . . ." I tried to force the words out but couldn't.

"I know that it's difficult," Rebecca said. She did something with the manual gearshift as we sped up. "You're like me in that respect—you think that it's better to keep everything bottled up inside. That's a mistake. People who think that they're immune to exploding are the most prone to it. Vulnerability makes us strong, Lexie. The Children of Murdered Parents support group has taught me that."

"I *was* vulnerable," I said defensively. "I shared a lot tonight."

"You were vague. I understand why you might not want to share everything with *them*, but I would hope that you could share with *me*."

She put her foot on the gas. I watched the speedometer on the dashboard climb up and up and up.

"Aren't we going a little fast?" I said. I wasn't usually wary of things like that. I didn't clap when planes landed successfully, or shudder when I was on a high ledge. But the roads were icy, and there was something about the look on Rebecca's face that told me she had no intention of slowing down anytime soon.

"Tell me what's going on, Lexie," she insisted.

"I can't. You wouldn't understand."

The car started to skid. I tried to press down on a brake that didn't exist on the passenger's side. I wanted to believe that I was in control of everything, but recent events had proved how false that was. I hadn't been able to save my relationship with Noah or keep him from dying. I hadn't figured out who'd killed him, and I couldn't stop the ache of grief in my chest. Most of all, there was nothing that I could do to lower the velocity of the car as it spun, out of control, into the opposing lane. I screamed, a recognizable thing, the sound of a woman about to die. Even though the sound came from my own mouth, it felt like I was observing the events from a distance. *Two friends went for a drive. They never came back.*

And then: *At least I won't have to feel heartbroken anymore, or worry about the police.*

The speed took us off the road and into a field, my body jerking with the movement. My seat belt pressed against my collarbone as it did its best to restrain me. There was a punch to my gut as the airbags inflated. Then, finally, we came to a stop.

The car was filled with the sound of breathing. I put my hand to my chest and felt for my beating heart, the same way that I had when the first organ was delivered to my house. It thumped wildly, too much of a good thing. I wiggled my toes, my fingers, and turned to look at Rebecca, who appeared to be doing the same sort of self-assessment.

When our eyes met—one blink, two blinks, *I'm okay, I'm okay*—a giggle inexplicably rose up in my throat. I worried that Rebecca might think I was crazy, until she began to giggle too, the two of us laughing like we'd heard the world's best joke. I laughed so hard that it sucked the air out of my lungs, a release like tearing the skin on a blister that was desperate to pop.

As we quieted, I opened my mouth.

"My fiancé left me for my best friend," I told her. "And I think he might be dead."

20.

Y OU POOR THING," REBECCA said.

I scooped another spoonful of ice cream into my mouth.

"It's been tough," I admitted. "Tough" didn't cover it. Noah's infidelity and death were like a cheese grater on the heart, but voicing such a feeling required a kind of vulnerability that I struggled with. That was on the long list of things that I blamed my mother for. She'd never listened to my feelings, had ridiculed me when I'd tried to go to her. Now emotional expression felt like trying to dance *The Nutcracker* without any ballet training.

Rebecca and I were sprawled across her king-sized bed, surrounded by a pile of snacks. I wore a pair of her pajamas. My wet hair smelled like her shampoo.

After my confession, Rebecca had called a tow truck to rescue us from the field. We'd waited outside, shivering, staring at the night sky.

"It's kind of beautiful out here," I said. There was a whole swath of stars that weren't obscured by the city's light here. They gave the darkness a cheery glow that had been missing from my treks through the woods.

"The bright side of a car crash," Rebecca joked.

"You didn't mean to," I said.

"The rode was icy," she agreed.

I got the sense that we were both lying, as though we were coming up with a cover story for a crime that we had committed.

"I see it all the time," the tow truck driver said when he arrived.

The two of us squeezed into the seat next to him. The cab reeked of marijuana.

"It's a pleasure to be able to help you ladies," he told us. I wondered what he was imagining we looked like beneath our jackets.

"Cars like that aren't meant for our weather here. Are you from somewhere else?" he quizzed, not pausing long enough to allow Rebecca to answer. "Snow tires are the thing. Snow tires and all-wheel drive. You'd be shocked if I told you about some of the stuff that I've seen." He proceeded to describe vehicles wadded up in little balls. I was relieved when we were safely in front of Rebecca's apartment building.

"Do you want to come up?" she asked. "I would offer to give you a ride back to your car, but, you know, I don't exactly have a car myself at the moment. We could have a sleepover."

A giggle escaped from my throat, residual from our earlier laughing session. Where that had been the result of a near-death experience, this laughter was all joy.

This was only the second time that I'd been invited to a sleepover at a friend's house. The first time, I was twelve, and the new girl in town had innocently invited me to her birthday party before the mother of one of the other guests clued her parents in to my identity; she'd shamefully rescinded the invite the following day. Later, she would become one of the girls who would torment me the most. I took her shift as proof that some people were born evil but others grew into it.

I'd always longed for a platonic sleepover. As I understood them from books and movies, sleepovers were sacred events during which girls painted their nails and confided in one another. Maybe that was why I couldn't tell anyone what had occurred between Noah and me: I hadn't grown up in the girlhood culture of confession.

"Sure," I said, like it wasn't everything to me.

———

REBECCA LIVED ON THE TWENTIETH FLOOR OF ONE OF THOSE towering apartment buildings that I looked at and thought, *I wonder who lives there*. The living room windows had a clear view of the city, and the walls were lined with colorful abstract prints. Everything was polished and sophisticated like no man's apartment ever was. It was the kind of place that I'd previously seen only in content from social media influencers.

"You must sell a lot of cars," I remarked as I looked around.

"I do okay," she said in the tone of someone who knew they excelled in their field. "Do you mind if I shower? I still smell like the tow truck. I have two showers. You can take the nicer one if you want."

I nodded. The tow truck reeked in a way that got stuck in my nose. There was something else there too—the scent of almost dying.

"Yeah, that would be great," I said.

The primary bathroom was a modern space with a cell-like

shower and a separate bathtub that was more of a decorative object than a pool in which to get clean. Rebecca supplied me with
a towel and pajamas.

"They're from a family Christmas," she explained, gesturing at
the snowman pattern on the pants.

I was familiar, from posts by influencers on social media, with
the ritual of matching family pajamas. I'd thought that the trend was
stupid and the people who engaged in it looked silly. Then Noah's
mother had given me an outfit of my own. I posed for pictures with
the family, and I liked how I blended in, my form indistinguishable
from theirs. Admittedly, I was jealous that Rebecca had a family like
that in spite of her father's murder. Selfishly, I wanted her to have a
past as fucked-up as mine. I was slowly realizing that that was too
much to ask of a friend—too much to ask of anyone at all.

My skin turned pink as the water returned the warmth to my
limbs. I hadn't realized how cold it had been in the field, my body
heated by adrenaline. I squirted a copious amount of expensive-
looking shampoo into my palm and massaged it into my scalp.
Though it was my first time in her condo, I felt at home in a way
that I hadn't in my town house since Noah left. I stayed in the
bathroom for too long, taking what Molly called a "sadness shower."
I wasn't sad, not quite, but I was processing.

When I emerged, Rebecca was on the bed with a variety of
chips, pizza bagels, and ice cream.

"I thought you might be hungry," she said.

"Did you just have all of this?" I asked. She didn't look like a
person who routinely ate things like pizza bagels.

"It's my emergency stash. You know, for when I really need it."

I settled awkwardly next to her on the bed. Platonic cuddling
was foreign to me. Through observation I was familiar with how

women touched one another, but casual touch had never come naturally to me. My parents hadn't been the kind of people to show affection. When I got in bed with someone, it was nearly always to have sex.

Rebecca pressed a button on a remote control, and the electric fireplace on the wall across from us burst into flame. A large television was mounted above it, and Rebecca clicked on the latest episode of *Love on the Lake*.

"Have you seen this yet?" she asked.

"No." I lied because I wanted to watch it again, with her.

I peeled the seal off a carton of ice cream. There was a particular way that women indulged together when there was no one else to watch, an implicit understanding of eating without judgment. As Rebecca had said, we *needed* it.

She paused the episode during a lull in the action and turned to look at me. From the way that she studied my face, it almost seemed as if she might be about to kiss me.

"I'm sorry I crashed the car," she started. "You weren't talking to me. Sometimes people need a little something to help them open up."

The popping sound when the lid of a jar of pickles finally released. It struck me then that the accident hadn't been entirely accidental. Rebecca had been trying to pry open something that was stuck.

"Tell me what happened with your fiancé," she continued.

I described the events of my birthday, how I'd anticipated a surprise party and arrived to find Molly and Noah together.

"He didn't even remember that it was my birthday. Molly, though—she knew. It's like she set up the whole night to hurt me as much as possible."

"Oh wow. What assholes."

"This is going to sound so stupid, but I was certain that things weren't over between us. I thought . . . well, I thought he was going to come crawling back to me."

The admission was humiliating and ludicrous. I recalled how Molly and I had judged the woman on reality television who'd taken her cheating ex back. I told myself that I'd been keeping the situation to myself as a strategy, but really I was trying to avoid the embarrassment of being cheated on. I worried that Rebecca would look at me with disgust or pity, but instead she let out a righteous "Of course you thought he would come back! Who wouldn't want to be with you?"

It was the exact thing that I needed to hear. I wasn't delusional or pathetic. I was normal. I was human.

"What happened next?" Rebecca asked.

"I tried to give him space. Men like that."

Rebecca laughed.

"It's the main thing they like. They like the shape of space more than a woman. Nothing is as sweet as the thing that you don't have."

"Exactly. When I couldn't take it anymore, I texted him and he came over, ostensibly to pick up his stuff, but we ended sleeping together."

"Whoa."

"Yeah. Things were weird when he left." I didn't tell her the part about sending the picture to Molly. If social media had taught me anything, it was that people always edited out the least palatable aspects of themselves.

Rebecca looked at me expectantly, and I realized she wanted me to tell her about the other part, the part where Noah was dead.

"I guess my former best friend found out what happened," I continued. "They had a fight when he got back to her place. He said he was going to stay with a friend. No one has seen him since."

"What the fuck? That's so messed up. What do you think happened?"

I took a bite of ice cream, a piece of chocolate crunching between my teeth.

Someone killed him. They're delivering him to me in pieces wrapped up like gifts of love. I can't tell anyone, because I'm afraid that someone's trying to frame me. I don't know what's more painful, that I had to dispose of parts of his body or that I have to keep it a secret.

"I have no idea," I told her.

"He could still be okay. Maybe he just needed a break," she suggested.

"Yeah, maybe."

I was so mad at him for what he did with Molly, but I would've forgiven him, because that's how much we were meant to be together. I still have a deposit on a wedding venue. I keep picturing him sewn together like a doll at the altar—you know, like those viral videos where people who are paralyzed learn to walk to surprise their bride.

Rebecca reached her hand out and grabbed mine.

"It's going to be okay," she said. "I'm here now. You can lean on me. Whatever happens, it will be all right."

There was a strange twinge in my chest. At first, I worried that there was something wrong with me. I'd read online that the most commonly referenced heart attack symptoms were the ones that were most likely to occur in men, while women might have a completely different experience. Was I dying? I was so used to the worst possible outcomes. No, whatever I was experiencing was positive. It was the ache that came with feeling warm and safe after years of loneliness and struggle.

"I'm so glad I met you," I told Rebecca. "I think I've been lonely for a very long time without realizing it. It's nice to make friends with someone new."

You showed up right when I needed you most.

"Same," she agreed. "I've been looking for someone like you for years."

Rebecca picked up the remote control and pressed play. The women on the show were getting dressed for a cops-and-robbers-themed party. Some of them dressed as police officers and others wore black-and-white-striped prison garb.

I fell asleep as two cast members argued about whether one was being supportive enough of the other's business. The bed was comfortable, my stomach full, and I felt safe in Rebecca's condo, with the knowledge that no one was going to leave body parts outside the door.

21.

——

I T WAS EASY TO be lulled into a sense of safety in Rebecca's orbit.
The intrusive thought *Noah's dead* still reverberated through
my skull, but her presence dulled it to a whisper. I hadn't realized
how much I'd needed someone—needed her.

I woke in the morning to find the bed empty next to me. It was
reminiscent of the night that I spent with Aidan—a connection
that disturbed me—until I heard the sound of pots and pans in the
kitchen. I wandered out of the bedroom and found Rebecca standing over a skillet, frying pancakes.

"Good morning, beautiful. How did you sleep?" she asked as
she handed me a cup of coffee.

"Great," I told her, not mentioning that I woke up several times
in the night with my brain going *Sleepover! I'm at a sleepover!* like
some kind of bad remix of the film *13 Going on 30*.

On one of the stools that lined the kitchen island, I took a seat
in front of a stack of pancakes and poured maple syrup over them.

"I got the recipe from someone I dated. He refused to give it to me for weeks, and then, as soon as he did, I ended things. It was worth it though, all the mediocre sex that I'd had to endure," Rebecca said.

I took a bite. They really were good. For some reason, breakfast was considered a "manly" meal, and a variety of men had made it for me as a form of proof. *Look at me! I can make an omelet! Would you like creamer in your coffee?* Noah, a noted noncook, was exceptionally proud of his ability to make eggs, a food that he ate regardless of the time of day. On the rare morning that he was still at home when I woke, he liked to present me with a plate of food before I left for work, an effort that I found touching. However, Noah's eggs were nowhere near as tasty as Rebecca's pancakes, which seemed like something that might be served at an expensive brunch. I ignored the sting that came with the thought that Noah would never make me—or anyone—eggs again.

The scene was exactly as movies had led me to believe breakfast after a sleepover would be, which was a rare feat, for real life to live up to film. Despite my carb-and-sugar-laden meal, I felt light as I headed into work. Sure, someone had murdered my fiancé and was delivering him, piece by piece, to my house, and sure, that someone was probably the psychopath who insisted that we were meant to be together, but the future was bright. In some ways, Noah's having been forcibly removed from my life made things easier, because it meant that I no longer needed to fixate on him. I would find someone new and better, the same way that I'd found Rebecca as a replacement for Molly.

That's why what I discovered when I arrived at the Better Love office came as such a shock.

I'd shown up late because I'd had to take an Uber to my car, and then drive to my house to change. Serena wasn't usually a stickler for punctuality, and after what had happened with Paul she'd told me it was fine to take time away from the office as needed. My grief over Noah was another, unspoken excuse. In any other circumstances, no one would've even noticed my late arrival, and everyone would have been in their offices, trying to finish up their work for the week in order to enjoy the weekend. As it was, every single Better Love employee was standing outside the building, and when I arrived, they all turned to look at me in a way that let me know that whatever was happening, I was somehow implicated in it.

"What's going on?" I asked.

"We had to evacuate. The police are on their way," Oliver told me.

"Why?"

"Because there are body parts inside," Nicole said. Her voice occupied a strange register between hysteria and glee.

"What?"

I suddenly regretted eating so many pancakes. My stomach roiled, and I could feel bile in the back of my throat. The night I'd spent with Rebecca had given me a false sense of security. When I'd gone home and found nothing new there, I'd hoped that Noah's murderer's reign of terror—whoever they were—was over. I'd been so wrong. While I lay in bed, eating snacks with Rebecca and telling her the saga of Noah and Molly, someone had been strewing the remainder of Noah's body parts around Better Love. It was only a matter of time before the police ran the DNA and discovered that the body parts belonged to the missing medical resident. There was little comfort in the fact that I'd spent the night with Rebecca, and therefore couldn't have planted the remains. The narrative was too good. I was the daughter of serial murderers and had recently been dumped. On top of that, I had actually buried other pieces of the corpse in the woods. I'd been careful, but it was impossible to have been careful enough when you were a suspect.

I debated my options. My first impulse was to flee. I thought of an episode of *Real Housewives* in which a cast member was arrested. She'd tried to run, which had made for excellent television and a poor defense. I imagined escaping was feasible only for millionaires, who had the kinds of funds that would allow them to relocate to countries that didn't extradite to the US. I didn't even know what countries those were. No, I would have to stay and fight. I tried to think of any lawyers I knew, and I couldn't come up with any. It was likely that the lawyers my parents had used had retired or passed in the years since the trial.

Then there was the mortification of being a grieving person. In a strange way, I found it less embarrassing to be thought of as a killer than to be seen as a wounded woman. I couldn't deal with the pity. It would all come out at once—Noah leaving me for Molly, my pathetic attempt to get him back, and his subsequent death. Everyone would know I was sad. It was possible that even my mother in prison would have access to the news and would bear witness to my downfall.

Just as I started to really panic, Oliver said, "I don't think they're real body parts."

"What do you mean, 'not real body parts'?" I asked.

"You'll see. It looks like a Ryan Murphy show in there."

"They could be real," Nicole said defensively as a police car, its lights flashing, pulled up to the scene.

Serena greeted the police, shaking the officers' hands like they were there to help. What would she do if they tried to take me away? Would she defend me? *I know Alexandra. She would never do something like this.* Or would she let them march off with me forever, the way that I had with my parents? I tried to reassure myself that Oliver was probably right, that the body parts were fake, the whole thing a prank.

"Whoever did it obviously has it out for you, Lexie," Nicole told me.

My head swiveled from the officers, now entering the building, to Nicole's face.

"What do you mean?"

"Well, they wrote 'matchmaking for psychopaths' on the wall. That's obviously about you, right?"

There was that stomach roiling again. No matter what was unfolding in front of me, I probably needed to use the bathroom sooner rather than later.

"Not necessarily," I replied, though I knew she was right.

Two police officers emerged from the building. Despite my efforts to will them in the direction of their car, they approached the huddle of matchmakers.

"How can we assist you, officers?" Nicole asked, her voice suddenly like a baby's.

I did my best to shrink, which was difficult inside my puffy jacket.

"We need to talk with Alexandra Smith," one of them said.

My parents were arrested twenty years prior, and in a different state, which meant that neither of the officers in front of me had been present. However, my brain interpreted them as the same officers as back then. The only difference now was that it was me they wanted to take away.

I coughed.

"What is it that you need?"

"It would probably be best to discuss this inside," one of the officers said.

I followed them to the door like they were the ones who worked in the office and I was a visitor. The carnage was immediately apparent. There was red paint thrown about the room, most of it still wet. Mixed in with the paint were plastic mannequin limbs. Though they looked wholly different from the real body parts that were delivered to my house, there was something unsettling about them. It felt like something human had been torn apart. As Nicole had mentioned, someone had written MATCHMAKING FOR PSYCHOPATHS in dripping red paint on one wall. The paint was blood for people who had never seen blood before.

"If you could keep moving, please . . ." one of the officers said.

"Sorry," I said.

We sat down at the conference table. I still needed to use the restroom, but I was scared to ask if I could go. The limbs in the lobby were fake, the blood obviously paint, and yet I couldn't shake the feeling that I was in trouble for something.

"We understand that, a few days ago, there was an incident with one of your clients," an officer began.

It took me a second to catch up. Paul. I'd forgotten about him. Could he have done this? He'd certainly seemed angry enough, but the messaging was confusing. He didn't know that I worked with psychopaths. He didn't know what he was.

"Yes," I confirmed. "I set one of my clients up on a date, and when she refused to go on a second, he got angry with me."

"Have you received any correspondence from Paul since then?"

"No. Nothing."

"Do you have any other clients that you think might've done something like this?"

Aidan. He knew what my clients were, what my job was. But I couldn't give his name up, because Aidan knew too much about me. He could tell the police my parents' identity, and if it was Aidan who killed Noah and delivered pieces of him to my house, he could point the finger in my direction. There was also the question of what else I'd said the night that Aidan and I met. No, I couldn't mention Aidan's name in such a setting.

"No," I said firmly. "I have no idea who might've done such a thing."

I stared into the eyes of the officer across from me as I spoke. Police officers had gotten much smaller since my parents' arrest. They'd seemed impossibly large then. My father had fought against the cuffs, and there was a moment—the tiniest of seconds—when I thought that he might get away. It took three men to wrestle him to the ground. I knew that if I ever spoke to him again he would call it an unfair fight, but I never did speak to him again. Later, I looked up some clips from his trial online, but I could watch for only several seconds before turning them off. I was afraid that, somehow, my father would climb through the computer screen and come back to life. I didn't want to be responsible for that—to be the person who uttered *Bloody Mary* three times in front of a mirror and then was shocked when she appeared.

Thankfully, my father was dead and I was a grown-up.

"Are we done? I just really need to use the restroom," I told the officers. I tried to say it like Nicole would. As a small child, I'd been obsessed with *The Wizard of Oz*. The man behind the curtain amplified his voice to make himself sound larger than life, and that was how he gained his power. Women did the opposite. They made themselves sound small and stupid to pull the wool over men's eyes.

"Just let us know if you see Paul again," the officers said. "We're worried that his actions are escalating, that he's spiraling out of control."

———

SERENA LET EVERYONE GO HOME, SOMETHING THAT WAS PREVIously unheard-of so close to Valentine's Day.

"Take a self-care day and come back Monday, ready to work," she said.

I didn't follow her instructions. The time for self-care was over. I needed to start practicing self-preservation. Yes, Noah was dead. Yes, I was wounded, but it wasn't fatal. I needed to buy a needle and stitch myself shut.

I closed myself in my office as a cleaning crew descended upon the lobby. Their job wasn't as simple as just scrubbing surfaces. They had to rip up the carpet, repaint the wall. Serena put a sign on the door that read TEMPORARILY CLOSED FOR REMODELING. Businesses were as apt to lie as people.

"I guess this is as good of a reason as any to update things," I heard Serena say through my closed door.

I texted Rebecca.

Have you heard from Paul?

The conversation with the police had made it clear that he was their primary suspect. They didn't realize how many psychopaths were in play. I wanted it to be him, because that would be an easy answer. I knew that it wouldn't be, for the same reason.

> No. I blocked his number. I think
> he's gotten the message by now.
> Did something happen?

Yeah, I'll tell you the next time I see you.

I wasn't prepared to discuss the dismembered mannequins with Rebecca yet. I wouldn't be until I had more answers.

I searched for any updates about Noah. That the limbs at Better Love were fake offered only a bit of comfort, because it had brought the police into my periphery. They had released me from their questioning that morning, but what would happen when they realized that there was a real body involved? I couldn't go to prison. Prison was where my father had been murdered. Worse, it was where my mother was still kept.

She's drawing you to her, a voice in my brain suggested. It wasn't the most far-out suggestion. My mother would go to any lengths to get what she wanted. What if she decided she wanted me? It seemed possible that after two decades behind bars she'd learned to strip the shadow off her skin and let it haunt the earth. I thought of the comment I heard her make shortly before the heart's arrival: *I hear it's cold there.* I'd let it go as a statement about the prison, but what if she knew where I was? I'd been naïve to ever consider myself safe.

During the time that I'd been with Rebecca, online conversation about Noah's absence had increased. In addition to posts from medical residents, one of the local media outlets had run an article requesting that people step forward if they knew anything about his whereabouts. People I'd never heard of in the three years that Noah and I were together were posting on his social media pages comments like *I know you'll be found. The world needs you!* For my sake, I hoped he never would be.

Alarmingly, two of his former colleagues had sent me text messages.

Do you need anything?

Tell us what we can do to help. I hope
that Noah is going to come home safe.

I wasn't sure how they'd gotten my number. I replied with a quick "thanks" to each of them, and then continued reading all the comments, hoping for something that would give me a sure answer as to who had slaughtered my former fiancé. It was difficult to read the effusive praise of a man who'd hurt me so deeply, first by leaving me for my best friend, and then by dying—though the second event wasn't his fault.

I got lost in the scrolling. Thumps and screeches came from the lobby as the cleaning crew worked as quickly as possible to cover up what had happened there. When things grew quiet, I glanced at the clock and realized that it was past five. I needed to go home, as unappealing as that sounded. At least the body parts that showed up at work were made of plastic. I was gathering the will to stand when I heard a murmur of voices coming from down the hall. The sound startled me, as I'd assumed I was alone.

As quietly as I could, I opened my office door and tiptoed toward the voices. I'd been trained in such movement when, as a child, I crept out of my room in order to watch my parents woo the women before they murdered them. It was impossible to predict exactly what skills would come in handy in adulthood.

As I made my way toward Serena's office, it became clear that the speakers were Nicole and Serena. How long had Nicole been there? I'd assumed that she'd gone home like everyone else.

"There's something wrong with her," Nicole said. "I know you don't want to see it, but she's messed up."

I hated that I assumed that I was the "she" in question. It was a luxury to hear such things and assume they were about someone else. My assumption was confirmed as Nicole continued to talk.

"I saw online that her fiancé is missing. Did you know that?" Nicole asked.

Oh no. She knew.

"Noah? He's missing?"

"Yes. He's been gone a week, and she hasn't mentioned anything to us. Don't you think that's weird?"

"Alexandra has always been an extremely private person, as is her right," Serena replied.

"But what if she did something to him? Or what if one of her clients did? Did you know that I saw her with one in public the other day? They were drinking coffee. It could've been a date. She's dangerous. You can't seriously be considering her as the next director. You need to take care of this situation before it's too late."

Serena was silent a long time. I wished I could see her face. I wanted to turn into air itself so that I could inhabit the room completely.

"Those are very serious accusations that you're making, Nicole. I'm going to be generous and ignore your suggestion that Alexandra might have hurt her fiancé in some way. Regarding the director position, I haven't made any decisions yet. Things are still in flux at the moment. I will let you know when I have more information.

In the meantime, I expect you to be respectful to all the match-makers at Better Love."

Nicole let out a huff of air so loud that I could hear it from the hallway. I crept back to my office before either she or Serena noticed me.

In some ways, Nicole's attempt to point the finger in my direction made sense. Nicole was a mean girl in high school. Just because she hadn't gone to *my* high school didn't mean that she couldn't sense the things that I'd hidden inside myself. That was a mean girl's power. No matter how a person dressed, who they were engaged to, or what they did, a mean girl could sense nonconformity. She'd seen it in me the first time that we met. I'd dismissed it because I'd believed that she didn't have the power to hurt me. I had bigger things to worry about, a wedding to plan. I'd been so stupid. Not only was she trying to get me fired, my position eliminated, but she was trying to implicate me in Noah's disappearance. A quick thought: *Could it have been her?* No. She wouldn't get her hands dirty like that. She didn't need to. My life was filthy enough on its own.

I desperately wanted to talk to Rebecca. It had been so nice to let someone into my world, if only a small part of it. If I was the earth, I'd allowed her to land on the moon. However, I couldn't tell her everything, because her father had been *murdered* and my parents were *murderers*. That would be like befriending Bambi and admitting to him that my parents liked to go deer hunting for fun.

There was only one person I could talk to, and coincidentally, that one person was my number one suspect. I picked up my phone and started to dial.

22.

"Y OU CAN'T STAY AWAY from me, can you?"

I stood in the lobby of Aidan's building. It was Saturday night, two weeks since our first meeting, and a week since Noah had disappeared. He had the face of someone I'd known forever.

"I need to talk to you."

"Is matchmaking always this dire?"

"It's not about that."

I followed Aidan into the elevator. He wore black joggers and a T-shirt, as though he'd just come from working out. He hadn't wanted me to come here.

"Let me fly you somewhere," he'd said on the phone.

I thought back to my drive with Rebecca. It was one thing for a car to skid across a road, and another for a plane to fall from the sky. I didn't trust him to take me safely back down from such a height.

"No."

"A restaurant, then. Somewhere nice."

"It can't be in public. I don't want to be seen."

"Your house?"

"Are you saying that you know where I live?"

"Not until you tell me."

"Let's meet at your place."

He'd hesitated.

"I don't usually bring women here."

"Why? What are you hiding?"

"Nothing. I just like my space."

His defensiveness made me curious. I was sure that Aidan's apartment—the physical manifestation of his psyche—would reveal the specific darkness of his soul, just as my parents' various homes had revealed their darkness. Once my parents had been arrested, forensic investigators combed through every one of my parents' addresses that they could find for evidence. They'd been shocked to discover that there was seemingly no attempt to cover their tracks. There was trace evidence of the women everywhere. Their failure to catch my parents earlier was an indictment of the entire investigative team. They hadn't even realized that serial murders were being committed. Slutty women, they thought, disappeared all the time.

I didn't think that Aidan was a serial murderer, like my parents, but he was something. *A psychopath.*

We took the elevator to the top of the building. *The penthouse.* The doors opened to reveal a sparse, clean space that wasn't entirely different from Rebecca's apartment, except that Aidan's was much larger. On the walls were representational paintings of men on horses and ships at war with the water. Next to a window was a telescope that was angled in such a way that I couldn't tell if it was pointed at the sky or toward his neighbors. I couldn't detect the stench of death in the air. If Aidan was holding on to the rest of Noah's body, he was doing a good job of concealing it.

"Do you want me to show you the bedroom?" he asked.

"You know that's not why I'm here."

"Actually, I don't know. You wouldn't tell me why you needed to come here." Aidan's tone was snippy, and I conceded that recent events had caused me to get a little hysterical. I needed to calm down. I wouldn't get anything out of him if I was upset.

"Let's sit," I said. I led him to the couch like it was my place rather than his. The comforting thing about being in the home of my number one suspect was that I was confident that no body parts would interrupt our conversation, because I was watching Aidan's every move.

He took a seat next to me. It was like we were back on that bed in the hotel room, except that I was totally sober and was wearing leggings and a sweatshirt instead of something tiny and sparkly. My brain locked into place. It came to me suddenly—a *repressed memory*—like on reality television, when things that had happened in past seasons were spliced with the current one. Suddenly it unfolded in front of me like a note passed from one hand to another in class.

———

"I TOLD YOU ABOUT MY PARENTS. NOW WHAT ARE YOU GOING to tell me?" I asked Aidan that night in the hotel. I hadn't really expected him to give me anything. I was used to the lopsided nature of confessions. I was so good at winning the worst kinds of competitions.

"I was a difficult child," Aidan began.

The room was spinning—or was it my head? I wasn't sure what

day it was. It felt like an eternity since Noah and Molly had told me of their affair, but it had been only eight hours. Now I was on a bed in a hotel room with a stranger—*the handsome man.*

"I threw these wild, uncontrollable temper tantrums. They came out of nowhere and there was nothing my parents could do to calm me down. They had me tested for the usual things, but I wasn't that . . . *usual.*" He spit out the word like it hurt him.

"I guess they figured that I'd grow out of it eventually. It was a phase. In the meantime, my parents would just have to deal with it. They were worried that I might hurt my siblings. I *did* hurt my siblings. It was all accidents—you know, sibling stuff—but after my sister's broken arm they decided to do something."

"What did they do?"

"They made a padded room."

"You mean, like, a cell?"

"Yes. They turned my bedroom into a padded cell that locked from the outside. Whenever I acted out, they put me in it. But I struggled to grasp exactly what actions would land me in there. I pushed the boundaries. I spent so much time in there that they ended up installing a slot for food."

The man next to me was so *handsome*, so *normal*, that it was hard to envision him locked away like a mental patient in the 1950s. No one went through something like that and came out totally ordinary. My own childhood loneliness had driven me crazy, and I hadn't been locked away; I had merely been abandoned for long stretches of time.

"Eventually I figured out how I needed to behave to stay free. It was like having a role in a play. I was someone else for a while, and then, when I was alone, I became myself again. In a fucked-up way, I started to like being by myself. Being around people was a lot of work. I constantly had to put on a different face in order to please them. In my head, though, I still thought I was like everyone else. How can you tell that you're different when you're the only person you've ever really known?"

"How did you find out?" I asked.

"You mean, how did I find out that I'm a psychopath?"

"Yeah."

"No one's ever diagnosed me, if that's what you're asking. I've made sure to stay far away from mental health professionals. I diagnosed myself when I was sixteen."

"What happened when you were sixteen?"

He paused, took a sip out of the bottle in his hand.

"I murdered someone," he said. "You're the first person I've ever told."

I should've run away then. He'd just confessed to murder. However, my parents were serial killers. A little murder didn't faze me the way that it might faze other women. Also, I didn't totally believe him. Murder could be a lot of things. It could be accidentally hitting someone with a car on a dark night. Handing peanuts to a friend, forgetting that they had a deadly allergy. I figured that Aidan's killing had been one like that.

"Did you really?" I asked.

His voice grew quiet; it was barely above a whisper, as if speaking softly enough would mean that the confession didn't count. I put my hand on his knee. I didn't know what to do about this pull I felt toward him now that he'd confessed to causing death.

"I had this girlfriend in high school. I thought we were in love. We started dating because everyone told me that we would be perfect together and I believed them. All my friends said she was the hottest girl in school, and it made me feel good that the hottest girl in school wanted me. She had this ex-boyfriend who went to a different school. He treated her horribly, or she claimed that he did. Later I realized that she was doing things to egg me on. She wanted me to be protective of her. She thought it was romantic. It's difficult for me to parse who I was before we started dating and afterward. It's a weak excuse, I know, to say that she messed me up, but she really messed me up. Or maybe I was already messed up. Maybe I'd been that way since birth and was looking for someone to pin it on. Anyway, I became obsessed with her ex. I started following him around. I actually stood up my girlfriend a couple of times in order to follow him. I thought I was doing it for her, that it was what she wanted."

We both flinched when the heater came on with a creak. There were so many red flags in what he was telling me, but it felt so good to really get to know a person like this. All of Noah's stories were like *The saddest day of my life was when my team didn't make the soccer finals.* I hadn't realized how much I'd missed emotional intimacy.

"He was on the cross-country team. He went for these long runs by himself. At first I couldn't keep up with him. It was humbling. People think that I'm joking when I say that following someone is the best way to get into shape. I'm not. I'd be lying if I said that I never thought about hurting him. I did, but I had no intention of acting on it. It was a fantasy. It was never meant to be real. Then, one day, he was running and he noticed that I was behind him. He shouted at me. 'What the fuck do you think you're doing? I know that you're dating my ex.' We approached each other. Neither of us were very big, as we were teenage boys who ran all the time. He probably thought we were going to have a fistfight, the kind of thing that boys do all the time. It surprised both of us when I picked up a rock and smashed him over the head with it. I thought I was doing the right thing by protecting my girlfriend. I needed to eliminate him for her, for us. That's the kind of thing that a good guy does, right?"

Aidan laughed. It wasn't the bitter laugh that I was expecting but something sincere, like he was telling a joke.

"It happened so fast. Once you realize how fragile humans really are, it's amazing that anyone survives until adulthood. A single hit was enough to take him down. I didn't mean to kill him—that's what I tell myself, anyway. I just wanted to make sure that he never hurt my girlfriend again. I didn't tell her what I did. I couldn't. I didn't want her to think of me like that—*as a killer.* The irony was that she was so distraught over his death that she told me it wasn't *fair to us to stay together.* It was confusing to me. I thought she wanted me to get rid of him, and instead, that was the very thing that came between us. It took me a long time to realize that she never really loved me. It was him that she was fixated on the whole time. He was the one she couldn't stop talking about. I was the stupid rebound who thought we were in love. I never told anyone what happened. I didn't want to give anyone the power to put me behind bars the way that my parents had."

"Why are you telling me now?" I asked.

He looked at me like I was a lit window in the middle of the night and he could see everything that was happening inside.

"I haven't been totally honest with you," he said.

"You made the story up, didn't you? You've never killed anyone," I said. The lie irritated me. I was ready to leave, to go home and win Noah back. What was I doing with this man?

"No, I did. The thing is, Lexie, I approached you tonight because I saw you across the room and knew exactly who you were."

"What do you mean?" I asked. I thought he meant "knew" in the way that similar beings could recognize one another across the universe. Aidan, however, had been literal in what he said.

"I knew who your parents were before you told me. I know all about Peter and Lydia Schwartz, their murders, their love story. You."

The room stopped spinning as adrenaline coursed through my veins, canceling out the effects of the alcohol I'd drunk. The handsome man had known who I was. He saw me in a bar and approached me, and now we were alone in a hotel room. I'd gone from being the child hiding in her room to being one of the screaming women.

Aidan didn't seem to notice my distress. He continued his monologue. Men could be so oblivious to the danger that they represented.

"I was fucked-up after that. Or maybe I was fucked-up before that and that's why I did it. Anyway, I was fucked-up. I'd worked so hard to fit in with the cool, popular kids, and suddenly I couldn't even pretend. I didn't care about their stupid parties or the girls who threw themselves at me. I was so fixated on how it felt to bash that guy's head with the rock. I wanted to do it again, which I knew was wrong. I couldn't tell anyone how I felt. I was completely alone. I started doing these searches online. Covert, of course. I couldn't type *I want to kill someone and don't know what to do.* Even as a high school student, I wasn't that stupid. Eventually I discovered your parents, what they'd done. I understood that they were like me. They took pleasure in something that wasn't supposed to be pleasurable. Unlike me, they didn't spend all their time trying to resist. They gave in. They were a warning. They were a love story."

As much as I wanted to tell Aidan that he was wrong, that they were total monsters, I saw truth in what he said. My parents did, somehow, truly love each other. There was something beautiful about that, that out of all the fish in the sea, they each found the one whose bite was equally vicious.

"How did you find me? Have you been *stalking* me?"

I pulled away, putting space between us on the bed. It disgusted me to think that he could be one of them, one of my parents' *followers*.

"No, no. It wasn't like that. I saw you in the bar and thought you were hot. I was looking for a hookup—that's all. Then I got closer and saw your face and just knew that you were the person I'd been searching for my whole life. My soulmate. The only one who can really understand me."

The confession made me sick. I thought we were having a metaphorical dick-measuring competition, only the length was a measure of childhood trauma. Instead, I'd discovered that the handsome man—someone I'd kissed—had killed someone and was obsessed with my parents. I stood up to leave, but the spinning of the room had increased and was like the worst kind of carnival ride. I ran to the bathroom, hurling up all that was inside me. It was my bodily functions that forced me to stay, but stay I did. It seemed fitting that other people's lives were changed when a butterfly flapped its wings and mine was altered when I spit up half-digested food in the toilet.

ON THE COUCH IN AIDAN'S APARTMENT, I STIFFENED.

"You knew who my parents were before we ever talked," I said.

I'd been unable to figure out why Aidan was so certain that we belonged together, especially since I'd told him that my parents were serial murderers. I'd thought that he was allured by the chase. He couldn't have me, and that made him want me more. But no, he wanted me *because* of who my parents were.

People liked to talk about nepo babies, the children of famous people, who were given a leg up in life because of who their parents were. Everything that they achieved was marked with an asterisk that noted that they came from wealth and fame. It meant that nothing could ever be their own, not really. I was the nepo baby of death. As long as I was affiliated with my parents, nothing would ever be mine.

There was also the fact that he killed a person, but that was a concern that I would get to later.

"It was never me that you wanted at all," I said. "It was my mother or my father. Which one is your favorite? People usually pick. Do you love the siren or the madman? You don't know what it was like growing up with them, how that kind of environment destroys a person."

"I do. You told me. I get it, Lexie. I really do. Don't you see? We're the same. You spend all your time setting up couples, and you can't see what's right in front of you."

"I was supposed to marry Noah. We were going to move to the suburbs. I was going to have ordinary children, maybe get a dog. That was what I wanted, not whatever this is."

Aidan grabbed my hand, and I was too startled to take it back.

"You can play this game all you want, but I see you, Lexie. I know who you really are. You're not this good-girl housewife married to a doctor. You would've been bored within five minutes. That's not the kind of love you want. You want passion, excitement. It's what I want too. We can do everything together—travel the world, eat the best cuisine, see the greatest works of art."

"Kill people," I added.

"No," he said.

"You did kill someone though."

"Just one."

"Really? Tell me the truth, Aidan. Am I really supposed to believe that you stopped with a single person? You idolize my parents. They're serial murderers."

"You idolize people on reality television, and I don't see any filler in your lips. That's not how things work. I idolized them because I was lonely. You understand that, don't you? Loneliness? I just wanted to be seen. I wasn't trying to be like them."

I pulled my hand away. All parts of myself belonged to me.

"Bullshit. I don't believe you. I've been through hell lately, *hell*. My fiancé left me for my best friend, and now he's dead. You killed him, and you've been delivering him to me in pieces. Isn't that what you do, Aidan? Protect women by killing their exes? Guess what. It's not a great way to woo someone! Every time that I think I'm safe, something new shows up. Do you even know how hard it is to bury things in the wintertime? Of course you don't, because you don't bury things. You keep them and deliver them to my doorstep in gift-wrapped packages. And what is with the stuff at work? The roses were one thing, but the dismembered mannequin went way too far. Nicole suspects something—I can tell that she does. She's trying to get me fired, and I can't let that happen. I'm a *matchmaker*. It's what I'm good at. I have nothing else left. Molly is gone, Noah too. What am I if not that?"

I talked and talked and talked. I might've gone on forever, but in a moment of clarity I realized that I sounded like my mother on the phone, the way that, when she'd gotten started on a perceived injustice, she couldn't shut up about it. It made me insane. I hated that I had the same impulse. It was Aidan; it had to be. He'd killed Noah, delivered pieces of him, and brought out the *mother* within me.

"I didn't know all of that was happening," Aidan said quietly. "I wouldn't do something like that, Lexie. I don't want to hurt you—don't you see? I want to *love* you."

I had no patience for his weak denial. The truth was so clear in front of me.

"But you have hurt me—don't *you* see? I'm not like my parents. I don't appreciate bloody objects wrapped in tissue paper. Murder isn't a love language!"

I stood up. I couldn't remember why I'd come. I needed to keep Aidan away. He was like my parents, an agent of death. But I couldn't call the police, because he'd implicated me in his crimes. It was smart, really. It was a common plot device in romantic comedies—two people, unable to avoid each other, finally realize that they were meant to be. That was what he wanted, but I refused to give in to his machinations. I was in charge of my own fate. Maybe I couldn't have Noah, but I could find someone else like him. Someone ordinary, with a mom who stayed at home and made casseroles. A kind of person who couldn't fathom how traumatic my childhood had been.

"If you care about me at all, you'll stay away from me and Better Love. No more packages, okay? I don't want to see a single fingernail. Do whatever you want with the rest of him. I won't call the police as long as you return the favor. Please, Aidan. Please. I want my life back."

Aidan followed me to the door.

"Please don't leave," he said. "I can he—"

"I've said all I have to say, Aidan."

A hand took hold of my arm, at once firm and gentle. Something about being held like that made me want to stay, to turn toward him. He was even more dangerous to me than I'd given him credit for.

"Just stay. Hear me out. You don't have to be alone anymore."

It was so like a man to create problems and then hold an unwilling audience captive to hear him rationalize them.

"I'm leaving, Aidan. Let me go."

He did as he was told. It annoyed me that I almost wished he hadn't. My arm burned with the memory of his touch, and I couldn't help but remember how it felt when our lips were pressed together on the night we met. I made myself stop. I couldn't think of him in that way. Aidan had hurt Noah—or at least I was pretty sure he had—and I wasn't about to let him do the same to me.

I left the condo. I entered the elevator and watched the doors close, and it felt like an ending. It was the kind of shot used to indicate the end of a season on television. I forgot about the documentarian's favorite move, the one where the screen went black and then words like *Two months later* ominously appeared to show that the end of the story was never where we thought it was.

23.

"HOW'S YOUR FIANCÉ?" MY mother's voice drawled through the phone.

I'd spent the day bleaching the town house. Now that he'd been reported missing, the search for Noah had ramped up. There was a grainy photo of him from the last night he'd been seen alive—the last time we'd had sex—and I recognized the background as Molly's apartment building.

It might be easy to assume that I was most haunted by the screams of the dying women, but one thing about ghosts is that no one gets to choose who they're haunted by. The thing that really kept me up at night was my parents' arrest. They didn't see it coming. Of course not. They thought they would get away with killing forever. My father had been caught in his crimes before. We'd been evicted from homes, kicked out of restaurants. I'd seen him screamed at on the street. But there were no lasting consequences. He ran out of money; he got more. Someone punched him in the face; the bruises healed. Everything that he did built up his idea that he was infallible. I'd watched him talk his way out of numerous traffic tickets, including once when we were in a stolen car. He started to let his guard down like the tiger's keeper who forgot that it had teeth.

I saw the whole thing. Probably someone should've made sure that I was out of the way, but the police were too distracted by the body. My parents came home earlier than expected. No one was prepared, least of all me.

"What are you doing in my house?" my father demanded when he saw the police.

It wasn't his house. It belonged to someone he and my mother had met in a bar and murdered. It wasn't in the kind of neighborhood where anyone noticed or cared about new neighbors.

The police pulled out their guns. For a moment, I thought they were going to shoot my parents in front of me.

"No," my mother said. "We don't mean any harm. We haven't done anything to anyone."

Another obvious lie.

They feigned cooperation until the police tried to cuff them.

"I'm a mother!" my mother cried. She didn't seem to notice me standing there. I wanted her to look at me, to really see me. Strangely, I thought she would apologize.

Viewing the arrest was like watching a nature documentary in which a beautiful beast was finally beaten by the elements. My father never stopped believing that he would somehow escape the charges. He acted as his own lawyer, which didn't go the way he'd hoped. He was lucky that we didn't live in a death penalty state, though he died anyway. My mother tried to claim police brutality. They'd hurt her wrists, her neck. She wore an oversized brace for part of the trial. People might've cared more if so many bodies hadn't been found. I was happy that she'd never really mastered using the internet, so that she didn't have to see how many people made rape jokes about her.

Two simultaneous truths were that they deserved to go to prison and that seeing it was traumatizing to watch. I used to fear the monster that devoured women in the house, but my new nightmare was the police who took my parents away. I couldn't shake the feeling that the officers were going to come back for me.

It broke my heart that Noah was dead. It broke my brain that his dismembered parts kept showing up at my house. I felt like the worm on the hook of a fishing line waiting for law enforcement to come take a bite. I hadn't killed my fiancé, but I wasn't sure that mattered.

"He's dead," I told my mother. "Someone is delivering him in pieces to my house."

She laughed.

"You've always been so dramatic, my darling."

"It's the truth. I think it was a psychopath that I work with. He brought me his heart, and I buried it in the woods."

"It sounds like he loves you."

"That's not what love is. You don't know what it means to love."

"Don't dump your teenage melodrama on me, Alexandra. I know more about love than you could ever comprehend. Your father and I had one of the greatest romances of all time. People have written books about it."

"They wrote those books because you killed people. Your life wasn't a romantic comedy."

"No. It was better than that. Your father and I are going to be remembered forever. No one is ever going to forget our love. I can feel his presence still, you know. He's always with me. He always will be. What we have lasts for an eternity."

"Why couldn't you love me like that?" My voice came out as a wound.

Another laugh. I couldn't figure out where the jokes were.

"What is this 'woe is me' act about, Alexandra? We gave you culture. What more could you want?"

"Sometimes you forgot to give me *food*. You left me alone for days on end. I was a *child*. I was *your* child, and you never cared. You were more worried about what you looked like or that you were having fun. Now my life is ruined. I'd almost gotten away from what you did. I was going to have a different life. But I can never escape, not really. People don't make themselves; they are made by the things around them. I was formed by you and Dad, by what you did. Why couldn't you just be normal parents? Get a stupid bob, wear frumpy clothes? Would that have been so bad?"

There was quiet on the line. After years of conversations, I'd finally silenced her. I hoped that she might apologize. *You're right, Alexandra. Your father and I were bad parents. We should've cared more. Better people would've suppressed their murderous urges for the sake of their child. We were weak. We took pleasure in brutality. We only really knew how to love each other.*

Then my mother's voice came through, sharp and poisonous.

"You greedy little bitch. You never wanted me to have anything for myself."

I recognized the beginning of a rant. My time to speak was over. It was her time now. She was letting me know that I'd gone too far—or, more likely, she hadn't heard me at all.

The way that I felt now wasn't entirely different from how I'd felt when I held the heart in my hands. I knew now that it belonged to Noah, but it had felt like mine. I just hoped that if—when—the police brought me in, I wouldn't end up in the same prison as my mother.

24.

———

I PUT EVERYTHING ASIDE FOR Valentine's Day. Several people
who didn't know about our breakup reached out to me about
Noah's disappearance. *This must be so hard for you.* It was, but not
in any of the ways that they expected. In a way, it was nice to be
a matchmaker on February fourteenth, because it didn't allow
me any time to think about his death.

The lobby had been refurbished. Serena had opted to paint the
back wall a cheery pink. Everyone complimented her on the choice,
but it made me think of the fake blood that had been smeared
around with the mannequin parts. My hands still smelled like
bleach from the day before. Nothing would ever be clean enough.

The conference room was turned into a "war room," with multiple people stationed at phones and on computers to process new
clients. The clients wouldn't be matched immediately, but Serena
understood that when people signed up on that date, they needed
the promise of love at the very least.

Married people, even those who'd had a difficult time landing
partners, forgot how much of society was designed to remind

people of their loneliness. Tables in restaurants were set for two. Wedding invites allowed for plus-ones. There were actors who made entire careers starring in made-for-TV movies about two people falling in love. During the month of February—a month when seasonal depression was at its deepest—stores were flooded with flowers and chocolate.

I'd thought that it would become easier to cope with Noah's death, but every sign of romance rubbed it in my face.

You're alone, hissed the heart-shaped boxes as people walked through stores.

You're alone, said the marketing emails delivered from every store they'd ever shopped at.

You're alone, said their parents, their friends, the silence of their phones.

You're alone, the mirror said when I got up that morning.

In my most despairing moments, I worried that I would never recover. I'd thought of trauma as a cup that, once full, couldn't hold any more. I'd misjudged; trauma was a limitless pool that expanded to contain whatever filled it.

I threw myself into my work. I matched clients, arranged dates, shoved chalky candy hearts into my mouth until I felt sick. Each accepted match gave a little rush of dopamine. I was good. I was kind. I wanted people to be together. I wasn't the grim reaper that my parents' actions had ordained that I would be. I'd buried the heart because I'd been forced to. I was only doing what I needed to in order to survive.

What are you doing tonight? I TEXTED REBECCA. I HOPED THAT THE two of us could watch a romantic comedy and eat junk food as single women. We couldn't replicate the times I'd spent with my mother, but she could be something better than my mother—a friend.

> Sorry, I'm going out with Tyler.
> We should hang tomorrow!

I frowned. I hadn't set up a date for them, and they were still several weeks away from graduating from the program. Rebecca was good at a lot of things, but complying with Better Love's instructions wasn't one of them.

Yeah, tomorrow! I replied. I hid my hurt. I'd been counting on seeing her that night, as I didn't want to be alone, and my only romantic prospect was with a psychopath who had probably murdered my ex-fiancé. Matching her with Tyler had been my own downfall. I was just happy that I'd never tried to pair her with Aidan. The two of them together would've been explosive.

I bought sushi for one on the way home from the Better Love office when it had finally closed for the night. I did a good job of pretending that it was enough. What did I need a man for when I had raw fish?

There was nothing at my doorstep when I arrived home, and nothing waiting inside. I should've felt relief, but somehow it exacerbated my feeling of isolation. I'd once matched a client who was into taxidermy. Personally, I found the practice disgusting, and before I set up her first match, I confirmed that the animals she stuffed had died of natural causes. However, those pieces of Noah were all that I had left of him, and they helped me understand the impulse to dress up something dead until it looked alive again. As gruesome as they were, they were a continuation of our story. One way of looking at the spot in the woods where I'd left them was as a dumping ground for remains; another way of looking at it was as a shrine. My empty doorstep was an indicator that not only had I lost Noah, but the person who killed him was busy that night. I was left behind, forever the forgotten child.

Hoping that it would relax my nervous system, I put on a romantic comedy that I'd seen dozens of times before. Based on the number of pieces of sushi that slipped out from between my wooden chopsticks, it was doing a poor job.

I dropped the chopsticks on the floor when my phone buzzed. In theory, smartphones made socializing easier. In lived experience, however, they did so only for people who were already sociable. For everyone else, their stillness emphasized how little anyone cared to contact them. That hadn't been a problem when I was friends with Molly, because she was needy and texted me constantly, even when she was at work. While Rebecca and I messaged each other frequently, it wasn't in the same rapid succession as with Molly. When Rebecca was in a room with someone, she liked to look at their face instead of the glowing rectangle in her hand.

Because Rebecca was on a date with Tyler, I knew that she hadn't caused the buzz, and the possibility of an unexpected text excited me more than I cared to admit. Maybe someone had reached out to confess their love on Valentine's Day.

I looked at the screen. The message was from a number that I didn't recognize. Despite this, I was unmistakably its intended recipient.

Want to find out what happened to Noah?
Meet me at Better Love at 10pm.

I didn't bother cleaning up my sushi or pausing the romantic comedy I was watching before gathering my boots, jacket, and hat and heading out the door. I knew there was a possibility that the message drawing me to Better Love was a setup, but I couldn't bring myself to care, because I wanted answers. If I was potentially going to prison, I needed to know who wanted me there. Also, I was lonely. Loneliness wasn't treated as a crisis, like drug addiction or depression, but I knew from my years as a matchmaker that it could make people act just as irrationally. That was why people gave up everything to travel across the world to meet strangers they'd only conversed with online, or agreed to go on reality dating shows on which they got engaged to someone without ever seeing their face. We were all so desperate for companionship. I was desperate enough that I was willing to risk my life.

I PARKED DOWN THE STREET FROM THE OFFICE. THE WORLD around me was frozen in more ways than one. The streets were quiet as couples shared romantic candlelit meals or snuggled together under the sheets. Outside, ice crunched beneath my boots, and I nearly tripped as I approached the entrance.

Better Love was dark. I slid my key into the lock and cautiously opened the door. The alarm system beeped in warning, and I quickly entered the code to silence it. There was no sign that there was anyone else in the building.

The lobby was decorated for Valentine's Day, with heart-shaped balloons floating around the room and paper Cupids stuck to the newly painted walls.

"Hello?" I called out.

Nothing.

I crept through the darkness, unwilling to draw too much attention to myself with the overhead lights. I walked through the corridor, doing checks in each room as I went. I couldn't escape the feeling that someone might be hiding somewhere, waiting to pop out and surprise me. The break room was empty, as was the conference room. I made my way down the hallway between the offices. Some matchmakers had left their doors open, and the blackness within glowed eerily.

In my own office, I grabbed the letter opener that Noah had given to me. It was comically small. Noah had never really known how to keep me safe.

I began to relax when I reached the end of the hall. No one was there. The message was a prank, a way to lure me out of the coziness of my home and into the chilliness of the night, and in my loneliness, I'd fallen for it.

My parents used to do extravagant things on Valentine's Day: expensive restaurants, shiny jewelry, murdered women. One year my father bought my mother and me matching diamond earrings. None of my shoes fit, and I was wearing last year's clothes, but I walked around with the equivalent of a car in each of my ears. Another year, he whisked my mother away for a vacation, both of them forgetting about me until they got home a couple of days later.

There were two wolves inside me. One of them wanted me to be loved as passionately as my father had loved my mother. The other went after men—had wanted Noah—only when it understood that my life with them would be devoid of that level of obsession. Noah and I would be safe. We would be good. No one would ever suspect that I was related to serial murderers. For now, I tamed both beasts with a sigh and walked back down the hallway. I would go home, finish watching my movie. I wondered how long sushi could sit out before it would poison me.

Back in the lobby, a hand reached out from the darkness and grabbed my wrist.

I jumped. The letter opener slipped out from between my fingers, fell to the floor, and disappeared from sight.

"I didn't mean to scare you," a female voice said.

It took my brain a moment to process what was happening. I'd been so prepared for Aidan that I didn't know what to do with this person, this woman. When my eyes had adjusted to the dim light, I realized that it was Nicole. The alarm hadn't beeped, which meant she'd been there the whole time, watching me grope through the dark.

"Nicole? What the fuck? What are you doing here?" I asked.

She was wearing one of her heart-patterned sweaters. A big red bow adorned the top of her head. She looked like a child.

"I asked you here," she replied, like it was obvious.

"What do you mean, you asked me here?"

"We need to figure this out, Lexie," she said.

"Figure what out? What did you do with Noah?"

"The situation between us. The future of Better Love. Right now, we're at an impasse. We both want to be director, and Serena is dragging her feet. It's that mother instinct in her. She doesn't know when to let go. She knows that I'm the right person for the job, but for some reason she doesn't want to hurt you. Meanwhile, you're pulling us all down. I had to show her how dangerous it was to have you around, the damage that she's doing by continuing to placate your feelings."

My jaw dropped. Of all the possibilities—Aidan, Molly, Paul, my mother, a supernatural monster—I'd thought Nicole was the least likely. I hadn't thought her capable of brutality. I disliked her, sure, thought her deranged in her normalcy. No one was cutesy like that on the inside. All of us were cynical, suffering.

"That was you?" I thought back to everything that had happened. The flowers, the destruction of the Better Love lobby, the pieces of Noah's corpse. "What did you do to Noah? Was it you who killed him, or someone else?"

"I have no idea where your ex-fiancé is," she said glibly. "I assume that he's off somewhere trying to stay away from you. I can't imagine what it was like dating you for all those years. I would need a break too. It was Ethan's idea to mention him in the text message. He said it would be a good way to get you here, and he was right."

My brain worked to parse what she was saying. Nicole claimed she hadn't killed Noah. Could it have been Ethan—her husband—who was responsible for his death?

"So you didn't"—I paused, trying to think of the right way to phrase the question—"send anything to my house?"

Nicole's nose wrinkled.

"Your house? No. I just sent you the flowers and redecorated the lobby. Did you like it? I hoped that it would remind you of your childhood home."

I tried to put the puzzle pieces of Nicole's confession together. I was so sure that everything was connected. They were too similar to each other to be a coincidence.

"Were you working by yourself?" I asked.

Nicole smiled coyly.

"I might've had a couple of little elves helping me out. Ethan, for one. He's here now too, helping me with a project outside. Isn't that the most romantic thing you've ever heard? He's willing to sacrifice Valentine's Day to help me with my career goals. You can only imagine what it feels like to be loved like this."

Nicole was becoming recontextualized in front of me. I'd thought her a boring, vapid woman. Perhaps it was wrong of me to judge another woman like that, but it would be unreasonable to expect me to like every woman solely because of my gender. Men weren't condemned for hating one another.

I'd taken Nicole's frequent comments about psychopaths, and the way that she cast shade in my clients' direction or asked intrusive questions about their private lives, as a sign of jealousy. I'd forgotten that the people who most liked to label others as psychopaths were most likely to be psychopaths themselves, the same way that people who said things like *I hate drama* were ultimately the most dramatic people of all. I hadn't thought of her in that way because I hadn't thought her capable of violence, and now I saw that I'd been wrong. She wanted to hear about my clients because she saw something familiar in them, like a wolf howling into the distance toward a mate that only it could see.

"You're a psychopath," I said. It was a statement that I was more certain of than that her hair was blond. However, Nicole refused to accept the diagnosis.

"I am not. You are. I know all about you, Lexie, all the things that you've been hiding. I know that you haven't been with Noah in weeks. I know that you've been forcing your clients to hang out with you as though they're your friends. It's pathetic—that's what it is. I tried to tell Serena, but she wouldn't listen. 'Alexandra wouldn't do that,' she told me. She doesn't know how deep your problems go. She doesn't know about your parents."

I froze. Nicole might not have killed Noah; I'd forgotten about the part where the note writer knew my secrets.

"My parents?"

"I did some snooping. Name changes are public record, you know. I discovered that you haven't always been Alexandra Smith. You used to be Alexandra Schwartz, daughter of Peter and Lydia Schwartz. Your parents were—what was the term? Oh yeah, 'serial lust murderers.'"

I listened to Nicole detail their crimes. She delighted in talking about them. She knew all the gory details. I could tell that she'd done her research, spent hours and hours of her precious life learning exactly how my parents seduced women before they slaughtered them. All this time I'd thought she hated me, and now I realized that she was obsessed. It could be argued that her obsession was something akin to love.

"Okay, Nicole. You know about my parents. So what? I was a kid. It had nothing to do with me. Yes, I changed my name, but not because I was hiding the truth. I just didn't want to be associated with them anymore. You can tell Serena. I don't think it'll get you the results you want."

It stung to think about Serena learning about my parents, but it wouldn't be the end of the world. It would be just another way in which I'd disappointed her, in a string of disappointments. There was nothing I could do to truly upset my own parents, like other people did with theirs, so I had to find new people to let down.

"I thought you might say something like that. Serena's biggest fault is that she's too forgiving, which is why I came up with a backup plan," Nicole said.

I recognized the tone of her voice. It was the same as Molly's when she told me that she and Noah were in love—the squeal of a person excited to deliver bad news.

"What? Are you going to release a herd of snails in Serena's office or something?"

"No," she said. "I'm going to burn down Better Love."

It was then that I identified the whiff of gasoline. I'd mistakenly thought that the chemical scent in the air was caused by the new paint on the walls. I was so bad at sniffing out danger.

I laughed. That's what I did when people made ludicrous statements about their intent to destroy me.

"You're going to burn Better Love down? Why? What is that going to do?"

"I need to convince Serena of the danger that you and your clients pose. It's nice that she's accepting and all that, but it's not the kind of business that the *investors* want. Serena might be powerful here, but she's small potatoes compared to who she's been talking to. They have real money. Have you ever flown in a private jet? Me neither. But I'm going to. Serena will make me director, and I'll show them who does the real work around here. I have a plan for Better Love. We're going to pivot, become more exclusive— a matchmaking service for the rich and the beautiful."

I didn't bother telling her that many of the rich and beautiful were psychopaths, and it was their money and power that allowed them to get away with their bad behavior.

"You didn't think this through," I replied. "What are you going to do? Burn down Better Love and tell everyone that I did it? Great plan, Nicole. I'll just tell them the truth."

"No," she said, and lifted her sweater to reveal a gun in a holster. "I'm going to shoot you and then burn the place down. Ethan's surrounding the building with gasoline right now. Everyone will think you were a victim of your own crime."

I'd forgotten that Nicole was one of those gun women. She'd told everyone in the office when Ethan had purchased her the firearm; she'd squealed like it was a diamond necklace. The two of them liked to go to shooting ranges together. She thought that made her hot.

Nicole took the gun out of the holster and pointed it at me. Even if she hadn't practiced at the firing range, it was a close shot.

"What about the cameras? There are cameras in the lobby," I said, and gestured at the device implanted on the ceiling.

"You really do think I'm stupid, don't you? I disabled the cameras. It wasn't hard. Serena's not exactly a tech genius."

"You don't know what something like this does to you, Nicole. It changes you. Everything you do for the rest of your life will be colored by this moment. You get to choose who you are tomorrow. Do you want to be yourself, or do you want to be a killer?"

I gave my final plea. Nicole's smirk showed that she was unconvinced.

"I want to be director," she said. She looked at me like I was a target. Point of view: I was a bull's-eye.

"I won't miss working with you, Lexie," Nicole said as the safety clicked off.

25.

T HERE WAS A CRASHING sound that I assumed was from a bullet being expelled from the gun, before I realized it was from
a window smashing. The alarm started to shriek. Nicole jumped
at the noise, the gun flying out of her hand.

Rather than a single foot on the floor, there was an entire body.
I didn't know whose it was until Nicole yelled, "Ethan! Ethan!"
and I processed that it was her husband's.

A figure, dimly lit by streetlights, stepped through the broken
window.

"Hello, Lexie."

Our eyes met through the dark. Even in pitch blackness I
would've known who he was, because we *knew* each other in a way
that didn't require sight. Glass crunched beneath his feet. He
seemed especially large, a hulking beast, but he wasn't a monster—
or he was, and I'd misinterpreted what the monster had wanted
all along. As a child I'd assumed that the monster was there to kill

and eat my family, but what if its real purpose had been to rescue me?

"I found this guy skulking around outside with a canister of gasoline," Aidan said, still gazing at me.

Nicole was next to her husband on the floor, trying to figure out if he was still alive. I'd met Ethan a few times, at various Better Love holiday gatherings. I'd once asked him what he did for work, and he was so boring that I'd tuned out before I got a real answer. The main thing I knew about him was that he was obsessed with sports and Nicole. Based off my knowledge, helping his wife set her workplace on fire was the most interesting thing he'd done in his entire life.

"Ah, I see. So you decided to throw him through the window?" I replied, still trying to process what was happening.

Aidan shrugged.

"It would be more accurate to say that he fell. Unfortunately, he lit a match before I could stop him. We probably shouldn't stay in here too long."

That explained why Aidan was growing increasingly visible. I thought it was an emotional effect, like I was really seeing him then, but it was the fire.

"You need to help me get Ethan out of here," Nicole cried from the floor. "He needs medical attention."

I pulled my eyes off of Aidan. I looked at Nicole, and then to the floor, in search of the gun.

"You just tried to kill me," I told her. "Why should I help you?"

"I can't get him out of here on my own. He's too heavy," she pleaded.

I thought about striking some kind of deal, one in which Nicole relinquished the director position to me and I made her kiss my feet each and every day she continued to work at Better Love. But how would I explain the fire to Serena?

Aidan watched me curiously, making no move to help Ethan.

"What do you want to do, Lexie?" he asked.

He knew. It was clear from the calmness of his tone. That was the last thing that I'd told him the night that we met: he wasn't the only killer in the room.

Ultimately, Nicole was right. She and I couldn't stay at Better Love together. Like having too many cooks in a kitchen, it was never good to have too many psychopaths in a single office.

———

"I DON'T ADVISE TRYING TO HURT ME," I'D TOLD AIDAN, IN BE-tween bouts of vomiting that night in the hotel room.

It was the final piece of the puzzle. The last part I'd forgotten, or had blocked out. The thing that I tried my best never to think about. That was a problem with pretending my life was a television show—it allowed me to separate myself from my actions. I watched myself performing scenes, like an actor on the opening night of a film.

"I'm more dangerous than I look," I said as I wiped my mouth. I wished I had a toothbrush. Despite everything, I was embarrassed by my bad breath.

He held back my hair.

"I'm sure you are, sweetie."

"Don't call me 'sweetie.'" I tried to stand up, but the room was spinning too quickly, the world's worst carousel.

"What would you like me to call you?"

"Nothing. Call me nothing. I don't associate with people who are obsessed with my parents. They're all fucked-up. I know because I've spent more time with my parents than anyone else, and I'm fucked-up."

"You're not fucked-up."

"Says the psychopath who killed someone."

"Fine. What have you done that's so bad? It's your turn, Lexie. Tell me all your secrets."

I started the story at the beginning. I had to. It was the same way I recounted the events to myself, because otherwise I'd sound too much like a cold-blooded killer. Worse, I'd sound like my parents' child.

Once I'd figured out that there was not, in fact, a monster in my house, and instead, it was my *parents* who were slaughtering women, I struggled with what to do. It seemed possible that all adults were secret killers and no one talked about it. From my perspective when I was a child, there were a lot of things like that. Adults were constantly trying to hide the truth from children. I'd known about sex from a young age, but when I tried telling my peers about it, they looked at me like I was crazy. Surely that wasn't what our parents were doing. Surely that wasn't the thing that brought about our births.

I'd learned my lesson from that experience, and I told no one about my parents' murderous exploits. Even before the screams started, I understood that my parents were quirky. Other parents all had the same haircut, wore the same unflattering clothing. They owned houses, had stable jobs, made dinner at night.

"You don't want parents like that," my mother assured me. "They're boring, and being boring is the worst thing."

I never knew how to reconcile the things that my mother told me and what my classmates said. That dissonance did help me learn at a very early age the importance of keeping secrets, of separating the private realm from the public.

Are my parents bad people? The question haunted me. My simplified understanding of the issue was that the world was separated into two groups, the good and the bad, with no gray space in between. Because I was myself and my parents were my parents, I naturally assumed that we were good. How could we be anything else?

Murder made things more complicated, but not in a way that was totally clear. There were, for instance, examples of when killing was allowed, or even encouraged. War was one of those examples. Superheroes in action movies frequently maimed or murdered, and no one seemed to mind as long as they were doing it for the right reasons. My parents weren't soldiers or superheroes, but I figured they must have had a reason for doing what they did, because if they didn't, then they were bad people, and, by extension, I was bad too—and I didn't *feel* bad.

Later, after my parents' arrest, I would learn that the sex part of things was more distasteful than the murder for a lot of people. *Of course those women deserved to die! They were engaging in group sex! Some of them were cheating on husbands or boyfriends! Why had they been in bars, looking beautiful, to begin with?* There were even those who believed that my father was some kind of prophet trying to morally cleanse the streets. My father encouraged such people, though he didn't have faith in any kind of higher being. How could he, when the only things he truly cherished were my mother and himself?

In the end, it was a TV marathon, not some cosmic sense of right and wrong, that pushed me to do what I did.

It was the summer after fourth grade, and since my parents

had neglected to enroll me in any of the camps that the other kids in my class attended, I spent my days watching television or wandering the city, hoping to come across enough quarters that I could afford to buy a bag of chips. My parents paid little attention to my whereabouts. They took it for granted that I would come home at the end of the day, though they might not have noticed if I didn't.

Sometimes I went back and they weren't there. They never told me where they were going or when they would return, and cell phones were only just becoming common, which meant that there was no way for me to reach them. Most of the time, though not always, they returned before I awoke the following day.

During a scorching week in August, when I went scrounging in the cupboards for something to eat and found them empty, I realized that they'd been gone for multiple days in a row. I tried to think of the last time I'd seen them, and I vaguely remembered the sound of a door opening and closing late in the night several days prior. At that point, I figured that they would come back. They always, eventually, came back. My immediate needs, primarily my need to eat, overrode my concern about their disappearance.

By then, I'd been stealing for years. I didn't like to do it, because I was a *good person*, and *good people* didn't steal. I did it because I needed to. Summer made things difficult, because it meant there were fewer places to hide things. I raided my mother's closet for oversized clothing that could help me conceal items. I was careful to avoid the stores closest to my house, because stealing from places where I might be familiar to the employees was a recipe for getting caught. My youth was an advantage. I wasn't yet old enough for people to consider me a suspect.

When I had enough food to sustain me—mostly candy bars,

single-serving granola bars, and other items that I could easily obscure—I returned home with my loot and settled in front of the television to wait for my parents to come home. I didn't quite understand the phrase "absence makes the heart grow fonder," but I noticed that the desire to see my parents was never stronger than when they were gone.

Something funny about my parents was that, regardless of our financial situation, we always had a cable subscription, because, in addition to movies, my mother *loved* television. This was before streaming networks were around, and I filed through the channels until I found something that interested me.

One channel was playing a multiday marathon of a crime show about investigating brutal murders. I started watching because I enjoyed the mystery element of it. *Who is the killer?* It was a nice distraction from my rumbling stomach and my growing concern that my parents had abandoned me forever. In addition to being lonely, I was dangerously close to running out of toilet paper.

In the third season of the show, the police realized that they weren't dealing with a run-of-the-mill murderer; they were looking at a *serial killer.* It took me a few episodes, but eventually I understood that my parents bore a remarkable number of similarities to the top suspect. The only difference was that, on the show, a single, isolated person had built beneath his house an unsanctioned bunker in which he committed his crimes. My parents didn't own a house or a bunker, nor were they isolated. They were the stars of every party they'd ever attended. However, they had killed several women.

I liked television because TV villains were irredeemable. *Yes, go to prison forever, you scum!* Things were a little different when the villains were my own parents. Aside from the screams of the women, which interfered with my sleep, their nighttime activities hadn't impacted me directly. But their continued absence caused me undue pain. There were days when I wondered if they'd simply moved and forgotten to take me, or if I'd done something wrong, causing my sudden abandonment. I became sure that I'd somehow *caused* my own suffering and deserved everything that I got.

I was watching the show when they finally returned.

"Oh, there you are, Lexie," my mother said. She was tan, wearing a bikini. My father said nothing to me at all.

"We were at the beach. We only planned to stay a night, but we were having such a good time that we decided to extend things."

By that time, they'd been gone for three weeks.

The show helped me realize that my parents were bad people, but their absence had done something greater—it helped me understand that they were *bad parents* and, like the villains on the show, they needed to be punished for what they'd done.

I didn't start with murder. Killing wasn't a natural impulse for me. I was gentle toward animals, and I didn't hurt my peers any more than an ordinary child. The first thing I did was tell my fifth-grade teacher.

"My parents are killing people," I told her.

School had been in session for only a couple of weeks, but somehow the social hierarchy in the classroom was already well established. I'd once again been marked as "the weird girl," a label I was used to. One of the worst things about being socially outcast was that it wasn't limited to being outcast by people my own age. Teachers wanted to be accepted by their students, and thus they distanced themselves from the stranger people in the class. Somehow, they knew that I didn't belong, and they treated me as such. When I told her what my parents were doing, my teacher, a tired woman who lacked all the softness I wanted her to have, looked at me and said, "Come on, Lexie. You know it's wrong to lie. There are better ways to get attention."

I knew then that no one would believe me, not without proof. I needed to make my parents' crimes impossible to ignore. I needed to create a situation that my father couldn't talk his way out of and my mother couldn't seduce herself free of. I needed a body.

After making this realization, I began to study the crime show, committing to memory all the dumb screwups that killers made. The mistakes seemed so obvious on television. In real life, particularly for a ten-year-old, orchestrating the perfect murder was more difficult. The victim had to be small enough that I could overpower them, but they couldn't be someone my own age. There were people in my class whose disappearance I wouldn't have minded, but killing someone I knew felt too risky. Something I'd learned was that people tended to murder people who were like them, and that serial killers' victims tended to be similar to one another. The other difficulty was that the murder had to be done in the house. Bodies were heavy! Detectives on TV mentioned that all the time. As strong and capable as I felt, there was no way I had the kind of power needed to lift a corpse. Also, I didn't want to kill just anyone. I needed my victim to be *bad*, because there was something redeemable about killing someone who was bad.

I considered waiting until my parents had completed another murder themselves. However, that would leave too many factors out of my control. I didn't want them just to be punished; I wanted their downfall to be a spectacle. *Look at this show that I put on for you!* I probably spent too much time envisioning the set design and not enough time considering what would happen if my plan worked, but I was ten—what did I know about consequences?

Every person I saw became a potential victim. Nearly all of them proved themselves to be unworthy. After several weeks of looking, I began to consider a woman who routinely walked by our house. Occasionally, she had with her a small dog that wagged its tail whenever it saw me. How precious it was to feel loved, even if it was only by a stranger's dog on the sidewalk. One day, I witnessed her kicking the dog. The action filled me with rage. It was the one thing in the whole world that loved me, and she'd caused it harm. After that, I noticed more slights. She tugged on its leash rather than letting it enjoy sniffing the grass. She grew irritated when I asked to pet the dog's fur. I understood her to be someone like my parents, the type of person who didn't deserve to have another living creature in their care. I would be doing the world a favor by getting rid of her. It was actually a *good* thing I was doing. I imagined a future in which the dog and I ran away together and lived a happy life.

One night, when my parents were out, I waited by the window until she came by; I hoped that it wasn't one of the occasional evenings when she skipped her stroll. As I waited, I realized that I was excited. I didn't get to look forward to birthday parties or Disney vacations like other kids did. Sure, my parents and I occasionally did nice things, but there was always something *unsettling* about them, largely because my father swindled his way into everything we had. Most of the time, I was lucky if there was food in the fridge. Finally, I had something to anticipate. I mentally ran through the scene again and again, like I might practice a speech for a presentation at school.

When she arrived, it felt like I'd summoned her. She was without her dog, and there was no one else on the street. We were actors. This was her role. *Lights, camera, action.*

I ran outside.

"Help! Help!" I cried. "My mom fell down and I don't know what to do."

The woman looked around. She wanted there to be someone else. There wasn't.

"Please come inside and help me!"

It took some convincing. After all, she was a *bad* person. I acted my little heart out until, finally, she relented and followed me inside, where I killed her. I had no gory details about her death to share with Aidan, largely because I didn't remember most of them. When I tried to think back, I could recall only the scene that I'd imagined in my head, rather than the reality of the blood.

After I finished, I called the police and told them I'd just arrived home to find a body in the living room. I'd sprinkled the corpse with evidence of my parents, rubbed their clothes against the mess, grabbed strands of hair out of hairbrushes. I gave the police incontrovertible proof. If anyone suspected me, I never heard about it. Still, as the police dragged my parents away, paranoia crept in, along with the sinking realization that, unlike the things I watched on television, all of this was real. A woman was dead, and my parents were going away, maybe forever.

"You think I'm disgusting. You want to get away from me," I told Aidan that night in the hotel room.

He shook his head.

"No, you were a child. You didn't know what you were doing."

"I did though. I planned the whole thing out."

"Then you were doing what you needed to in order to survive. No one can blame you for that. Or at least I would never blame you for that."

"I've been trying to avoid men like you for my entire life," I told him.

"What kind of man is that?" he asked.

"The kind of man I could love," I replied.

———

IF IT HADN'T BEEN AIDAN STANDING THERE, IF IT HAD BEEN Noah or Molly, I would've considered calling the police. But it was Aidan, and I knew that he wouldn't judge, because he understood what I needed to do. You can justify almost any action as a matter of self-preservation if you try hard enough.

As long as Nicole was alive, I would never be able to relax. She'd labeled me as the enemy, and I knew from my years of watching reality television that feuds between women didn't come to an end until one person left the show. Besides, she was a *bad* person. The police would never see that. They would look at her and see an innocent baby-woman. That was her power and her weakness.

As soon as I spotted the gun, I recognized what I was going to do. Before Nicole realized what was happening, I grabbed it off the floor and pointed it in her direction.

"You would've been a terrible director," I said, and then pulled the trigger.

26.

———

M URDERING A SECOND PERSON was easier than murdering the first. My father would've said using the gun was cheating. If I really wanted to feel something, I needed to do it with my hands.

But who cared what my father had to say? He was dead, and I was in a burning building.

Nicole didn't die immediately. Unlike her, I had little experience with firearms, and despite the close range, I had managed to hit her leg, which was bleeding profusely.

"Ow! Fuck, that hurt, you bitch!" she said.

The fire hadn't yet reached the lobby, though smoke was starting to pour in. The alarm continued to blare, and I knew it was only a matter of time before the security company arrived to check things out. I intended to be long gone by the time that happened.

Nicole was trying to get up. She'd gone from being concerned about her husband to caring only about herself. Pain revealed us all.

"I never liked you," I told her. "But I think that you're right about me. I am dangerous."

I shot her again. This time I managed to hit her squarely in the head. Ethan, who'd been silent since crashing through the window, moaned from the floor, as though he could sense his wife's passing. Without asking for it, Aidan took the gun from me and completed the job. There was something romantic about Nicole and Ethan, soulmates, lying dead on the floor, in a pool of each other's blood. Nicole thought that Ethan's committing arson for her was the ultimate sign of devotion, but she'd forgotten about death. In the end, the two of them would be together forever.

Aidan approached me. The gun was still in his hand. In the midst of Nicole's death threat, I'd forgotten what she'd said about not killing Noah, meaning that the murderer continued to roam free. Aidan was dangerous, a psychopath, and he was approaching me with a gun. His jaw was tense. His eyes were hard. I didn't run or fight or scream. When he leaned down to kiss me, I took all of it in.

I knew what this moment was. The kiss in the rubble, when two people finally decided they were going to be together.

"We need to get out of here before the security company comes," I said, reluctantly pulling away.

Flames were licking the side of the building, not caring about the cold. I glanced down the smoky hallway, toward my office. Was there anything I should try to save? My computer, the picture of Noah and me, the threatening notes I'd tucked into my desk? No, I needed to leave that stuff behind. The things that I'd thought were important meant nothing.

"What should we do about them?" I asked, gesturing at the bodies on the floor. If I was going to prison, I didn't want it to be because of Nicole. Even from death, she would view it as her own personal victory, and I couldn't have that.

Aidan took a tissue from the box that the receptionist kept on her desk, and he carefully wiped down the gun with it. He placed it in Ethan's hand, pressing his pointer finger over the trigger like Ethan had pulled it himself, making the lobby look like the scene of a murder-suicide. The cameras were off. As far as anyone else knew, Aidan and I had never been there. Whatever had occurred between Nicole and Ethan, they took it with them to the grave.

I coughed, my lungs aware of the gathering smoke in a way that my eyes couldn't yet register. In the distance, a wail of sirens was starting to gather. I took one last look at Nicole and Ethan lying on the floor. I hadn't really believed that they loved each other until that night. I thought they'd gotten together because Nicole was the pretty cheerleader and Ethan the hot jock, and that they stayed together because it was the path of least resistance. I'd considered Nicole too shallow to experience the depths of true love, an assumption that was a kind of internalized misogyny that was difficult to excise. Now I recognized the passion that they'd felt for each other even after all the years they'd been together. It hung in the air, clinging to the particles of smoke. Ethan was so supportive of his wife that he was willing to spend Valentine's Day burning down her workplace with her rival inside. That was the kind of grand gesture that my mother would've approved of.

I didn't regret what I'd done. After all, Nicole hadn't given me any choice in the matter. One of us was going to burn, and it wasn't going to be me. However, I did regret not taking her more seriously while she was alive. I'd allowed her baby voice and her over-the-top clothing choices to woo me into a sense of complacency. It was the type of mistake that my parents had made all the time. They couldn't fathom that there were people cleverer, better-looking, or more in love than they were. That was their weakness, the reason why they were ultimately taken down by a child.

I was almost taken down by Nicole. Then someone saved me.

Aidan grabbed my hand and pulled me through the hole that used to be a window.

We ran to his car and peeled away onto icy streets. The sirens grew in volume and intensity as more and more vehicles made their way to the Better Love building. First the security company arrived, then firefighters and paramedics, and finally the police. I was glad that I'd left my car far from the entrance, inconspicuous in the night.

My brain felt as if it were being swarmed by bees—in a good way. Nicole was dead and Better Love was burning, and I didn't care.

Aidan parked in an unfamiliar covered lot.

"Where are we?" I asked.

"You'll see," he said.

It quickly became clear that we were at the airport, but not in the place from which I flew coach. We were in the area where people kept their private jets.

He brought me to a small plane. Shortly before she died, Nicole had mentioned a future in which she was going to ride in private jets. Her prediction hadn't been totally off base; she'd simply missed whom it applied to.

While Better Love burned below, Aidan and I ascended into the sky.

"You can ride in the back," he offered, "or you can sit in the cockpit with me."

It was in that moment that I realized I didn't want to leave him, not even for a few minutes. To tell the truth, I hadn't really believed in soulmates. Whether I believed in soulmates was a question that people frequently asked when they found out I was a matchmaker, and I changed my answer depending on the audience. To the religious crowd, I suggested that God had created matchmakers, just as he'd created love. To skeptics, I said that all of us were compatible with a multitude of people, and it was just a matter of finding them. As for myself, I thought that love was about creating an image of the life that I wanted: a hot, successful husband; his mother, who could become mine. I was trying to create a movie scene that I could live inside.

Aidan was all wrong. Sure, he was hot and successful, but he was also a psychopath who had killed at least two people and was obsessed with my parents. The main problem that most people had with being in love with killers was that killing was morally wrong, which made it easy for me to overlook another problem, which was that Aidan might someday be taken away from me. My mother and father had loved each other so intensely, and yet, when my father was murdered, they hadn't seen each other in a decade. It was inconceivable to me that anything could be worth all that drama—until I found myself flying through the sky with Aidan.

When we reached cruising altitude, he turned to me. We didn't need words to explain what was about to happen. He ran a finger along my cheek and it was over. I stripped off my boots, my pants, and my underwear, leaving my thick socks on, as my feet were cold. He undid his own pants and pulled me on top of him.

"You have no idea how long I've wanted this," he said.

Normally, I found it a turnoff when men desired me so much. Part of the appeal of Noah was that, because he was frequently at work, it was impossible for the two of us to get too close. He would always be at arm's length, and that was where I'd wanted him. I'd thought that I wanted a man who didn't know the truth about me, about my parents, but as Aidan and I stared into each other's eyes, I had to accept that it was possible that I'd been wrong about everything. He looked at me like he wanted to destroy me, and I opened my legs to let the destruction in.

We fucked like two people who needed sex to live. We fucked like two people who'd committed murder and set their lives on fire. It felt so good that I couldn't even loathe myself for it.

Soulmate. The word hit my brain as I orgasmed. Aidan had been trying to tell me for weeks, and I hadn't listened. But then, if love came easily, there could be no movie. The story was about the struggle to come together.

"HOW DID YOU KNOW WHERE TO FIND ME?"

We were in a hotel room, lying naked on the bed. We'd flown several hours, through the night, and landed at an airport surrounded by palm trees. I wasn't sure what state we were in— Florida?—and I didn't care. After years of stability, a path planned and plotted, the unknown was exhilarating.

"I've been following you," he said plainly. He didn't look ashamed of or embarrassed about the admission. "You gave me access to your location the first night we met, because you didn't want us to get separated. I take it you forgot about that."

"So all these weeks, you've been stalking me?"

"Well, no. I do have a job. I was concerned about you after we talked. You mentioned that your fiancé—your *ex*-fiancé—was being delivered to your door in pieces. I was hoping to catch whoever was doing it in the act."

"But that was you. You killed him. You cut him into pieces and brought him to my house."

"No." He shook his head. "I told you before, I didn't have anything to do with his disappearance. He was never my competition. His presence was no threat to me."

His voice was unwavering. He spoke as a man without doubt.

I'd listened to so many of my clients describe what it was like when they had a successful match.

Don't tell them that I said this, they'd confide in me, *but I think I'm in love.*

I realize that my other relationships were never real, because this one is, they said.

What's that phrase? 'When you know, you know'? Well, I know now.

I'd nodded along, happy that I'd done a good job. I'd considered it a workplace accomplishment, assuming that I understood what they meant because I had a fiancé. *Yeah, yeah, love, whatever.*

I hadn't known though. I could see that now, lying in bed next to Aidan. Everything else had been a shadow of the real thing, a simulacrum of love. I watched it on TV and thought I'd understood, when I'd merely been watching a cast.

That was the whole thing about being human. It was impossible to gauge which experiences were universal. My college roommate hadn't known she was color-blind until the third grade, when she did a class project on the condition and discovered that she couldn't see the numbers embedded within circles that everyone else could. I hadn't known until I felt the real thing with Aidan that I wasn't really in love with Noah. How could I? Love is like one of those islands that can be found only by people who already know where they are.

I'd spent so long running. I thought that I could steer my life in a particular direction to evade destiny. In the end, no lifestyle changes I could make would alter my DNA. I was born a killer, a psychopath, or I had been made that way by my parents. Ultimately, nature or nurture became irrelevant. I was who I was.

Marrying a man like Noah wouldn't have turned me into a happy housewife. Eventually, we would've divorced or killed each other, whichever came first. His mother would never have replaced mine, because I'd never learned how to be mothered. Even if Noah's mother had sincerely cared for me, I wouldn't have known how to accept that type of kindness. My muscles were tired from contorting my body into unnatural shapes. What a relief it was to embrace myself. What a pleasure to give into a man who loved me so much that he would kill for me. He hadn't killed Noah though, just Ethan, and who cared about him? He was a side character, not even in the supporting cast.

"I can't figure it out," I said. "If it wasn't you, then who was it? I think someone is trying to frame me. Nicole did the stuff at work, but there's someone else."

"Who might want to kill Noah?" he asked.

"No one. He was a doctor. A great man. Everyone online is saying so."

He scowled.

"People will say anything online. They're all playing pretend."

"Is that why you don't have any social media accounts?"

"Are you saying that you looked me up on social media?"

"You're a psychopath who showed up in my office claiming that we were meant to be together. Of course I looked you up."

"I was right though, wasn't I?"

"You were right," I conceded. "Noah was a good person in some ways though. Not so great in others. Mostly, he wasn't great to me.

To Molly either. I think she thought she'd 'won' when he left me for her, but he wasn't a very good boyfriend. It went bad so quickly between them. When I saw her, she looked so rattled."

"Do you think she could've killed him?"

"No. I don't know. I didn't think she would steal my fiancé either, and she did that. It's so hard to know another person, isn't it?"

"You can't ever really know someone else. All you can do is put your faith in a person and hope they don't hurt you," he replied.

I looked at the man next to me—the *psychopath*. I realized that I was no longer frightened. I'd mistaken my fear of embracing something real, something forever, for a fear of the man. Sure, he'd killed people. But I had too. And despite all that, we had each other. What a gift.

"I don't know if she had anything to do with Noah's disappearance, but she's the only one who would make sense working with Nicole. The two of them met a couple of times, and they follow each other on social media. It wouldn't have been difficult for Molly to reach out to her. On top of that, Molly knows my secrets. She must've told Nicole. It makes me mad. She stole my fiancé and tried to sabotage me at work, and Nicole paid for it with her life. Aside from losing Noah, Molly hasn't paid for any of the things that she's done."

"Do you want me to kill her for you?" he asked.

I worried that Aidan was serious until I saw the joking look on his face.

"No. We can't just kill everyone who's inconvenient. There'd be no one left."

"Fair enough."

"I have something else in mind for Molly. Something better," I said.

27.

I N THE MORNING I woke to a text from Serena.

No one is coming to the office today. More information to come.
Sending us a text message gave away the urgency of the situation,
as Serena abhorred text messages. Real connection, she liked to
say, wasn't built that way.

After we finished our multiple lovemaking sessions, Aidan and
I showered together, wiping off all evidence of our crimes. Aidan
was tender as he scrubbed my back. I wasn't self-conscious in front
of him. For the first time in my life, I was romantically involved
with someone who knew my darkest secrets. With the right person, it was a comfort to be seen.

I'd always wondered how my parents managed to sleep after
their violent acts. Aside from imprisonment, insomnia was one of
the main concerns in connection with immorality, hence the question *How do you sleep at night?* As I collapsed back onto the hotel
bed, I got it. Murder was exhausting, even when it was done with
a gun.

After Serena's text, Aidan and I got breakfast, and then went to the mall for a shopping spree, to buy replacements for the clothes and outerwear that we'd worn the night before. I wasn't about to leave anything to chance. I still wasn't sure where we were—somewhere with strip malls and diners and beach-themed restaurants with names like Dickie's Crab Leg.

Midmorning, I received a link to a virtual meeting. I took the meeting in the hotel room, using a filter to hide the background.

Serena wasn't wearing makeup. In all my years of working for her, this was the first time that I'd seen her real face. It was astonishing how much her bare face aged her. I was someone who often pretended to be someone she wasn't, and it turned out that I wasn't the only one. All of us were pretending in our own way.

"Something horrible has happened," she said. "I wish there were some easier way to say this, but there's not. I need . . . I need to get it out before I can't. There was an incident last night at the Better Love office. Unfortunately, Nicole was injured and killed in the course of this incident."

The receptionist hadn't muted herself, and her gasp was loud and disruptive.

"The police are investigating what happened," Serena continued. "They think . . . they think it was a murder-suicide, as her husband, Ethan, was also found at the scene. Effective immediately, Better Love is on hiatus while I evaluate the future of the company. Now I'll do my best to answer any questions you might have."

The other matchmakers sought comfort from our mother duck. They murmured condolences, which I echoed in an effort to appear sad, though when I prodded my emotions, I discovered that I wasn't.

Since I'd gotten the job, I'd told everyone how much I enjoyed being a matchmaker.

"You know, it's refreshing to find someone who actually enjoys what they do," Noah's mother had told me after explaining that Noah thought women should stay at home and raise children.

I realized, however, that something had changed when I realized I wasn't getting the director position. There was no room for me to grow. I would continue to match people, and the matches would work out or they wouldn't. Maybe I was using other people's love to make up for the lack of it in my own life. In any case, the job no longer fulfilled my ambitions. I needed something more.

The building hadn't burned down completely, but from an insurance position it was a total loss. Serena didn't mention the investors. I suspected that they'd been scared away. Matchmaking wasn't a business for the faint of heart. I refrained from asking about the state of the bodies, though that was what I really wanted to know. Had Nicole's pretty little face been burned to a crisp? It was strange to consider that, after all the hours that I'd spent there, I would never sit at my desk again, that the office no longer existed as I'd known it. Perhaps I could've done more to save it if we hadn't been so busy trying to frame Nicole and Ethan for their own deaths, but a girl needed to take care of her own self first.

"I HAVE TO GO HOME," I TOLD AIDAN.

He nodded.

"Whatever you need," he said, and I believed him.

We went straight from the airport to the woods. It didn't escape me that that was the sort of thing that my parents had done together. The difference was that they'd had bodies in the back of their car. Aidan and I were doing the reverse of what my parents had done. We were going to the woods to get parts of a person back.

I expected it to be difficult to figure out where I'd left Noah's body parts, but a map to the location was burned into my memory. The various body parts had held up surprisingly well, due to the cold.

"What is this?" Aidan asked, picking up one of the organs.

"I don't know. A liver maybe? Noah was the doctor."

"Do you really think it's him?"

I held up one of the fingers.

"This is how I knew. It looks like him. Does that make any sense?"

"Yes. I would know your fingers. I would definitely know your heart."

I smiled.

"It's okay, you know, if you feel sad. You were engaged to someone, and now he's in pieces. That's a weird thing for anyone to go through."

"I was lonely when he left," I admitted. "I was in denial after I found out about the affair. I couldn't let myself be sad, because if I was sad, then it was real, and I couldn't accept that. I was so certain that he was going to come back. I thought that I was this grand master of love, and instead, I was just like everyone else. His death made me see that. This might sound horrible, but sometimes I wonder whether I was mourning the loss of *him* or the idea of our relationship. I wanted to be the person that he thought I was so much, and then I just wasn't."

"It's not horrible. That's what loss is. The death of a person you love turns you into someone else, and grieving them becomes a grief for the person you used to be," Aidan replied.

Strolling through the woods was almost like a date—"almost," because I was still so close to Noah's death that being with Aidan felt like a betrayal. It was funny—I'd killed two people and could move through the world without issue, but Noah continued to be sticky. The difference was in the choices that I'd made versus the ones that were made for me.

"I'm thinking of going back to school," I told Aidan.

"What for?"

"I want to become a therapist. That's what I wanted to do originally, and I lost focus somewhere."

"No more matchmaking?"

"No. I think I've accomplished all that I can in that particular role."

"I'm not sure there's a higher pinnacle than this," Aidan agreed. "You might as well go out on top."

ONCE WE'D RETRIEVED NOAH'S PARTS, WE DROVE BACK TO THE city.

"I have an address for you," I told Aidan, and showed him where Molly lived.

Rebecca had been blowing up my phone all day. Better Love had sent an email to all of our clients, notifying them of the fire and the "temporary" closure. There was nothing about Nicole and her husband in the email, though it didn't take much digging in the local newspaper to find information about them.

> OMG I heard what happened. Are
> you okay?

> Wasn't Nicole the coworker that you
> hated? It's so wild that she died.

You better answer me soon or I'm getting
in my car and driving over there.

"Who are you texting?" Aidan asked as I responded to the flurry of messaging.

"My best friend," I told him, and then amended, "My new best friend. She actually started as a client of mine. I thought about matching her with you."

Talking about that made me uneasy. I was suddenly paranoid that Rebecca and Aidan *were* meant to be together and I was simply a stand-in until they met. That was one of the many difficulties of being hurt by someone close—it made it impossible to really trust anyone ever again.

"Her father was murdered," I continued. "We go to this support group together, Children of Murdered Parents. That's where I realized I want to be a therapist. There are people out there who need me."

"Do the other group members know who your parents are?" he asked.

I shook my head.

"They know how my father died."

One of the nice things about Aidan was that I didn't have to explain anything to him. At first it scared me how much he knew about my parents, as if I were a mere fetish for him, but in practice, I found that it equated to understanding.

"You're the only person in my life who knows the whole truth," I told him. "Molly knows part of it, everything up to the arrest. And we're about to take care of her."

28.

———

B ACK WHEN MOLLY AND I were friends, I used to watch her cat
when she went on vacation. Felix was deranged, and I adored
him. He had a huge, poofy tail like a squirrel's and performed
death-defying acts of acrobatics across the apartment. Occasionally, he went into attack mode, in which he decided our legs were
the enemy and left deep scratches in our skin.

"Why don't you get your own cat?" Molly asked me once.

"I don't want my own cat. I just want Felix," I told her.

One of the subtler stings in the end of our friendship was that
I lost access to Felix, and thus, when I opened Molly's door with
the key that she had given me all those years prior for the purpose
of pet sitting, I was delighted when Felix immediately rubbed his
furry body against my legs.

I made Aidan wait in the car. I told him it was because I was
worried about him being caught. I explained that my DNA was
already embedded in the seams of Molly's couch from all the time

we spent lying on it, watching reality television together. His DNA, however, was foreign. His presence could only be nefarious.

In reality, I wanted a quiet moment in which to say goodbye. When it was all said and done, I'd probably spent more hours with Molly than I had with Noah. Romantic breakups were the subject of countless great works of literature and film, but friendship breakups didn't receive the same treatment. I'd jumped so quickly into my relationship with Rebecca that I hadn't given myself time to mourn the loss of Molly. Mourning, I thought, was something that other people did.

As I stood in Molly's living room, something unlocked within me. Her apartment had an open floor plan, which allowed me to view the whole space in a single glance. There was the kitchen where we'd prepared meals that spanned from frozen pizza rolls to complicated cuisine. There, the couch on which we drank wine and watched television. There, the stain from when I spilled a glass of red wine on the floor, which still hadn't come out.

A part of me wished that Molly were there so that I could tell her everything I was thinking.

I made a new best friend. It's amazing how easy you were to replace. She watches all the same shows that you and I do. She drives a really nice car.

I've finally realized that you were correct about one thing, that Noah was wrong for me. To be fair, I don't think he's right for you either. I wish he'd gotten the chance to live as a person on his own before he was chopped into a million pieces.

I've started seeing a new guy, who knows about my parents. Actually, he's obsessed with my parents. I think that maybe this one will stick.

I'm not sure if you're the one who was working with Nicole. I'm not sure that I care. You can't really think that I would let you get away with what you did.

I miss you. I think I always will. You were supposed to be a different kind of forever. I'm sorry that we didn't last, but I'm not sorry for what I have to do.

Another part of me was glad that she wasn't there, because if she were I might've had to kill her. I was no longer pretending that there were things that I wouldn't do.

Felix trailed behind me as I made my way deeper into the apartment. There were traces of Noah throughout.

A pair of gym shoes by the door.

A laundry basket with boxers and scrubs.

A telltale glass of water on the bedside table, gathering dust.

I wondered what the days they'd spent together had been like, the glorious high of announcing a long-secret affair, followed by the comedown. That was one of the problems with affairs. They were built on the thrill of the secret rather than on true compatibility. Of course, there were strong relationships that had started that way, but they were the exception rather than the rule.

How quickly did Molly realize that Noah was everything that I'd said he was, the absentee boyfriend who cared more about his work than about the people around him? A nearly immediate shift? When she was a secret, he'd had to schedule her in. When she became his girlfriend, she became another part of the background.

I imagined the way that she must have raged at him when he'd returned to her apartment after sleeping with me.

How could you? I thought you loved me. You told me you didn't want Lexie anymore. Which is it, Noah? Who do you want?

Noah didn't know how to handle a woman's tears. That was one of the reasons that he liked me. I never cried, or asked anything of him. I was easy. It was possible that I'd gone too far in that direction. Maybe he liked how vulnerable and human Molly was. He liked how much she needed him, until she needed him to be a good boyfriend, and then he didn't like her anymore.

He packed a gym bag full of things and left. Where had the bag gone? Where was the rest of his body? I thought of the night that Molly showed up at my doorstep, asking if I knew where Noah was. In retrospect, I thought she was trying to create a trail of plausible deniability. Sooner or later, the police would come knocking on both our doors, and she wanted me to vouch for her goodness—but I couldn't, not anymore.

Molly must've colluded with Nicole. Nicole had referenced having a "couple of elves," which implied that she was working with more than just Ethan. Molly must've been the one to tell her about my parents. Molly's part in conspiring with Nicole was hurt on top of hurt. She knew how much I disliked Nicole, and she'd gone to her anyway. She must've really hated me. I couldn't believe that I'd never sensed her animosity.

It seemed so unfair that, outside of losing Noah, Molly had emerged unscathed. She'd stolen my fiancé, murdered him when he wouldn't stay, deposited his body parts at my house, and sabotaged my work. I needed to show her some degree of the pain that she'd caused me. I wanted her to be forced to sit and evaluate all the things that she'd ever done, to be broken down until she realized she wasn't any more worthy of love than me.

That was why I hid the body parts throughout her apartment.

Molly was messy, a shopaholic. She fed my own worst monetary impulses. Why save when I could buy something new? She liked to buy fast-fashion hauls that she wore once and then never again. Her square footage wasn't enough to hold everything she bought; her apartment was bursting at the seams. It wasn't difficult to find places to hide the body parts. Now that they were no longer in the freezing cold, they would start to decompose, a process that would cause a stink. Likely, that wouldn't matter, as Molly was prone to procrastinating on taking out the garbage. More than once, I'd walked into her apartment to find it reeking. She didn't seem to notice. To her, the odor emanating from the trash just smelled like home.

"HOW DID IT GO?" AIDAN ASKED WHEN I GOT BACK TO THE CAR.

"When it's done, we have to come back for Felix," I said.

I stripped off my gloves and dropped them into a garbage bag.

"Who's Felix?"

"Molly's cat. He doesn't deserve to be caught up in all this. He hasn't done anything wrong."

"Projection" was another term that I'd learned in my college psychology courses. I couldn't help but see myself in Felix, a victim of his mother's wrongdoings. That Felix was feline seemed insignificant.

Aidan nodded.

"We'll come back. Felix shouldn't be left alone," he said.

If I had any doubts about being with Aidan, they were erased in that moment.

We drove to a gas station, where I picked up a cheap burner phone. I'd never done such a thing before, but I'd learned quite a few tricks from watching movies. Whoever claimed that television wasn't educational clearly hadn't spent enough time watching it.

I called in a bomb threat. It was a practice known as "swatting," and in several states it was illegal in itself. Here was how it went: someone called the police to tell them there was a bomb planted in a particular location where, almost always, there was none. The police swarmed said location, sometimes harming innocent people in the process. I didn't care if Molly got hurt, because Molly wasn't innocent.

I made my threat—"There's a bomb! Come quick! She's a psychopath!"—then disconnected the call, dismantled the burner phone, and deposited it in a dumpster.

I found out later what happened next.

The police hurried to Molly's building. They were aware of swatting as a practice, but they still needed to take bomb threats seriously. Their arrival coincided with her return home from work. She looked awful, worse than the last time I'd seen her. Every day since Noah's disappearance ate away at her a little more, probably because she'd killed him.

There was no bomb in her apartment, of course. The police canines determined that quickly enough. Molly was grateful for their presence. She thought they were protecting her. Though they didn't find any bombs, they did find an assortment of human body parts. A heart, a foot, a liver.

"What the fuck are you doing?" Molly screamed as they cuffed her.

Tests confirmed that the body parts belonged to a man. Further tests confirmed that they belonged to Noah. The police did an investigation into who had made the call, but their search came up empty. Did it matter? Did it matter that they had only scattered bits and pieces of Noah?

"Where is the rest of him?" they asked.

"I don't know! I didn't do this. Someone is setting me up. I don't know where he is!" Molly insisted.

No, they decided. It didn't matter. She was the last one to see him. They'd fought, and he'd disappeared. Then parts of his body were found in her apartment. How could she be anything other than guilty?

Meanwhile, I brought Aidan home to the town house.

"This isn't your house," Aidan said.

"It is," I insisted.

"No, this is the home of the person you were pretending to be," he said. "The two of us will get something better."

I thought of my favorite house, one where my parents and I had lived when I was a child, the one where my parents had murdered the first woman. It had been so nice until she died.

That was what I wanted. A house like that. Something that stood out from its neighbors. A place that people walked past and said things like *I wonder who's lucky enough to live there. They have amazing taste.*

"You're right," I said.

I looked around the space that now appeared foreign to me, at the gray walls, gray floors, gray carpet. I couldn't remember who I'd been when I wanted that. I was trying to fit in with all the women I'd gone to high school with. They had bland homes, husbands, and children. But I was wrong to think I could pull it off.

"I'm thinking of a nice Victorian," I told Aidan. "Something big enough that I could have an in-home therapy practice when I finish school."

"Sounds perfect," he said.

And it did.

29.

———

I FINALLY FOUND SOMEONE WHO really gets me," I announced at the COMP meeting a couple of weeks later. Everyone clapped. They were so happy for me! Death didn't need to mean an end to life after all.

Aidan was now my official boyfriend. We'd celebrated the label by returning to Molly's apartment to fetch Felix the cat after Molly was denied bail. He started purring the moment that I let him out of the cat carrier, which I took as proof that he was pleased with his new living space.

"I didn't realize how lonely I was until I wasn't anymore," I continued. "For the first time in my life, I have the right amount of love."

I glanced at Rebecca, who smiled at me. I'd made sure to keep her a priority as my relationship with Aidan blossomed. I wanted them both, the boyfriend and the best friend.

Rebecca and I had plans to get together with Aidan after the meeting. I was nervous about introducing them. I worried that they would hate each other, a common concern with a best friend. Molly hadn't liked Noah to begin with. More than that, though, I worried that Aidan and Rebecca would like each other too much. There was something similar about their energies, Rebecca with her fast cars and Aidan with his planes. Before Molly stole my fiancé, I never would've guessed she had the capacity to do such a thing. Rebecca, on the other hand, went after her desires with the brutality of a woman who was used to competing with men.

We joined Aidan at a table at a sushi restaurant where plates of food traveled by on a conveyor belt and diners grabbed what they wanted to eat. When he saw her, he did a double take, gazing at her, then looking away, and then looking at her again. There was a spark of envy in the pit of my stomach. So what? Rebecca was beautiful. That was one of the reasons that I'd gravitated toward her. I needed to get myself under control. Rebecca wasn't Molly, and Aidan wasn't Noah.

"So, you're Lexie's new boyfriend," Rebecca said.

"It's nice to meet you," he replied.

I took a plate of sushi off the conveyor belt as they shook hands. I tried not to be bothered by their touch. I reminded myself that Molly was in jail, awaiting trial. I couldn't be jealous of everyone forever.

"How did the two of you meet?" Rebecca asked. She took a plate of her own. Her fingers were adept with chopsticks, in a way that mine were not. "Lexie's been vague."

"We met at a bar. I saw her across the room and thought she was the most beautiful woman I'd ever seen," Aidan told her.

Had he told the truth: *I saw her and thought, "That's the daughter of those killers I'm obsessed with."*

"Aw, that's so sweet. I love it when people meet in real life like that. It's great that you can be like, 'We met in a bar,' rather than 'We met on a dating app,' like the rest of us."

"It was great. It was fate," Aidan said.

The word made me flinch. That was one of the ways that my father justified the killings. *It was fate that those women died,* he said. What he meant was: *Is something really a crime if it's bound to happen anyway?* I never bought it. People said things were destined to be when they were convenient to them. Still, I loved that Aidan thought this about the two of us. It made it seem like everything bad that had ever happened had happened in order to bring us together. *Was it worth it?* a small voice within me asked. *Of course it was worth it. Love is always worth it,* I replied.

Rebecca took another plate off the conveyor belt. She ate a lot when we were together, which made me think that she didn't eat much the rest of the time. My parents were like that too. They either binged or starved.

"What is it that you do, Aidan?"

Both of them were prone to unsettling stares, and the table around me was all eyes. It was unusual for me to be in a position where I wasn't one of the more dominant people in a room, but their energies overpowered me.

"I'm a pilot."

"A pilot?" Rebecca glanced in my direction. "That's interesting."

Aidan shrugged.

"I like it. It pays the bills. And what about you? Lexie tells me that you sell cars?"

"Luxury cars," Rebecca clarified.

"I'll have to contact you next time I'm looking to buy," he said.

There was something unspoken in the air between us. I could

feel it, though I wasn't certain what it was. I looked from Aidan to Rebecca. I wondered if my parents had ever dined with the women before they killed them.

What do you do?

I'm a teacher.

What is it that you teach?

History.

It must be tiring dealing with kids all day.

It is. Do you have children?

Yes, we have a daughter. She's at home, waiting to listen to you scream.

"Not to be blunt," Rebecca said as she popped a piece of sushi into her mouth, "but what are your intentions with Lexie? She's been through a lot, you know. She likes to present herself as a tough girl. There's something else hiding in there though, something soft. Are you going to take care of the soft parts, Aidan?"

Aidan stared Rebecca down as he finished chewing a piece of tempura.

"I want to take care of all of Lexie's parts," he said.

She met his gaze.

"Okay, okay. I don't want to be too hard on you. It's just, Lexie is like a sister to me, and I don't want to see her get hurt. Her last boyfriend—he didn't treat her right."

"I'm aware of the deficiencies of her ex," Aidan said, with an edge to his voice.

Sitting there with them wasn't dissimilar to watching my parents from the balcony in my favorite house, the one that overlooked the living room in which they danced with the women, kissed them, and fed them drinks before they took them to the bedroom. The problem was that I couldn't quite figure out who was supposed to be whom.

Was I my father? The charismatic man who spouted off philosophy that sounded good, but in practice was simply an excuse for his own behavior. Or was I my mother? The beautiful temptress who was the accomplice—or leader?—in a multitude of murders. I refused to accept the third possibility. I was never the woman who was about to die.

It was possible that I was a secret fourth thing, the child watching from above as her parents circled their prey.

"I have no intention of hurting Lexie," Aidan continued. "I'm not a perfect person, but I will be good to her."

Rebecca leaned back, settling into her seat. She smiled, dropping her accusatory posture. She appeared friendly, nice.

"Sorry for the protective-father act. I just want to make sure that you're taking care of my girl," she said.

"I get it," Aidan told her. "She's my girl too."

I LEFT THE RESTAURANT WITH AIDAN. HE PAID FOR ALL OF OUR food, even Rebecca's numerous plates, which had started to tower into the sky.

"She's a force," he said when we'd gotten into the car.

"She is. That's why I like her."

"How did you say you met, again?"

"She was actually a client of mine at Better Love. I looked her up online, and that was how I found COMP. Why?"

"There's something about her that's familiar to me, like I've seen her before or something."

"Maybe the two of you hooked up."

He shook his head.

"No, that's not it. I would remember her."

He leaned over and kissed me, an action that cleansed any lingering jealousy from my palate.

"It doesn't matter," he said as he started the car. "If she's your friend, then I like her."

"In a platonic way," I clarified.

The car paused at a stoplight, and he grabbed my hand and kissed my fingers.

"In a platonic way," he agreed.

30.

One month later

AIDAN AND I WERE seated at a metal table that was bolted to the floor. It was designed that way by people who understood that anything could be used as a weapon.

I sensed her presence before I saw her.

Mommy.

It was the kind of charisma that couldn't be taught. Anyone who'd spent time with politicians or celebrities knew what it felt like, a force stronger and more inescapable than gravity.

"I knew you would come eventually," my mother said as she took a seat across from us at the table.

The prison was located in the middle of nowhere. Most prisons were. Entire rural economic systems were built on locking people up. Aidan flew us to a nearby airport. It was in a different plane than the one he flew on our first ride. I knew better than to question where he'd acquired it.

I wore a plain black dress, a long-debated choice. I wanted my mother to think I was pretty. I wanted my mother to understand how I'd suffered for what she'd done. Ultimately, clothing that said what I wanted it to didn't exist.

"I have someone I want you to meet," I told her.

The mother from my memories was the most beautiful woman in the world. I'd learned that a lot of people thought that of their mothers. *But mine really is*, I wanted to insist. Prison had aged her. Or time. Were those different things? A sentence always meant a number of years taken away. Deep wrinkles were imprinted on her face, her dark hair streaked with gray. I missed who she'd been before, the movie star who lived in my brain.

When she looked at Aidan, I saw that she still had that same gaze, the one that made men fall to their knees and made women agree to leave bars with two strangers. *He's mine.* I wanted to snatch him away, put him in my pocket.

It had been my idea to visit my mother. Meeting-the-parents was a whole genre of romantic comedies. There were wild mishaps, such as when the new partner accidentally caused structural damage to homes, destroyed cakes, and wounded siblings, only to become a beloved member of the family by the end of the movie. Because my mother was in prison, I'd never been able to share such moments with Noah. Because Aidan was a killer who was obsessed with my murderous parents, something new opened itself to me.

Or that was what I told Aidan. That was the nice version of my motive to see my mother. A part of me was still stuck on Noah's dismembered body. Nothing new had arrived since Better Love had burned down with Nicole inside of it and Molly had been arrested for Noah's murder. Most of the time, I assumed that I'd solved the murder—it was Nicole and Molly, case closed. But then there were those small moments when I couldn't shake the feeling that my mother was somehow involved in the killing.

———

"YOU FINALLY BROUGHT HIM," MY MOTHER SAID AS SHE DRANK Aidan in. She had immediately forgotten the conversation in which I'd told her that my fiancé was dead and had been chopped into pieces. She was always doing stuff like that—forgetting inconvenient truths in order to remember the world how she wanted it to be.

"How's your fiancé?" she had asked during our next conversation. I was in the middle of a *Vanderpump Rules* rewatch with Rebecca and had excused myself to take the call outside. Eager to resume our viewing, I'd neglected to remind my mother of the bloody truth.

"He's great," I told her.

Now I was in front of her with a different man.

Noah would've folded beneath my mother's gaze, but Aidan was unflinching. They measured each other up. I was grateful that he was seeing her this way, in an aged state. The last thing I needed was another rival for my mother's love.

Watch this, I said to my parents as I crossed the monkey bars.

Watch this, I told them when I'd learned to read and write.

Watch this, I said as I misbehaved for the sole purpose of getting their attention.

It didn't matter what I did. My father had eyes only for my mother, and my mother paid attention to me only during those hours when she wanted a daughter to do things with. The rest of the time, I was invisible. Naturally, I'd assumed that it was my proximity to multiple murders that had warped my brain chemistry, but maybe the shift had occurred earlier.

Please love me, I'd begged and begged my parents. I couldn't understand why they weren't like the parents I saw in the movies we watched. Good. Wholesome. Frumpy, in a comforting way. No one wanted the people who raised them to be beautiful and powerful.

"You weren't lying when you said he was good-looking," my mother told me. She talked as if Aidan were a picture on the wall that both of us were looking at rather than a man in the room.

"This is exactly who I imagined you ending up with. Look at those arm muscles. That face. Smart too, a doctor. The two of you will have amazing children, the future of the species."

"I'm a pilot, actually," Aidan said.

My mother looked accusatorily in my direction.

"I thought you said he was a doctor."

I scanned the room for vending machines. I needed something to put in my mouth. Being in the same room as her made me want to swallow my tongue. Sometimes I questioned myself. *How bad could it really have been?* The answer revealed itself clearly: *Bad, so bad.* I needed to escape. The room, however, was void of distractions. There was only one visitor aside from Aidan and me, a man who wept as he told a jumpsuit-clad woman about their children.

"The doctor's dead," I reminded her.

My mother smiled at Aidan. There was a glimmer of the person I remembered, the woman so beautiful that she could put anyone under her spell.

"Has my daughter ever told you how I met her father?"

"No," Aidan said.

I rolled my eyes, settling in to hear the same story that I'd heard again and again. The romantic comedy of my parents' lives. The horror story of someone else's.

"I was out to dinner with my husband, and Peter—"

"Your husband?" I interrupted. "I thought it was just some guy you were dating."

"I mean, he was just some guy. Being married doesn't mean that he was important."

All that lore that I carried around in my head . . . It was jarring to learn that part of it was wrong. There was a phenomenon, the Mandela effect, of people collectively remembering details about the past in a particular way, only to find out that they had those details wrong. Nelson Mandela didn't die in prison, the Berenstain Bears always had 'stain' in their name, and my mother had left a man she was legally linked to in order to be with my father. Had she lied or had I misremembered? How many times had I interpreted the world, myself, as I wanted it to be rather than the truth?

"I thought that you and Dad eloped three weeks after you met. How did you do that if you were married?"

She grinned at me. I could almost swear that her teeth were sharp like a vampire's. I attributed that to prison dental work.

"Well, because my husband was dead, of course."

Her eyes locked onto mine. No wonder she hadn't cared when I told her that my ex-fiancé had been chopped into pieces. It was the same thing that had happened to her first husband. The generational curse—the generational gift—repeating itself again and again. Trying to change the outcome was like going to a fortune teller, then doing everything possible to avoid the predicted fate, only for the avoidance to be the very thing that brings the predicted fate about.

I'd been so determined to be with someone ordinary, to be

ordinary myself. I hadn't realized that my mother had done the same thing. The tornado could only be a tornado. The snake, a snake.

I understood what had happened without needing my mother to elaborate. My parents met that night at the restaurant and knew they were supposed to be together, and they'd eliminated the person who was standing in their way. Everyone assumed that they murdered only women. That was because of a bias that wasn't limited to my parents' crimes but extended to death as a whole. Didn't people recognize that men were mortal too?

Do you really want to be with me? Then prove it.

It was a grand gesture. The grandest of gestures.

Would you kill to be with me?

Better than a public declaration of love, it was an act of violence that irrevocably tied them together. No wonder my mother sneered at other women.

They think they know love, but they don't.

Up until that moment, I had doubted her viciousness. Mothers weren't murderers. They were nurturers, victims, but never killers. It had been easier to pin the killing on the father who hadn't loved me the way that I wanted to be loved. Lots of people had terrible fathers. Having a monstrous mother was more difficult to comprehend.

My mother didn't go along with what my father wanted to do; rather, she pushed him to do what she wanted. My father might have written a manifesto, but behind every manuscript penned by a man was the woman supporting him. The first kill had been about my father proving his love to my mother. It was possible that all the other ones were too.

I only love you, Lydia. I only want you, Lydia. This woman means nothing to me. I will kill everyone in the world if that's what it takes to show the depth of my devotion.

They hadn't escalated to killing later in their relationship. Their relationship had *started* with death. It was the only way that they knew how to process things, their method of showing devotion.

"Did you kill Noah?" I asked.

"Don't be rude. Didn't I teach you not to interrupt me when I'm telling a story? So, I was in a restaurant, and Peter came up to me—"

"Did you chop him into little pieces and leave him at my house? Are you trying to frame me? Or is this how you show your love?"

"I don't know why you're talking about something so gruesome when I'm trying to tell this lovely gentleman here a story," my mother snapped.

I saw now that it had been a mistake to come here. There was nothing that my mother could give me. I'd continued to talk to her out of a sense of obligation. I'd continued to talk to her because I wanted her to *love* me. More than any of that, I'd talked to her because I felt guilty about what I'd done. I was responsible for her incarceration. She would never be released, and I'd never paid for what I'd done. The least I could do was tolerate a weekly phone call.

As I looked at my mother, her face twisted into a snarl, I decided my debt was paid. I was done. I was never going to get the answers I was looking for, and my mother was never going to be the mother I wanted her to be. I needed to say the thing that I'd been putting off for all those years. As long as it was unspoken, I'd forever be in my mother's grip. If I voiced it out loud, then I could finally be free.

"I framed you," I said, interrupting her depiction of the first time she and my father had sex.

That got her attention.

"I was mad at you and Dad. You were bad parents. It hurt me when you left me alone. And I knew you were killing people. How could you do that while I was home? Didn't you care about me? Never mind. I don't care. I killed that woman, the one the police found. That's what you and Dad taught me, killing as problem-solving. I hope that you're happy with yourself. What's that saying? 'You reap what you sow.'"

Another phrase: "Fuck around and find out."

My mother wasn't quiet, but neither was she forming words. Instead, garbled vowels emerged from her mouth. Her face grew so red that I thought she might explode. She stood up, and finally the sounds arranged themselves in the correct order.

"Guards! Arrest this woman! She framed me! My daughter framed me!"

She screamed. It wasn't all that different from the sound of death. After all, something *was* dying—the house we'd assembled together, dismantled brick by brick.

The guards didn't care. They'd heard it all before. They weren't the judge or the jury. Their only duty was to keep my mother locked up. And she was locked up, I reminded myself, taking a deep breath as the heavy metal door of the prison released me back into the world with a jarring beep. There was only so much she could do to hurt me.

"I THINK YOU DID THE RIGHT THING," AIDAN TOLD ME WHEN WE were back on the plane.

"Was she everything that you hoped?" I asked.

The distance between us and the ground made me feel safe. I

was willing to risk the wrath of gravity if it meant escaping from my mother.

"I told you, I don't care about her. She led me to you, and now that I'm here, you're the only thing that matters."

I still hadn't fully adjusted to Aidan's predilection for speeches about how devoted he was to me. Noah had been more of a silent Midwestern type. I hoped that eventually I would be able to believe fully.

"There was one thing that I wanted to do while we were there that I didn't get to," Aidan said.

"Did you want a prison tour?"

"No, I wanted to give you this."

He whipped a box out of his pocket. My heart started to thump. I didn't trust gift boxes. Anything could be inside. A toe. An ear. A finger.

Aidan opened the box.

It was a ring.

"I'm sorry that flying the plane makes it impossible to get down on one knee. I don't want to wait to do this. Alexandra, you're the most exciting woman I've ever met. I know that we've only been together for a short period of time, but I don't want to wait to start my future with you."

He was a psychopath who'd become obsessed with my parents after committing a murder of his own, everything that I said that I didn't want in a man. I was supposed to marry Noah, who'd been perfect on paper. He was a doctor, handsome, and fit, and yet our relationship hadn't worked in practice. Things were wrong before Molly interfered. Things were wrong before he was chopped into pieces.

I'd always thought that love was a conscious choice. People fit together because of their temperaments, their likes and dislikes, and their goals. Looking at Aidan, I realized how wrong I'd been. I loved him in spite of all his flaws. I loved him so much that his flaws no longer seemed so wrong. He'd *killed* for me. We'd killed together and covered up the crime. There was no part of myself that I had to hide from him, no aspect I needed to make more palatable. He wanted me for who I was: the daughter of serial murderers. A murderer myself. A psychopath.

"Yes, yes, yes," I said.

That was when the tears fell down my own cheeks. Aidan had cracked me open, the box in my brain where I kept all my feelings in shards on the floor. It was beautiful and painful at once. My path to true love hadn't been ordinary, but then, they didn't make movies about ordinary people.

Aidan slid the ring onto my finger. It fit perfectly, unlike the one that Noah had given me, which needed to be resized because it was too large. Normally, I would've said that didn't mean anything. It wasn't a sign. In that moment, though, the ring became a symbol for everything. Aidan and I were meant to be.

31.

I T'S PERFECT," AIDAN SAID when he saw the wedding venue on a nature reserve overlooking a lake. Across the water, woods stretched for miles. I wondered how many bodies the trees hid.

"You're not bothered that this was where I was supposed to marry Noah?" I asked.

"No. Noah's part of our story. I think it's good that he's included in this," Aidan said.

That was one of the things that I liked about him. He wasn't threatened by other men, or anyone, really. His total faith in us made it easy for me to be faithful too.

It seemed like a miracle that, in the end, it was all going to work out for me.

Rebecca helped me put together the bits and pieces of the wedding that had been neglected after Noah left me for Molly. I called on the connections that I'd made as a matchmaker to secure a last-minute cake, catering, photographer, and DJ. I put Aidan in charge of the invitations, because he had more people to reach out to than I did. I invited only Rebecca, Oliver, Serena, and a couple of acquaintances from college, who sent their regrets.

I met Aidan's family at the rehearsal dinner the night before the wedding. His father spent the evening talking about the Ironman competition that he'd recently completed, while his mother complained about the food. They were the type of people who didn't know how to express positive emotions.

"I hope you're ready for him," his mother warned, gesturing to her youngest son. "I thought I knew how to raise children, and then he was born."

I watched Aidan's siblings—a brother and a sister, with kids of their own—move about the room. Physically, they resembled him, though their auras were different. Aidan had something that they didn't, something intangible.

"At first, we thought he was the perfect baby. He was so calm and relaxed all the time. And then he learned to talk, and we knew we had something else on our hands," his mother continued.

She said such things as if I might agree with her, or even feel bad for her. Either she didn't realize that Aidan had told me about the padded cell his parents had kept him in, or she thought I'd understand. All choices seemed rational to the people who made them.

BY THE END OF OUR CONVERSATION, IT WAS CLEAR THAT THERE would be no Christmas celebrations with matching pajamas. While Noah's mother had worshipped the ground Noah walked upon, Aidan's mother didn't even seem to like Aidan. I mourned the relationship that I wouldn't get to have with my mother-in-law, and then I let it go. I didn't need an extended family, not when I had Aidan. We would create our own little world.

"Are your parents going to be here? I would love to meet them," Aidan's mother asked when she'd finished complaining about her son.

"No, unfortunately they couldn't make it," I told her.

"That's too bad. We'll have to get together with them another time."

"Yes, another time, for sure."

———

AFTER THE REHEARSAL DINNER WAS FINISHED, THE BEST MAN and the maid of honor gave their speeches. I'd been to enough weddings to know the way that speeches could dominate the night, and thus I relegated them to the evening before. Plus, I didn't want anyone to notice how few people were present to say things about me. Aidan had loads of friends, while I had almost none. Even Serena had sent her apologies. She didn't give a reason, but I could guess why she didn't want to come.

The previous week, she'd announced that she'd decided to close Better Love for good. I'd expected as much. The business had been shuttered for three months. Most of the matchmakers had found other employment, the clients other dating prospects. The investors, I assumed, had moved on to other projects. People continued to fall in and out of love without us, though perhaps it was more difficult. Serena claimed the closure was because of her age, her grandchild, but we all knew the decision was because of Nicole's and Ethan's deaths, which had been officially ruled a murder-suicide. She felt that she somehow should've seen what was coming, been able to tell who Ethan was on the inside.

"Did Nicole say anything to you?" she asked when she called me. "I keep thinking back, wondering if there were signs that I missed."

"No. She didn't say anything to me at all," I replied.

I wished I could tell her that Ethan was a man who'd loved his wife so much that it killed him. I couldn't tell her anything though, so all I said was that I understood why she needed to close the business, and I wished her the best.

It stung that she didn't want to attend the wedding. She was quiet for a long time when I'd told her that I was engaged to a former Better Love client so soon after my former best friend was charged with murdering my ex-fiancé.

"Are you sure this is what you want? Sometimes people rush into relationships when they're in an emotionally vulnerable place. There's nothing wrong with taking your time."

"I've never been surer about anything," I told her defensively.

It didn't matter. Serena had no control over my life. She wasn't my boss or my mother. I didn't need her at the rehearsal dinner or the ceremony. Love existed before her, and it would continue to exist after her.

Aidan's best friend gave the first speech. He'd been there the night we met.

"Does he know about you?" I asked Aidan.

He shook his head.

"Men don't talk about things like that," he said. "We get together and watch basketball, go to the gym, drink. It's not complicated, like your friendships," he said.

Men liked to present their relationships with one another as simple, easy things. Another way of looking at their lack of drama was that they kept a lot of secrets from one another.

"I wasn't surprised when Aidan told me he was getting married to someone he'd just met," his best friend said. The room tittered with laughter. "He's a person who goes after exactly what he wants, without hesitation, and since the night that they met, what he's wanted is Lexie."

Our glasses clinked, and Rebecca stood up. She looked gorgeous in a pink floor-length dress. I saw the way that the people in the room eyed her—*Who is she?*—as she walked among them. I was proud to have such a friend, even if she was my only one.

"Lexie and I have a strange history. First she was my matchmaker. Then she became my best friend. The thing about Lexie is that it can take her a minute to open up, but once she does, she'll do anything for the people she loves."

She made eye contact with me as she spoke. I thought of all the things that went unmentioned. The COMP meetings during which I'd told near strangers more than nearly anyone else in my life. The tragedies that marred both of our lives. I'd known that Rebecca was going to be my maid of honor before I knew that Aidan was going to be the groom. In some ways, our friendship was as much of a case of love at first sight as my relationship with Aidan.

While Rebecca talked about our shared love of messy reality television, I assured myself that she would never betray me the way that Molly had. That was something about love of all kinds. I could build up walls, and fortify them with concrete and metal, but at the end of the day I was lonely in a way that mere sex or acquaintanceships couldn't fill. If I wanted to love and be loved in return, I needed to allow myself to be vulnerable, to carve out a door in the fortress I'd built in my head, to allow others to come in. I needed to trust them not to hurt me. I needed to trust them to kill for me if that's what it came down to.

"Cheers," Rebecca said.

There was a shattering as she and I clinked our flutes together.

I realized that my glass had somehow broken in the process, and there were shards of it floating in the champagne.

"Oops," she said. "I must've hit you too hard."

We laughed about it as the restaurant staff cleaned up the mess. They assured us it was no problem, and promptly replaced my drink. The rest of the guests looked briefly startled, and then resumed conversation like nothing unusual had happened.

I looked around the room. The normalcy of the night overwhelmed me. Finally, the party that I'd been waiting for, a night built for me. I'd found my groom, my maid of honor, enough friends and family to fill a room. People who had never experienced true loneliness couldn't appreciate how good it was to be loved. They took it for granted, the same way that people who'd never been hungry didn't know what a privilege it was to eat. I enjoyed every morsel of food, every drift of Aidan's hand against my body.

Despite everything, I'd done it. I'd made it to the end of the film.

32.

___

The wedding

I ALWAYS KNEW THAT NOAH would attend my wedding; I just thought that he would be the groom. As I rooted through the box that was delivered to the bridal suite, my fingers met hair. Despite the humanlike texture, I hoped that the object was a stuffed animal until I spotted the skin below. That was when I shrieked.

It was his head. It was my wedding day, and someone had delivered me the head of my ex-fiancé. Had I misjudged Aidan? I'd known him less than five months, and there we were, legally binding ourselves together forever. If it was Aidan, he'd done an exceptional job of hiding the body part. Since the night that Better Love burned down, we'd spent nearly all of our time together, excepting when he was at work. When I'd gone into his freezer for ice cream, there were no frozen heads. There were no bones in the linen closet. Would it change things if he had been the one to wrap up my ex-fiancé's skull with a pretty bow and deliver it to my door? When two people who'd committed murder were engaged, what kind of thing was bad enough to be a deal-breaker?

Rebecca burst into the room.

"I heard you scream. Are you okay?"

"I got a gift," I said, and gestured to the box.

She looked down at it.

"Something good?"

"It's Noah's head."

I expected Rebecca to express surprise or confusion. *What do you mean, it's Noah's head?* She did none of that. She stared at me and raised an eyebrow.

"Well? Do you like it?"

I got the same feeling I'd had when we were skidding off the highway in her car. I tried to apply the brake, but I wasn't the one who was driving. My mouth was dry. I didn't want to voice it. I wanted to shove the truth into that metal box in my brain and lock it away forever. But some things were unavoidable, particularly when those things were standing right in front of you.

"It was you," I said. "You were the one who killed him. You were the one who left pieces of him at my door, and broke into my house."

Rebecca grinned at me. She was proud. How frustrating it must have been for her to watch me spin my wheels when it was her the whole time.

"I did it for you. As a gift."

"Why would you do that? You didn't even know him."

I looked back down at the head. It was well-preserved. Noah must've been kept in a freezer. I recalled the night when Rebecca and I had eaten ice cream in her apartment. Was it body-freezer ice cream, or had he been somewhere separate? What a thrill that must've been for her, comforting me over the death of a man she'd killed herself.

"Noah was all wrong for you, even before he left you for Molly. I couldn't believe it when that happened. What a fucking joke," she said.

"But how did you know?"

I tried to assemble the timeline. Noah had left me for Molly on a Saturday. I was first introduced to Rebecca's existence at the intake meeting on Monday. When Noah disappeared the following Saturday, she was still under the impression that we were engaged.

"Lexie, come on. You didn't really think that I went to Better Love because I wanted a boyfriend, did you? I can get a boyfriend anytime I want, which I don't. Who wants to be tied down like that? I mean, I guess Paul did. Don't worry—I took care of him after he harassed you at work. That was so rude of him."

Paul? I hadn't thought of him in months. Compared with the staged murder-suicide of Nicole and Ethan, his appearance had been an unsettling blip. He'd been so destroyed the last time I saw him, so eager to see Rebecca again. "I'll do anything," he said, and she took it literally.

"I went to Better Love because I wanted to meet you officially," Rebecca continued. "Imagine how delighted I was when you showed up at COMP later in the week."

No. All of that was wrong. I'd been the conductor of our relationship. I'd been vulnerable the week that Rebecca arrived. I needed a friend, and there she was. I'd combed through her social media in an effort to learn more about her life. Was it possible that she'd done the same thing with me?

"Why would you do that?"

"I can't believe you haven't figured it out yet," she said. "It was so obvious to me from the moment that we met. You're my sister."

I laughed. She laughed too. Could laughter during uncomfortable moments be a genetic trait?

"No, I'm not. I'm an only child."

There were many things that I was uncertain about in the world, but one thing that I knew for sure was that I'd been the single child in the house with my parents. No one had been with me when I heard those women scream.

"Come on. Put it together," she said.

"Your father was murdered when you were a child."

"Yes."

"My father didn't have any other children."

I said it, though I wasn't confident. My father was the kind of man who might've had numerous children and not cared about their existence. It was my mother who kept him tethered to me. Still, the math didn't add up.

"My mother," I said.

"My mother," she echoed, those eyes of hers boring into my skull.

"No. I would've known."

It wasn't possible. My mother had never mentioned having another child. When I was small, I'd begged and begged for a sibling, and my mother said that she refused to ruin her body like that again. I tried to recall what Rebecca had said about her mother in our previous conversations, and I came up empty. Our talks had always been about only her father. He'd been murdered, so that made sense. Often the dead were discussed more than the living.

Her first husband, I realized. *She had a baby with her first husband, and then my father killed him.*

Before there was me, there was Rebecca. She'd had a normal family. Then, within weeks, it had all fallen apart.

"She left you," I said.

Stupidly, there was some satisfaction in the statement. My mother had picked me. Well, she'd picked my father, and then I'd come along. As messed up as my childhood had been, at least my mother was around. She hadn't left until I'd forced her to go. Surely that was an indication of a kind of love.

"For a while, she did," Rebecca said. "But the mother-daughter bond is unbreakable."

My head spun. I'd left the visit with my mother convinced that she'd been rendered impotent. She was going to be in prison forever, slowly turning into a sad old woman who grasped at the smallest of things for joy. How wrong I'd been. I was the daughter my mother talked to on Sundays. It seemed possible that she had one for every day of the week.

"Did you always know about me?" I asked.

"I didn't know about you until the arrest. You were a side comment, the child raised in a house of killers. My family never mentioned your name. I didn't figure that out until years later. I hated you then, because I thought you were my replacement. Our mother left me behind, and then got you."

"You were the lucky one. You didn't see what she was really like. She abused me. She—"

"Shut up," Rebecca said. Her voice sounded different. Nicole had driven me crazy with her baby voice, but it hadn't occurred to me that Rebecca might be similarly using an affect. "You got to have her to yourself for years. I was by myself with a family who looked at me and only saw my dead father. How can you call that lucky? They wouldn't let me talk to her. They pretended she didn't exist, but I never forgot. I reached out to Mom as soon as I was old enough to afford my own cell phone. We picked up again like we'd never been apart. She made me whole, understood me in a way that no one else ever has. Have you ever missed someone before you met them? It was like that. Her absence hurt me daily."

I fixated on how casually she said "Mom," like it was an easy word to push out of one's mouth.

"How did you find me?" I asked.

"What's that word you like? 'Serendipity.' That's what it was. You might find it interesting that Mom rarely talks about you. It was years before she ever mentioned your name, and that wasn't partic-ularly helpful to me, since you'd changed your last name like a cow-ard. I found that picture online, of course, the one of you as a teenager, which also proved to be useless, though I was glad that all of Mom's good looks were passed down to me. I gave up the search. I told myself that if you didn't want to see me, then I didn't want to see you. But you found me, Lexie. I was in the Twin Cities for a car show, and there, on my phone, was your face. It was an ad for Better Love. So I got a job in the area and, well, the rest is history."

The ad. I hadn't thought much about it. Serena was so good at stuff like that. Most of running a business was less about what that business did and more about understanding how to sell it. She used advertisements to hit targeted demographics. She increased spending during holiday seasons, because that was when potential clients were at their loneliest. I wasn't featured in most of the ads. They didn't even show my whole face. But my sister—*my sister*—had recognized me.

"Why didn't you just tell me?" I asked.

"Initially my plan was to kill you." Rebecca didn't blink as she made the statement. "You got to have her for all those years, while

I was left behind. It wasn't fair. You had everything I didn't—a mother, a father. You never appreciated it, not how I would've. Mom told me how you treat her. I told her to stop talking to you, and she wouldn't listen. I thought it best to take care of the issue for both of us. But then I started following you, and I really liked you."

Rebecca was following me. Aidan was following me. There had been a whole parade on my tail and I hadn't even noticed.

"So you decided to kill my fiancé instead?"

"To be fair, I killed him after he left you. He wasn't really your fiancé anymore. It made me mad that you slept with him after what he did. I had to do something. Have some self-respect, Lexie. It doesn't matter who a man is; he shouldn't be allowed to get away with things like that."

The excuse was weak. Noah had died before Rebecca had known what he'd done. She'd killed him because she wanted to. Even if she had somehow known, I resented her judgment. Rebecca might be my sister, but she hadn't grown up in the same house as me. She didn't know what it had been like. She didn't understand why I wanted someone like Noah, a milquetoast man who loved his family. Was it settling if it got me what I wanted?

"He wasn't hard to kill. I followed him to Molly's apartment—that bitch—and watched him storm out a little while later. He went straight to a bar and got drunk. I swear, he nearly peed himself with excitement when I invited him to come home with me. Boy, was he surprised when I stabbed him. Don't worry—I made sure that his death was slow. I wanted him to suffer for what he did to you. He kept saying 'Why, why, why?' like he couldn't possibly fathom anything he'd done wrong in his entire life. If only he'd stayed loyal, then he might be getting married today."

Rebecca shook her head as though she truly thought it was a pity. She didn't. She would've killed Noah even if he hadn't hurt me. She didn't need a reason to do what she did. That was the difference between us. I killed to save myself, and she killed because she loved it, just like my parents.

The box still rested on my legs. Sometimes, when Noah had had a really long shift at the hospital, he'd come home and lay his head on my lap and I'd run my fingers through his hair to comfort him. *Mmm, that feels good,* he'd murmur. The current situation wasn't so different from that, aside from the fact that he was dead and could no longer feel anything.

"Fine, you killed him to protect me. But what about leaving his heart on my doorstep? The display on my mantel? And the stuff that happened at Better Love—was that you too?"

"You did get one thing right. The stuff at Better Love was Molly's brainchild. She's pretty fun, for a terrible person. It's good that she's in prison now. She doesn't need to be out in the world, with the rest of us. Molly, Nicole, and I struck up a friendship for a while. Or, they thought I was their friend. Nicole, as you know, was insufferable. I wasn't sad to hear that she died."

Rebecca narrowed her eyes at me.

"You didn't have something to do with that, did you? She really hated you, Lexie. She hated your clients too, all your little psychopaths. That's what she called them. She told me, 'I don't mean you, Becky.' But I knew she did. She just wanted me around so that she could use me. Anyway, I killed Noah because I was mad that he cheated, and I wanted you for myself. You were so *comfortable* in that little life you created. It's like you couldn't even tell how unhappy you were. No one really changes unless they're forced to. I needed to get you away from your stupid fiancé and that matchmaking job. I wanted to remind you of where you came from, who you really are."

I thought of my cold fingers pawing at the frozen ground in an attempt to cover up part of Noah's body. Was that person my authentic self? More real than the woman who was engaged to a doctor, worked as a matchmaker, and lived in a town house adorned in gray? Both Rebecca and Aidan had seen it, the cage that I didn't realize I was trapped inside. Was I supposed to thank her for giving me freedom, or had I simply been placed behind bars of a different kind now?

I shook my head.

"That's not who I am. I'm not a killer."

Rebecca strode to the snack table, her maid-of-honor dress swishing as she walked. She picked up a petit four and popped it into her mouth.

"I heard something interesting from Mom a couple of months ago."

I wanted to yank the word "mom" out of her mouth and cut it into a million pieces. That wasn't who she was. She was Mother. Something threatening. Something that could devour us all.

"She said that you confessed to killing the woman the police nailed her for. You set her up. What a sneaky little bitch."

Rebecca's tone had changed from friendly to venomous. Reluctantly, I put Noah's head on the floor and stood up. I wasn't totally sure what was happening, but I wanted to be ready.

"I had to do it. They were killing people." My voice was weak, unconvincing. The line between *need* and *want* was so thin.

"Did you *have* to, Lexie? Mom's never going to be free, you know. She's stuck in there because of you."

"What is it that you want, Rebecca?"

It occurred to me that that might not be her real name.

"I used to want a sister, someone who really *got* me. We did get each other, didn't we, Lex? I had these stupid fantasies about the two of us traveling together to see Mom." She shook her head. "Practicality isn't a strong suit in our family. All of us are living in our own imagination. When Mom told me what you did, I realized the error of my ways. I didn't want a *sister*. I hate competition."

I watched Rebecca's face as she spoke. Now that she'd said it, I recognized how she was similar to my mother. Our mother. The sharpness of her gaze. The high cheekbones. I saw too the part of me that couldn't help but love her even as she explained that the world wasn't big enough for us both. I couldn't believe that I hadn't seen it before.

There was that other side of me though, the part of me that loathed my mother, had devoted the entirety of my existence to being anyone other than her. I *had* needed to take my parents down, or they would've done the same to me. They might not have killed me, but they would've rotted out my core. There were days when I wondered whether it had been too late. Maybe I'd already turned bad. But I recognized something within myself, a tendril of goodness. Someone who wanted love.

"This wasn't supposed to happen," I said. "This isn't how the movie is supposed to go."

"What movie?" Rebecca asked.

"The one where I get what I want," I said as I grabbed from the snack table the knife that had previously been used to slice bagels and I stabbed it into her gut.

33.

——

I need your help, I texted Aidan.

The ceremony was supposed to start in half an hour. Guests were filling in the chairs that were lined in rows in the garden outside.

Aidan showed up at the door of the bridal suite almost immediately.

"Isn't it bad luck to see the bride before the ceremony?" he asked as he took me in.

The fabric of my dress, once a creamy white, was stained red with blood. There was blood on the carpet, the walls. Rebecca was a rag doll on the floor.

"I think we're past the point of considering luck," I told him.

It had been like the first murder. I remembered grabbing the knife, but not the look on Rebecca's face as I turned on her. I must've taken her by surprise, because she was taller and stronger than I was. When I resumed consciousness, Rebecca was dead and the room destroyed. So much for my security deposit.

"What happened?" Aidan asked as he surveyed the scene.

"Rebecca's my sister," I told him. "She was the one who killed Noah, who sent all that stuff to my door. She helped Nicole and Molly plant the stuff at Better Love. It turns out that she was following me before we even met."

"That explains why she was so familiar to me. We must've run into each other at some point while I was following you."

I rolled my eyes. "I really need fewer psychopaths in my life," I said.

"You'll never be free of us. We're everywhere," Aidan said. He was joking, but like with every joke, there was truth buried in it.

Reluctantly, I took off my stained dress. We used the layers of fabric to wrap up Rebecca's body.

"What about the mess?" I asked.

He pulled me close to him. I was wearing my underwear and bra, which were miraculously unstained. Aidan had thrown on my robe that said *Bride* across the back in order to protect his suit.

"I don't want you to worry about that right now. It's your big day. I have someone I can call. They'll take care of it."

Previously, I thought the greatest act of love was killing for a partner. In this moment, I realized the true greatest act of love was taking care of the cleanup after the murder was done.

The body would have to wait. Every minute, more guests filtered into the hall below. Rationally, I understood that I should feel sad about the death of my sister, and worse that I'd been responsible for it, but I felt utterly calm. I'd spent two decades training myself to turn off my emotions, particularly when it came to my family, and my heart had barricaded itself before the first stab. All the feeling that I had left was reserved for Aidan and the life we were going to build together.

We stuffed Rebecca's body into a closet and did our best to tidy the room.

Aidan texted friends—how I loved that he had people to count on—and they managed to procure something new for me to wear. The new dress was a deep red, and through some miracle, it fit me perfectly.

"You know it's bad luck to see the bride before the ceremony," I reminded Aidan as he eyed the outfit.

"Fuck luck," he said. "We have something better. We have love."

He was right. I could feel it in the air as I walked toward the altar. No one seemed to care that I wasn't wearing a white dress. The red suited me. It was a little quirky, a little out there, just like I was. I got lost in the moment. My father was dead, my mother imprisoned, and I'd just killed the sister I'd never known I had. None of that mattered. All that was important was the man in front of me.

"I vow always to be there when you need me. I vow to keep you safe. I vow to let you watch your favorite reality shows even if they drive me crazy." There was a roar of laughter at that one. "I vow to keep our lives adventurous. Most of all, I vow to love you for who you are."

My parents' wedding had been a small, rushed affair. There was an urgency to it, as though they knew their time together was limited. As they had alienated their family members, the only witnesses were two fleeting friends. My mother had made it sound romantic, but when the crowd cheered as Aidan and I kissed, cementing our union, I understood how lonely her life ultimately had been. I was getting married to a psychopath, yes, a man who had killed people, but he was a psychopath with friends.

The rest of the night was just like in the movies. The photographer took shots while the guests drank signature cocktails and ate hors d'oeuvres. Our entry into the reception was met with a round of applause. We ate dinner, and then hit the dance floor. Drinks appeared in my hand without my asking for them. Guests came up to me to tell me how beautiful I looked and how happy they were that Aidan had finally found someone to tame him.

"Oh, I'm not taming him," I told them. "He finally found someone who could keep up."

We cut the cake. I threw my bouquet backward over my head, and Oliver caught it and groaned. I realized as I danced with my wedding guests that I was never again going to try to seek out a best friend, the way that I had with Molly and Rebecca. One had stolen my fiancé, and the other had murdered him, delivered his dismembered body parts to my door, and turned out to be my secret sister. I'd spent so much time longing for that type of connection, the kind that I'd witnessed in the shows that I watched, only for it to go so horribly wrong. As it turned out, reality television wasn't a good instruction manual for how to be a human.

The revelation that I would never again have a best friend didn't bother me the way that it once might've. I had a husband with an active social life, and I had a cat. We'd just closed on a house, and we were talking about having kids. In the fall, I was going back to school to start a PhD in psychology. I didn't need Molly, Rebecca, or even my mother. I'd excised the toxic parts of my life and, in doing so, found the life that I'd always dreamed of. Finally, I was being true to myself.

At the end of the reception, the guests lined the doorway with sparklers as Aidan and I made our way to a golf cart, which I'd thought would be a cute way to leave instead of the usual limousine. Rather than driving to the nearby hotel where we'd reserved the honeymoon suite, we drove to the back of the venue and snuck up the stairs.

Rebecca was still waiting for us in the closet. I guess I did have a family member at the wedding, even if she wasn't alive to watch it. Aidan was strong, and the two of us carried her corpse down the stairs without much difficulty, then loaded it onto the back of the golf cart.

We drove her to the far side of the lake. The woods weren't spooky when Aidan was by my side. We got into the water, which was still cold in late spring, dragging Rebecca along with us. We weighed her dress down with stones—how she'd bragged about those pockets!—and watched as she sank to the bottom.

Presumably, there were people who would notice her absence—my mother or Rebecca's coworkers—but I was the only one she was really close to. She'd even held the other members of COMP at a distance. I used to be lonely like Rebecca was, but Aidan had changed things. We did stuff together. His friends were my friends. We went to barbecues, attended sporting events and concerts. For all intents and purposes, we were ordinary, friendly people.

The dip in the lake was cleansing, a type of purification. I washed myself free of Molly, Noah, and Rebecca. I let go of my grievances with my mother. I was with Aidan now, my soulmate. We had it all planned out. Our lives were going to be perfect. Perfect, that was, as long as we could keep ourselves from killing too many people.

ACKNOWLEDGMENTS

First and foremost, I want to thank Katie Greenstreet, Jen Monroe, and Leodora Darlington, who helped me through the second-book process.

To Daniel Bernal, Joe Loye, Carolyn Browender, Blair Jones, Elizabeth Blyakher, Elizabeth Deanna Morris Lakes, Brandi Wells, Tessa Carter, Gloria Feltman, Sal Pane, Theresa Beckhusen, Krista Ahlberg, Julia Austin, Kim Caldwell, Theresa Pappas, Mary Lauda Crenshaw, Julia Ricciardi, Jason McCall, Zach and Susan Doss, Patti White, Michael Martone, Robyn and John Hammontree, Jim Robinson, Sarah Howard, Patricia and Edward Oliu, Pamela Klinger-Horn, and everyone in both Minnesota and Alabama who have been so great about sharing my work.

To the baristas who got me hundreds of cups of coffee.

To the bag of popcorn that got me through the final draft.

To the reality show cast members who serve as friends on my loneliest days.

ACKNOWLEDGMENTS

To my dad, brother, and the entire Coryell family.

To Summer the greyhound, who passed away while I was writing this book. To Husker the greyhound, who arrived just in time.

To Brian and Ronan, who are the closest thing I have to soulmates.